TARGET!

Winston pulled out a glass bottle. He thought at first the cheater had filled it with beads or rocks. Then he realized what he was looking at: The bottle had been filled to the neck with glass shards from other broken bottles. The world's most terrible soft drink. This was how the cheater delivered flat tires with such ease.

"There's more," Jake said. "Look at the memo pad."

"Memo pad?" Mal asked. "What was he going to do, give us all paper cuts?"

"Just look," Jake said.

Something in Jake's tone made Winston dimly alarmed. He reached into the plastic bag and found a perfectly ordinary memo pad. He flipped through the pages, many of which were crumpled and mussed. He didn't find anything exciting. "Carburetor from Mack" read one note. One page had strings of meaningless numbers, and there were doodles all over. Winston looked up at Jake questioningly.

"The last couple of pages," Jake said.

Winston turned to the last page of writing, and for a moment, he wasn't sure what he was looking at. At first all he saw was a bunch of letters and numbers. Then his glance settled on something he couldn't quite believe. Written in the cheater's memo pad was his own name: BREEN.

OTHER BOOKS YOU MAY ENJOY

The Big One-Oh	Dean Pitchford
Black Duck	Janet Taylor Lisle
Edenville Owls	Robert B. Parker
Encyclopedia Brown, Boy Detective	Donald Sobol
Encyclopedia Brown Cracks the Case	Donald Sobol
From Charlie's Point of View	Richard Scrimger
The Mystery of the Third Lucretia	Susan Runholt
The Puzzling World of Winston Breen	Eric Berlin
Something Rotten: A Horatio Wilkes Mystery	Alan Gratz
The Westing Game	Ellen Raskin

The Puzzling World of
Winston Breen

THE POTATO CHIP PUZZLES

ERIC BERLIN

PUFFIN BOOKS
An Imprint of Penguin Group (USA) Inc.

PUFFIN BOOKS

Published by the Penguin Group

Penguin Young Readers Group, 345 Hudson Street, New York, New York 10014, U.S.A.

Penguin Group (Canada), 90 Eglinton Avenue East, Suite 700, Toronto, Ontario, Canada M4P 2Y3
(a division of Pearson Penguin Canada Inc.)

Penguin Books Ltd, 80 Strand, London WC2R 0RL, England

Penguin Ireland, 25 St Stephen's Green, Dublin 2, Ireland (a division of Penguin Books Ltd)

Penguin Group (Australia), 250 Camberwell Road, Camberwell, Victoria 3124, Australia
(a division of Pearson Australia Group Pty Ltd)

Penguin Books India Pvt Ltd, 11 Community Centre, Panchsheel Park, New Delhi - 110 017, India

Penguin Group (NZ), 67 Apollo Drive, Rosedale, North Shore 0632, New Zealand
(a division of Pearson New Zealand Ltd)

Penguin Books (South Africa) (Pty) Ltd, 24 Sturdee Avenue,
Rosebank, Johannesburg 2196, South Africa

Registered Offices: Penguin Books Ltd, 80 Strand, London WC2R 0RL, England

First published in the United States of America by G. P. Putnam's Sons,
a division of Penguin Young Readers Group, 2009

Published by Puffin Books, a division of Penguin Young Readers Group, 2010

7 9 10 8 6

THE LIBRARY OF CONGRESS HAS CATALOGED THE G. P. PUTNAM'S SONS EDITION AS FOLLOWS:

Berlin, Eric.

The potato chip puzzles / Eric Berlin.

p. cm. — (Puzzling world of Winston Breen)

Summary: Winston and his friends enter an all-day puzzle contest to win fifty thousand dollars
for their school, but they must also figure out who is trying to keep them from winning.
Puzzles for the reader to solve are included throughout the text.

ISBN 978-0-399-25198-6 (hc)

[1. Puzzles—Fiction. 2. Contests—Fiction. 3. Mystery and detective stories.]
I. Title.

PZ7.B45335Po 2009
[Fic]—dc22
2008033698

Puffin Books ISBN 978-0-14-241637-2

Printed in the United States of America

For Rita and Joel Berlin

*Also, a world of thanks to
Katherine Bryant, Ana Deboo, Francis Heaney,
Dan Katz, Susan Kochan, Lance Nathan,
Trip Payne, Scott Purdy, William Reiss,
and Will Shortz.*

ABOUT THE PUZZLES IN THIS BOOK

This book contains quite a few puzzles. You can solve them if you want, although you don't *have* to solve them to enjoy the story. Most of the answers can be found in the back of the book. Some of the puzzles are so important to the story, however, that the answer will appear on the next few pages. You'll see which ones those are when you get to them. Note that you can't really skip those puzzles and come back to them later, because you'll learn the answer almost immediately. Take a few minutes to try them, and then continue reading.

And if you don't want to write in this book, just head over to **www.winstonbreen.com**. There you can download and print out all the puzzles. Happy solving!

C
H
A
P
T
E
R

O N E

WINSTON BREEN DIDN'T know why it was called "study hall." They weren't in a hall, and hardly anyone studied. Sometimes you'd find kids finishing homework due the next period. You could tell that's what they were doing—they had a wide-eyed, racing-the-clock air to them, and they gripped their pens so hard that blood stopped flowing to their fingertips. But this was the last week of school, and there was no more homework. Kids sat in little clusters, talking semi-quietly, occasionally bursting into laughter, which would attract a glare from Mrs. Livetta, the study hall monitor. A couple of kids were reading, and one girl, with hypnotic concentration, was covering her desktop with elaborate graffiti.

Winston, of course, was solving a puzzle. He kept a couple of puzzle books in his schoolbag at all times. There had been a day earlier in the year when he found himself puzzleless in study hall, and Mrs. Livetta refused to let him go to his locker. With nothing to read and nothing to solve, he sat there for a while in utter boredom. In fact, that was the day he discovered that the letters of BOREDOM can be scrambled to make the word BEDROOM. That was a pleasing discovery, at least.

Now he was always prepared. He clicked a few times on his mechanical pencil and doodled in the margin while he thought.

In a word square, words read the same both across and down. In the following two puzzles, solve the clues to create the word square.

1	2	3	4
2			
3			
4			

1. Badly behaved child

2. Competition for runners

3. There are four of them in a deck

4. Pop quiz, for example

1	2	3	4
2			
3			
4			

1. Secret way of writing

2. Kitchen appliance

3. Card in Monopoly

4. Odds and _____

This last word square has five letters in each word . . . and the clues aren't given in order, so you'll have to figure out which word goes where.

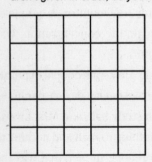

• "Great White" fish

• What's in the fireplace after a fire

• Questioned

• Abruptly to the point

• Spaghetti or ziti

(Answers, page 239.)

"Winston!" Mrs. Livetta all but screamed in his ear.

Winston jerked like a freshly caught fish, nearly falling out of his chair. The other kids in the study hall laughed. Mrs. Livetta was standing in front of him, hands on hips.

"Wh-what? Yes?" Winston tried to regain his wits. He knew what had happened. Sometimes he became so absorbed in a puzzle that the world around him simply faded away. Mrs. Livetta must have called him once or twice from the comfort of her chair and then, when Winston didn't answer, said his name louder, and then louder still, and then she finally came over and yelled at him. The next step might have been to hit him with a textbook.

The kids laughed again, but Mrs. Livetta wasn't laughing. "You are wanted down at the principal's office. Didn't you hear the announcement?" She pointed at the loudspeaker on the wall.

Winston reddened. It was worse than he thought. The loudspeaker, which was indeed loud, had barked his name, and he hadn't heard it at all. Wow. That had to be some kind of record.

Wait a minute—the principal's office wanted to see him?

"Why does the principal want to see me?" he asked.

"I don't know," Mrs. Livetta said. "It's a loudspeaker—you can't have a conversation with it. Ask when you get down there. Now go!"

Was he in trouble? He couldn't see how. Was something wrong at home? His mind reached in every direction at once as he walked through the empty hallways down to the main office. As he rounded the corner to the school's large central lobby, the intercom system crackled and chirped. The school secretary said once again, in the voice of an old lady robot: "Winston Breen, please report to the principal's office. Winston Breen, to the principal's office." Boy, whatever the reason was, they sure wanted to see him. He bit his lower lip and tried to prepare himself.

When he reached the main office, Mrs. Lembo was still returning to her desk from the PA system. "Ah, there you are," she said.

"Yes, sorry," said Winston.

"Well, go right in. Mr. Unger's expecting you."

The principal's office was down a short hallway, ending in a door you never wanted to open. Winston had never had a reason to knock on this door, and that was fine with him. He was still trying to figure out some way he might be in trouble. He took a deep breath and knocked softly. "Come in," said a brusque voice. Winston creaked the door open.

Mr. Unger was not behind his desk. He was up and pacing. "Ah, Winston. Good. Thought maybe you were absent today. Or cutting class!"

Winston recognized that as a joke but had no idea how to respond. "Yes, no, um, I was—"

But Mr. Unger wasn't looking for any explanations. "You're still the puzzle person, right?"

"Sure. . . ." Winston had shuffled entirely into the room now. He watched the principal pace back and forth, glancing occasionally at a piece of paper in his hand. When Mr. Unger walked the halls in his gray suit and shiny shoes, he was a severe, frowning authority. Now he didn't look stern at all. In fact, he looked rather like—Winston could hardly believe it—an excited little kid.

"All right. All right. Good," he said. "I want you to look at this. Here." Mr. Unger thrust the paper into Winston's hands.

It was quite fancy—stiff and crackly, and the color of rich cream. On it were a bunch of letters and numbers, written in ink:

C3	J5	S2	Q1	W3
A4	P2	L3	D1	E4
B5	F2	S1	O4	C2
Q5	D1	L2	B4	N1
R3	N4	B3	H1	E2
D4	R2	N5	F3	W1

(Continue reading to see the answer to this puzzle.)

This was not at all what he had expected from a visit to the principal's office. "What is this?" asked Winston.

"I was hoping you could tell me."

"It looks like a code of some kind. Where did it come from?"

Unger shook his head. "Don't know. It was in my mailbox this morning, but there was no return address."

"Was there a postmark?"

Mr. Unger stopped pacing. "The postmark! I didn't think of that. I knew you were the right person to call on this." He sat down in his chair, leaned over, and dug through his garbage pail, looking for the right envelope. "Aha, here we go," he said. The envelope was fancy, too. Mr. Unger brushed it off and looked at it, frowning.

"What does it say?" said Winston.

Mr. Unger didn't respond. He just handed the envelope over.

Winston looked at the front. There was no postmark. There was no stamp. "Oh," he said. He decided to sit in one of the two chairs in front of the principal's desk.

"Someone must have come in and slipped it into my mailbox," said Mr. Unger.

"I guess that means it's from someone nearby," said Winston.

Unger nodded his head. "I guess so. I guess so. I'll ask if any of the secretaries saw anything. But the main office is busy all morning. Anybody could have come in and put something in my mailbox. Can you figure out what it is?"

"I don't know," said Winston. "It could mean anything. Maybe it has something to do with a map."

"A map," the principal repeated, not understanding.

"You know how maps have letters across the top and numbers down the side? So you can find locations on them?"

"Ah, yes," said Mr. Unger, sitting back in his chair. "Coordinates. So we need a map . . . a map of what? The town?"

"I don't know," Winston said again. "Maybe."

"I can have Mrs. Lembo bring one in."

Winston shook his head. "The problem is, which map? The map in the phone book, the map in the road atlas? They're all different."

"Hmm," said Mr. Unger, frowning.

Winston added, "And do we need a map of the town or the state or the country? We could be staring at maps the rest of our life."

"All right," said the principal. "Then what do you suggest? Maybe it's not a code. Maybe it's something else."

"What?"

"Another kind of puzzle, maybe. A connect the dots."

Winston blinked. "What?"

The principal leaned forward. "Can you connect these letters and numbers in some way? Draw lines between them? Start at A1 then go to A2 . . . ?"

Winston thought about it. It didn't sound right, but it was more than he'd come up with. But then he noticed something. "There *is* no A1," he said. "Or A2. The first pair alphabetically is"—he scanned the paper—"A4. And then there's no A5."

"Hmm," said Mr. Unger.

Winston said, "I still think it's a code." He stood up and started pacing, just as the principal had been when he arrived. "Each letter and number pair is going to stand for a letter. Or a bunch of letters. Or . . ." He drifted off, staring at the paper. A wisp of an idea had breezed through his mind, fluttering just out of reach. "There's no A5," he said again.

Mr. Unger said, "Do you think that's important?"

"Maybe," said Winston, rubbing his forehead. The first pair was C3. If that represented some other letter, what letter could it be? Maybe it was three letters past C . . . which meant F.

Winston's eyes widened.

Mr. Unger saw that. "You have an idea, don't you? Did you just solve it?"

"I think so," Winston said, and told him his idea.

The principal took the paper back. "So then J plus five is the letter O . . . S plus two is the letter U . . . and Q plus one is R."

"That spells FOUR," Winston said, getting more and more excited.

They went through the whole code, counting out the alphabet again and again like students in a very strange nursery school. When they were done, they sat back and looked at what they had written:

FOUR ZERO EIGHT SEVEN FOUR EIGHT SIX

Winston was elated, but the principal was frowning at the answer. "Seven numbers," said Mr. Unger. "That's not a very satisfying solution. What does it mean?"

Winston said, "Maybe it's a phone number."

Mr. Unger rubbed the top of his balding head. "What *is* this? If somebody wanted me to call them, why not just give me the number? Or, heck, why not call *me*? What's with all this spy movie stuff?"

"I don't know," said Winston. "Let's call it and see."

A look of bewilderment on his face, Mr. Unger reached over and hit the speaker button on his sleek black telephone. A dial tone filled the room. The principal booped in the seven digits. There was a long, tense pause as the phone rang several times, and then a gentle click, followed by a booming megaphone of a voice. Mr. Unger hastily lowered the volume a couple of notches.

"You did it!" said the voice. "You, my friends, have broken the code! And now I would like to warmly invite you to a very special contest. I am Dmitri Simon, the president of Simon's Snack Foods. And I am going to give fifty thousand dollars to one lucky school." Mr. Unger's jaw dropped open. "You've solved the first puzzle, but there will be many more puzzles to solve. On this Friday, May 18, at ten A.M., send three students and one teacher to Simon's Snack Foods, 1 Livingston Avenue, in Maplewood. At the tone, please tell me the name of your school, so that I know who to expect. And congratulations on making it this far. I will see you soon!"

There was a sudden beep, and the principal leaned in and said quickly, "Walter Fredericks Junior High, Glenville. Bernard Unger, principal."

Mr. Unger turned off the phone. His eyes were wide open and dazzled. "Fifty thousand dollars. Did he say fifty thousand dollars? If we solve a puzzle contest?" He gripped his armrests as if he thought his chair might suddenly fly. "Can this be real?" he said.

"You can call the company and find out," Winston said.

The principal nodded. "I will. I definitely will."

A slow smile crept to Winston's face. "If it *is* real, I volunteer to be one of those students," he said.

"What? Of course you do. You *better*," said Mr. Unger. "Get two more kids. Whoever you want. Fifty thousand dollars!" The principal stood up, his eyes full of wonder. He looked like he had just seen a magician do the most amazing trick ever. "I'll find a teacher to go with you," he said. "It's the day after school ends, and technically, everyone will be on vacation. But I know a few of them won't mind. Yes. Let me think. . . ." He gazed thoughtfully up at the ceiling. After a moment, he began pacing again.

Winston got the feeling his meeting with the principal was over. Mr. Unger now looked positively giddy, like a man who has just arrived at his own surprise birthday party. "We can't lose, can we? We just can't lose!"

"I don't know," said Winston. "I don't want to *promise* anything—"

"Oh, I know, I know," said the principal. "But I can feel it. Go! Get your team together! We don't have much time! Just a couple of days! We're going to win!"

Winston nodded enthusiastically and backed out of the office. He didn't tell the principal that he didn't need to get his team together— he knew exactly who his teammates were going to be. All he had to do now was tell them. Winston took off running down the hallway.

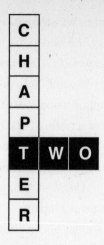

THE NEXT PERIOD WAS social studies, the one class he shared with Mal and Jake, his two best friends. The bell rang, and the hallway filled with kids. Winston ran as fast as he could through the crowd, weaving between groups of kids like someone in urgent need of a bathroom. That wasn't the problem, but it sure felt like *something* might explode, if he didn't tell his friends the exciting news.

When he reached the classroom, Mal and Jake were already sitting there, laughing about something. Winston started talking even before he reached them. He barely knew which wonderful thing to share first, and he wound up saying something like, "There's a puzzle thing, and we can be the team! And all the money's for the school!"

His friends gawked at him like he was insane.

"Was that English?" said Mal.

"I heard the word *puzzle*," said Jake.

"There's a surprise," said Mal.

Winston took a breath, sat down at his desk, and tried again. This time he managed to tell the story in something resembling a logical order, though he had to speed up the ending a little as their teacher, Mr. Nelson, breezed in, shutting the door behind him.

Tossing his briefcase onto his chair, Mr. Nelson said, "All right, all right, the school year may be coming to an end, but this is still my time, and we have work to do." There was a murmur of disapproval from Winston's classmates but no real surprise. Mr. Nelson wasn't one of those teachers who played games with the kids during the final week of school. He intended to teach them right up to the last bell on the last day. Indeed, if the bell system in the school ever broke down, Mr. Nelson would likely keep lecturing until the end of the world.

Winston tried to squeak in the conclusion to his story. He whispered, "And I can choose whoever I want for the team. You guys in?"

Mr. Nelson pegged him with a chilly stare. "Winston Breen, who should be speaking?"

Winston sat a little more attentively. "Not me," he said.

"Kee-rect," Mr. Nelson said. He turned to the class at large. "We're going to go over your final essays today. How have some of you managed to get through this entire school year without learning how to write? Let's take a few examples here. . . ."

Winston was still vibrating like a tuning fork. He'd blurted out his story about the puzzle hunt, but he didn't know if his friends would be able to join him. He looked at them, eyebrows raised in a querying *Well . . . ?*

Jake glanced over at him, saw his expression, and nodded, smiling. He was in. Mal saw the exchange and nodded too. Winston sat back, pleased beyond measure. He had his team. Friday was going to be a great day.

*   *   *

The next class was science, but Winston wasn't there for very long. In a way, he was *never* there. He was off in daydream land from the first minute, wondering what would happen on Friday. Would they simply be handed a bunch of puzzles to solve? Would they have to run around looking for things? He envisioned a hundred kids set loose in the Simon's Snack Foods factory, dashing between giant popcorn poppers and potato chip fryers, dodging splashes of hot oil in search of a vital clue.

How many other schools had received the code, and how many had cracked it? Would some of the teams have bigger kids from high school? Winston thought he could stand his ground in a puzzle competition against kids his own age. He wasn't sure if that would be true against high-schoolers.

He was brought back to reality by a knock on the classroom door.

Mr. Garvey, a math teacher who taught the advanced kids, peeked in. "I wonder if I might speak to Mr. Breen for a moment," he said. The class turned, and everyone gave Winston a look that was half curiosity and half pity.

The science teacher nodded, and Winston followed Mr. Garvey out into the cool, empty hallway. Mr. Garvey was a tall man with salt-and-pepper hair and thick matching eyebrows. He had a series of wavy, wrinkly lines in his forehead, as if he had gone into deep thought one day and had never come back out. Mr. Garvey smiled down at him, adding a few more wrinkles to that wide forehead. "Well," he said, "Winston Breen. I don't think we've officially met."

"In the cafeteria a couple of times," Winston said, "when it was your turn to watch everyone."

"Ah, yes," said Mr. Garvey. "You'll excuse me if I don't recall. That must mean you're one of the good kids. I spend those shifts in the cafeteria making sure the troublemakers don't start using the chicken fingers and fish sticks as deadly weapons. I'm sure eating them is deadly enough." Mr. Garvey laughed at his joke.

Winston smiled, but with some effort. Mr. Garvey's laugh didn't sound altogether real. It was the laugh of a dentist looking to lighten the mood before he stuck something sharp in your mouth. Winston thought he knew why Mr. Garvey was here.

Sure enough, Mr. Garvey said next, "So, our principal has shared a fascinating story with me."

"Oh?"

"He's asked me to accompany you on this puzzle expedition on Friday. And of course, I agreed."

Winston nodded, not daring to let his smile falter. This was exactly what he'd been afraid of. Mr. Garvey was nobody's favorite teacher. The students in his advanced math class dreaded being called upon—if they got an answer wrong, Mr. Garvey was more than happy to make fun of them in front of the whole class. It was even rumored that Mr. Garvey once made his entire Mathletes team cry after they had lost a crucial match.

Winston was on track to be in Mr. Garvey's class the following year and wasn't looking forward to it. Now it looked like he was going to get the full Garvey Experience a few months earlier than expected.

Mr. Garvey said, "I'm looking forward to working with you on this, Winston. Of course, I'm aware of your reputation as a puzzle lover. Quick! Why did the chicken cross the road?"

Winston looked startled. "Uh," he said. That was a riddle from first grade. Was Mr. Garvey serious?

Mr. Garvey smiled even more broadly and smacked Winston lightly on the shoulder. He said, "Just kidding. I'm sure you're light-years beyond silly little riddles. Indeed, I think you'll prove to be the cornerstone of the team, and I applaud Mr. Unger for bringing you on board." Mr. Garvey beamed down at him. "Say, I've got a little puzzle for you, if you want to hear it. A *real* puzzle. Nothing to do with chickens."

Winston nodded. "Sure."

"A math puzzle, of course, since that's my field. Ready?"

"Sure," Winston said again.

Mr. Garvey cleared his throat a little and said, "I went to a horse race, and I counted all of the horses' legs plus all of the jockeys' legs. The total came to 108. How many horses were in the race?"

(Answer, page 239.)

After Winston had solved the puzzle, Mr. Garvey said, "I wanted to talk to you about who the other teammates should be. There are a few sharp kids on my Mathletes team. I don't know if you know them. . . ."

Winston looked surprised. "I already chose my teammates," he said.

Mr. Garvey stared down at him. His fatherly smile tightened but did not fade. "You did? Don't you suppose we might have collaborated on this?"

"I didn't know you were going to be the chaperone."

All at once, Mr. Garvey's smile collapsed and vanished. Without it, Mr. Garvey's face took on a chiseled-from-stone look. He said sharply, "I'm not going to be a chaperone, Winston. I will be a coach, mentor, and guide. It's not my job to drive you around. It's my job to see that we win. You understand that, don't you?"

Winston nodded and tried not to look as sick as he was starting to feel. "Yes. Sorry," he said.

"And part of that job," Mr. Garvey continued, "is making sure we have the best possible team. Who is it that you've chosen to join us?"

"My friends Mal and Jake."

The math teacher took a deep breath. "Would I know either of these young men?"

"I don't know. Mal is in the drama club. And Jake is on the baseball team."

"An actor and an athlete," said Mr. Garvey.

"Actually, Mal works backstage."

Mr. Garvey nodded and flicked a hand in the air, not caring if Mal worked onstage, backstage, or collected tickets. "I'm sure they're very good at what they do," he said. "But I don't think there's going to be much call for moving props around or tackling the other team."

Winston couldn't believe it. Mr. Garvey wanted to kick Mal and Jake off the team. He tried not to let panic show in his voice. "They're good puzzle solvers. They both are."

Mr. Garvey sighed and stared at Winston thoughtfully. "Winston, do you want to win this thing?"

"Yes. Sure I do."

Mr. Garvey found his smile again. "I believe you. I really do." But he shrugged, and the smile turned doubtful. "You also, I imagine, want to hang out with your friends and have a good time. Don't you?"

"Well, yeah."

"That is my point," said the teacher. "You have the whole summer to have fun with your friends. I think it would be better if you considered Friday's adventure to be an important job you've been asked to do. That *we* have been asked to do. You and I."

A job? Mowing the lawn—*that* was a job. This was a spectacular event that he could hardly wait to begin. Still, he understood what

Mr. Garvey was getting at, and he said, "We're going to take it very seriously. We're not going to goof around. I promise. We all want to win."

Mr. Garvey nodded, that doubtful expression lingering on his face. "I'm sure. I'm sure. And you say your friends are good puzzle solvers. Maybe that's so. But I teach the advanced math classes here and run the math club, as well. We have some very bright students who I think might be a better fit on something like this."

"I already told my friends they could come along."

"Yes, yes. That is regrettable. I tried to contact you quickly so that we might work together to build the best possible team. You work fast."

"Mr. Unger said I could choose whoever I wanted," Winston said.

Mr. Garvey's eyes flared. "And maybe he got a little caught up in the excitement of the moment. Perhaps he forgot to consider what was best for the school."

Winston shook his head. "I can't just tell them they're not invited."

"No, no, I wouldn't make you do that," Mr. Garvey said with sympathy. "You leave that to me. I'll tell them it was a misunderstanding and that you didn't have the authority to invite them in the first place. They'll get over it, I promise. I'll have the main office page them right after class. What did you say their names were again?"

Winston was frozen. All he could do was blink stupidly at the math teacher. The simple act of saying his friends' names felt like a betrayal. How had everything fallen apart so quickly?

And who would replace Jake and Mal? The advanced math kids were all older—Winston hardly knew them. He'd be solving with strangers instead of with his best friends. In no time flat, Mr. Garvey had ripped all the fun out of a one-of-a-kind experience.

Mr. Garvey said, "Winston? Hello?"

Not really thinking about what he was about to do, Winston said slowly, "That's all right. I'll tell them. You're forming your own team."

Mr. Garvey looked surprised. "Are you sure? I know they're your friends. I don't mind breaking the news to them. If they're going to be angry at someone, let them be angry at me."

"No, I'll do it. I'll tell them all three of us are being replaced."

"What?" Now it was Mr. Garvey's turn to blink. "No, no. You're still on the team."

Winston shook his head. "I don't want to do it without my friends," he said. Which wasn't exactly true. He wanted to do it very much, and he could hardly believe the words that were coming out of his mouth. But in some way he couldn't explain, *not* going was more important than going without Jake and Mal. He'd read about it afterward, or call up the company and see if he could get the puzzles when the event was done. It wouldn't be the same thing, but he couldn't invite his friends and then just as quickly cut them out. They would understand, and they probably wouldn't hold it against Winston. But they would also remember.

Mr. Garvey, frowning, stared at Winston. He said, "I thought solving puzzles was your favorite thing to do."

"It is."

"But you're going to pass up a full day of solving puzzles, simply because your friends can't come along? That seems a little foolish to me, Winston. If you don't mind me saying."

Winston shrugged. He gazed off down the hallway—he couldn't look at Mr. Garvey full in the face. "I think I'd feel bad all day long," he said, keeping his voice calm. "I told them they could come, and then if they're not there . . . I guess I just don't think it would be fun."

Mr. Garvey said, "Maybe it wouldn't be fun. Maybe it would be hard work. But at the end of the day, you'd bring home a large financial reward to your school. Doesn't that make it worth it? Why don't you think of it *that* way?"

Winston said nothing. He was afraid Mr. Garvey would talk him out of quitting. Part of him was *hoping* this would happen.

Mr. Garvey continued, "I think you have a responsibility, Winston, to attend this event and do your best at it. No matter who your team-mates are."

A new, small realization poked its way through Winston's anger and disappointment. In fact, it felt a little bit like solving a puzzle: He'd picked up on the clues that were right in front of him and under-stood how they fit neatly together. Mr. Garvey had an entire class of smart kids to draw from, and yet he was trying quite hard to convince Winston to stay on the team. Quite hard.

"This is an opportunity for you," Mr. Garvey said, "to give some-thing back to your school. Do you understand?"

Winston said, "You really want me to be on the team."

Mr. Garvey gave a small bark of laughter. "That's what I'm trying to tell you."

"You don't think you can win without me."

Mr. Garvey looked surprised and then turned stony again. "I wouldn't go that far. I teach a lot of bright students. Some of them like puzzles very much."

"This will be more than math puzzles, though," Winston said. "It'll probably be all kinds of puzzles."

Mr. Garvey nodded slowly, aware he was being backed up against a cliff. "You're probably right. That's why I think it would be best if you stayed on the team."

Mentally crossing his fingers, Winston said, "I'll stay on the team if my friends can stay."

The math teacher crossed his arms. "And if not?"

Winston shrugged again.

The stony look on Mr. Garvey's face intensified. He shook his head in disbelief. "Are you playing hardball with me, Winston?"

"No," Winston said, although he knew the answer was yes. "I'm just saying that we already have a good team. That's the team I want to be on."

The teacher gaped down at him for several moments. He blew out a long breath and said, "Look at this from my point of view. Who are these friends of yours? They aren't elite students, or I'd have heard of them. One of them may be a fine athlete, but athletes don't tend to be master puzzle solvers." He searched around for some new way to salvage the situation and settled on, "Did I mention to you how much I want to win this thing?"

"They're both good thinkers," said Winston. "We're a good team. You'll see."

Mr. Garvey thought about it, shook his head briefly, and threw his arms out wide in a gesture of surrender. "I guess I will. You win, Mr. Breen."

Winston was hugely relieved. "Thank you," he said. He almost extended an arm to shake Mr. Garvey's hand in gratitude but stopped himself from doing that. "It'll be fine, I promise."

Mr. Garvey nodded, not wanting to discuss it any further. Winston was happy, but Mr. Garvey clearly was not. The teacher dug through the leather bag he was carrying and brought out a piece of paper and a pen. "Give me your address," he said. "I'll pick all three of you up at your house at eight thirty on Friday morning."

Winston wrote his address and handed it to the math teacher. Mr. Garvey glanced at it, then said, "Okay. I'll see you in a couple of days. Be ready." He stalked off down the hall, all in a rush.

No, he definitely didn't look happy.

"YAAAGH!" cried the knight as the blade of a sword separated his head from his body. The headless knight fell to his knees and turned to dust. Then the dust itself vanished. When things died in this video game, they died *permanently*.

"You did it again!" said Jake, frustrated. "How did you do that?"

"When you just stand there gaping, you make it real easy," said Mal.

"I don't just stand there!"

"You do, all the time! I can tell when you're trying to push the buttons for a special move. You take your eyes off the game and look at the controller, and your knight stands there like he's birdwatching or something."

Jake stood up, aggravated. "This joystick has more buttons than an airplane cockpit," he said. "Who can keep track of them all?"

"Yeah, yeah," said Mal. He turned to Winston, who was on the couch waiting for his turn. "Win! You're up. Your turn to take on the master." He blew on his knuckles like his hands were registered weapons.

They'd been addicted to *10,000 Swords* for a few weeks now, and even though it was Winston who owned the game, Mal had become the undisputed champion. Winston was passable, but Jake, considering his dexterity on the baseball field, was surprisingly hopeless. He once impaled himself on his own sword before his opponent could get a swing at him. They couldn't even figure out how Jake had done it. They'd spent half an hour trying to do it again, with no success.

Jake moved to the sofa, and Winston picked up the controller. Mal pushed the start button, and two warriors prepared to duel in a bleak castle dungeon.

As the swords clanged together, Jake said, "So is there anything we have to do to get ready for this contest?"

Winston shook his head, focused on the game. "I can't think of anything. I wish there was. I hate waiting."

Mal's knight jumped around, baiting Winston into making a move. Mal said, "And we're stuck with Mr. Garvey as our chaperone? Can't we get anybody else? I mean it—anybody else on earth?"

"I wish," said Winston. "But Mr. Unger chose him, so that means he's the guy. There aren't that many teachers willing to give up their first day of summer vacation."

"I never thought of it as *their* summer vacation," said Jake.

"Yeah, me neither," said Mal. His fighter lunged forward.

The phone rang. "KATIE, GET THE PHONE," Winston yelled up to his sister, while his fighter ran away from his opponent. The phone rang again. "KATIE!"

"Want me to get it?" said Jake.

"Yeah. Ugh!" Mal's fighter smacked him a good one.

Jake picked up the receiver. "Hello?" He listened for a moment. "No, he's in a swordfight right now. Who is this?" He listened for a moment and then said, "Who?"

Winston glanced over and saw confusion on Jake's face. That was all the opening Mal needed, and a moment later, Winston's knight was a pile of dust dissolving on the castle floor. "Oh, nuts," said Winston. "That's not fair. I got distracted."

"That's why you're dead," Mal pointed out.

Jake waved the phone and said, "He won't say who he is."

Winston stood up. "Huh? What do you mean?" He took the phone. "Hello?"

"Winston Breen?" It was a deep male voice.

"Yeah?" said Winston.

"Did you break the code?" This was said in what Winston guessed was supposed to be an ominous, mysterious tone. It didn't quite get there. And now that the voice had said more than two words, Winston thought it might be a kid lowering his voice to sound older.

"Who is this?" he said.

His question was ignored. "Did you break the code?" whoever it was asked again, in the slow, deep voice of a summoned demon in a horror movie. Except this voice cracked a little on the final word.

Well, he must be talking about the principal's code—the one that got them into the puzzle event. What else could he mean? Winston said, "Yes, I did."

"Then . . . I'll be seeing you," said the voice, dropping to a dramatic whisper. There was a click as the mystery caller hung up.

What was *that*? Winston, baffled, slowly hung up and stared at the phone as if another bizarre call might come through at any second.

Mal and Jake were looking at him. "So who was it?" Mal asked.

"He didn't say."

His friends glanced at each other. "Well, what did he want?"

"He wanted to know if I cracked the code. And he wanted to tell me that he'd be seeing me."

They considered that.

"Okay. That's really creepy," said Jake. "Do you know who it was?"

"I just told you. He didn't say his name."

"Yeah, but you're Mr. Puzzle Solver, so maybe you figured it out anyway."

Winston shook his head. "I have no idea."

Mal flopped back to the floor and picked up the video game joystick. "Eh. Crank call," he said. "If he'll be seeing you, I guess we'll know soon enough. Who wants to play? Jake, you're up."

Jake looked disgusted. "Forget it. I'm done."

"Win?" said Mal.

"Yeah, sure. One more game." But he couldn't shake off the strange phone call. Who *was* that?

Frowning and distracted and knowing that Mal was about to wipe the floor with him, he nonetheless sat down and started a new sword-fight. Jake threw himself back on the sofa.

Winston shook his head and tried to move the phone call to a holding cell in his brain, to think about later. "Hey, Jake," said Winston as he took the controller. "If you don't want to play this anymore, I know something else you can do."

"What?" said Jake.

"There's something fun that you can do that contains the letters of SWORD in that order, but has nothing to do with swords."

Jake nodded, unsurprised. Puzzles popped out of Winston with no notice. "And I have to figure out what that is."

"Well, I'll tell you later if you can't get it."

(Answer, page 239.)

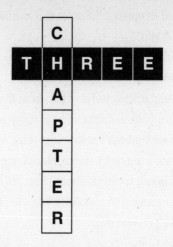

THE LAST TIME Winston participated in a large-scale puzzle event, he'd woken up at dawn and spent several hours wandering around his house, urging time to go faster. Time refused. Winston had pulled his hair out in frustration as he watched the minutes crawl, crawl, crawl.

When Winston opened his eyes on Friday morning, he knew immediately that the same thing was going to happen again. The light in his room was wrong—instead of bright summer sun, it was a pale mixture of daylight and darkness. Bracing himself for the worst, he rolled over and looked at his clock. Five forty-five. All year long he'd gotten up at seven o'clock, groaning and wishing for ten more minutes of sleep. Now, on the first day of summer vacation, he was awake and raring to go before full sunrise.

There was nothing to be done about it. He was awake like it was high noon. Winston got up and wandered around the house. There was nobody to talk to—his parents and sister were still asleep. He flipped through the television stations, but the only things on were news shows, infomercials, and cartoons for babies.

On one channel, though, he came across a commercial for Simon's Potato Chips. He knew it was unlikely to contain any clues for today's event, but he still had to stop and watch it. The commercial showed a bunch of young people, supposedly at a party, except that everybody was standing around, bored and glum. Suddenly a guy with a wide smile showed up holding a bag of (new!) Simon's Potato Squares, and the party was transformed: The music began thumping, and guest after guest grabbed handfuls of chips, which were indeed perfectly square. Fueled by this magical new snack food, everyone began dancing and chatting and having fun. "Think square!" said the guy who had brought the chips, his teeth flashing white as he held up the bag for the camera.

Winston turned off the television, amused. Did people really believe this? That a bag of potato chips could turn a boring party into New Year's Eve? Winston guessed that commercials like this must work at least sometimes, since it seemed like every other ad followed the same script.

The commercial gave him an idea, though. He went back to his room and went online to look up information about Dmitri Simon, the founder of Simon's Snack Foods and the guy whose voice they had heard on the answering machine.

The company Web site had most of what he wanted to know. A page marked "History" showed a big picture of Dmitri Simon's pudgy, smiling, bearded face. Simon had started his company after being fired from five jobs in a row. He made the first batches of his now-famous potato chips in a pizzeria's kitchen. He started off by selling them to delis and other stores out of the back of his car.

People loved them, and he soon had more requests for his chips than he could handle. He borrowed money from everyone he knew and opened a small factory. Now he was one of the richest men in the state.

He was also one of the *oddest* men in the state, as Winston learned while searching the Net for more information. Simon had more money than he knew what to do with, and he gave a lot of it away. Rather than merely writing a check, however, Simon enjoyed attaching the money to crazy stunts. He funded a local museum for a full year but insisted on an exhibit of "potato chip art," whatever that was. He built a playground for a children's hospital . . . but only after the doctors at various hospitals had competed in some kind of nutty Doctor Olympics, with track-and-field events. The winning team of physicians got the playground. And Dmitri Simon got tons of coverage in the newspapers and on television.

Would any of this help today? Winston didn't know. But he doubted he and his friends would be handed a bunch of word searches and pencil puzzles. Dmitri Simon enjoyed stunts that were big and goofy. Winston would try to remember not to be surprised by anything: With this guy's money and wacky ideas, anything was possible.

Winston looked at the clock again and sighed—6:05 A.M. He'd killed twenty minutes. He had another full hour before he even needed to get dressed.

He wandered the house a while more and then finally grabbed a puzzle magazine and stretched out on the sofa. It was going to be a long wait, but at least he had a puzzle to solve in the meanwhile.

WIS	AKE	ACK
AST	COL	ARK
CHO	DEM	ATE
PAR	ECR	AUT
QUA	LIF	ETS
TRA	RON	IED

You can take a three-letter puzzle piece from each of the three columns, and read across to make a series of nine-letter words. If you write these words in the order shown below, you'll find an extra phrase reading down in two places.

WIS __ __ __ __ __ __
AST __ __ __ __ __ __
CHO __ __ __ __ __ __
PAR __ __ __ __ __ __
QUA __ __ __ __ __ __
TRA __ __ __ __ __ __

(Answer, page 239.)

*   *   *

Jake and Mal were dropped off shortly after eight o'clock. Winston's mother had already left for work. His dad worked at home in the summer—soon he would go edit magazine articles, but right now he was cleaning up breakfast. And Winston's little sister, Katie, was sitting on the sofa, her arms crossed in an exaggerated mope. Her school wasn't participating in the big contest. Perhaps her principal never figured out the code, or elementary schools weren't sent the code in the first place. Either way, she was ticked.

She spent the morning trying to convince Winston to take her along. When that didn't work, she tried getting her parents to *make* Winston take her along. That didn't work, either. Now she wasn't talking to him, and instead of being happy that it was the first day of summer vacation, she was acting like she was locked in a Siberian prison.

"Hi, Katie," said Jake as he walked in.

"Hmmph," Katie said back, crossing her arms tighter.

Seeing that she was angry about something, Mal instinctively had to make things worse. "Katie!" he shouted. "Give me a hug!" He advanced toward her, his arms outstretched.

Katie was shocked right out of her mood. "Gah!" she said, leaping onto the back of the sofa and jumping off the other side. "Get away from me! Gross!" She ran up the stairs to her room, slamming her door as hard as she could.

Winston's father poked his head in. "What was that?" he said.

"Your daughter loves me," said Mal.

"Oh." Nathan Breen was used to Mal. He went back to whatever he was doing in the kitchen without further comment.

The wait continued, although at least now Winston had his friends with him. The three boys briefly considered playing their video game, but they were too restless. They paced around and tried to guess what might happen today. Winston told them about the oddball publicity stunts Dmitri Simon had pulled off in the past.

"So it's impossible to say what we'll be asked to do," Winston said.

"We should bring a bunch of random stuff with us. Maybe some of it will come in handy," said Jake.

"A box of paper clips," said Mal. "A birthday cake. A scuba diving suit."

Jake stared at Mal. "I meant random stuff that's not completely crazy."

"What's crazy about a scuba diving suit?" Mal wanted to know. "You'll apologize when we have to swim to the bottom of the river to get a clue."

They bantered and bickered a while more. Winston wondered, not for the first time, if he should tell Mal and Jake how close they had come to getting kicked off the team. He'd gone back and forth on that over the last several days. Ultimately, he decided to keep his mouth shut. He only hoped that Mr. Garvey would do likewise. But Winston could practically hear the teacher sighing and saying "My *smart* students would have known that" as they all faced a tough puzzle.

Winston wished again that he had been able to choose the team's chaperone. And he supposed that Mr. Garvey still wished he could have chosen his own team. Well, they'd all have to find a way to work together.

Mr. Garvey pulled in at eight twenty-five. The three boys and Winston's father filed onto the porch to meet him. "And here's my team," said Mr. Garvey, smiling as he got out of his car. There were hellos all around. Mr. Garvey and Nathan Breen shook hands. The two men made a minute's worth of small talk. If Mr. Garvey was still upset at Winston's insistence on including Mal and Jake, he kept it well hidden.

"Shotgun!" Mal called, so he took the passenger seat while Winston and Jake got in the back. There was a small cargo area behind them, holding a baby seat (it was always strange to be reminded that teachers had families of their own), a couple of grocery bags containing snacks, and a small cooler.

"What's with the food?" asked Jake as Mr. Garvey got into the driver's seat.

"Ah," said Mr. Garvey, starting the car. "That's called thinking ahead. I'm guessing this is going to be an all-day affair, so I've loaded up on supplies. If we don't have to stop for food, we'll have that much more of an edge on our competition."

"Do you have a Porta Potti back there?" Mal asked.

Mr. Garvey gave Mal a sideways look. "We might take a little break now and again, if need be," he said. "Here," he continued, handing Mal a piece of paper. "You just volunteered to be the team navigator."

"I did?" said Mal. "Oh. I did." He took the paper and unfolded it. It was a map. "Okay," he said. "Step one: Leave the driveway."

Mr. Garvey did as he was told. As they drove along, Mr. Garvey said, "Let me explain a few things about how today is going to work." Winston already didn't like the sound of that. The teacher continued, "I know you all think summer vacation has started. As far as I'm concerned, however, today is a school day. This is a field trip, and I'm the guy in charge. All right?"

"All right," said Winston. He and Jake shared a bemused look.

"I told Winston a couple of days ago, and I'll tell you two right now: We're here to win. And if you boys stay serious and focused, and if you listen to me and do what I say, we *will* win." Mr. Garvey drummed his fingers on the steering wheel. "I hope we have fun today, don't get me wrong. But our first priority is not to have fun. What did I just say?"

Mal said, with a tone of disbelief, "We're not supposed to have fun."

"You can have fun," Mr. Garvey corrected him. "Of course you can have fun. But that is not the main reason we are here. We are here to get these puzzles solved. We're going to do it quickly, we're going to do it efficiently. That . . . *that* is what we're here to do."

As pep talks went, this was more alarming than inspiring. Sure, Winston wanted to win, but he was troubled by Mr. Garvey's fervor, and he was sure that Mal and Jake were, too.

Mr. Garvey seemed to sense that. He said, "Jake, I'm sure your baseball coach says something like that before every game. Right?"

"Something like that," Jake said. He made a face at Winston that said, "Not even close."

The math teacher wanted to close the subject. He said, "All right. Let's warm up our brains a little. Winston, do you have any puzzles for us?"

Winston looked around. They were coming up to a red light near a small row of stores. He studied the stores for a few moments and said, "You see that store where you can buy kitchen stuff?"

"Yeah," Jake said.

"You might go there if you wanted to buy a PLATE."

"Okay. . . ."

Winston continued, "You can add a letter to the word PLATE and then scramble all the letters. You'll wind up with something you can buy in the art supply store right next door. Then you can add a letter to *that* word, scramble the letters again, and get something you can buy in the office supply store. Then you can do it one more time—take the item from the office supply store, add a letter, scramble, and you'll get something you can buy in the garden center. Can you get them all?"

"Holy moly," said Mal. "Not before the light turns green."

| Kitchen | Art Supply | Office Supply | Garden |
| Store | Store | Store | Center |

(Answer, page 240.)

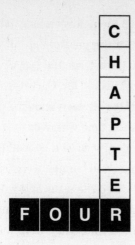

CHAPTER FOUR

SIMON'S SNACK FOODS was in Maplewood, the next town over. The factory was huge, with pipes jutting out of the walls and roof. Every pipe emitted smoke or steam in various shades of gray. Winston imagined that Dmitri Simon would have a crazy, Willy Wonka–like factory, but this was a disappointingly normal brick building. Also, Winston had expected an overwhelming odor of frying potato chips, but the air here was just air.

The office building, on the other hand, was more eye-catching. It was glass and steel, and had been designed by someone with a sense of humor. It went off at all kinds of odd angles and had shiny metal beams sticking out for no particular reason. The office was attached to the factory, and the effect was that of a flashy sports car towing a dump truck.

In the parking lot, there was a section roped off for visitors. As they got out of the car, Mr. Garvey said, "I want us all to stay together." The universal command of teachers escorting students on a field trip.

The pretty receptionist pointed them down a long hallway before Mr. Garvey could even speak. "All the puzzlers are meeting in the main conference room," she said. "You'll see the signs."

"How many puzzlers are there?" asked Mr. Garvey.

"I have no idea. You'll meet them all soon enough." She pointed again, all but declaring that question time was over.

They passed a number of small offices as they walked down the hall. Phones were ringing, and men and women were at their desks doing who knew what. They followed the signs and wound up outside a closed door with a sign that said "Puzzlers Welcome." Winston felt an electric tingle in his bloodstream. They were minutes away from the true start of the day.

Mr. Garvey said, "All right, boys. Best behavior. No spitballs or flamethrowers."

"I left my flamethrower at home," said Mal.

"Mine's broken," said Jake.

Mr. Garvey nodded, accepting this bit of humor. He opened the door.

The main conference room had a hundred seats or more. Groups of three or four seats were fastened to their own little tables facing a small stage. The stage, at the moment, was empty.

There were a couple dozen kids here with their adult chaperones. Some kids were pacing, while others sat and chatted with their teammates. There was a tension in the air, the kind that precedes an exciting event you know is supposed to happen at any moment.

Mr. Garvey led his team to one of the empty tables. Nearby teams eyed them curiously. Winston saw that all the kids were about his age—no little kids from an elementary school and no high-schoolers, either. So Dmitri Simon must have restricted the contest to middle schools, after all. This was good.

"I wonder how many teams there'll be," said Jake. He swiveled back and forth in his chair, restless. A lot of kids were swiveling.

"They must be coming from all over the state, don't you think?" said Winston.

"I hope not," said Mr. Garvey. "The fewer the better." Something across the room caught his attention. "Oh, no," he said.

"What's wrong?"

"Lincoln is here," Mr. Garvey said with quiet horror.

"Abraham?" asked Mal.

The math teacher set his jaw, as if jokes were not appropriate at a time like this. "Lincoln Junior High. Well, of course they would be here. That's Rod Denham, their Mathlete adviser. I bet he has three kids from their math team here."

"Are they good?" Jake asked.

"They're very good. In fact"—there was the slightest pause before Mr. Garvey said, "we've never beaten them." He shook his head, as if this news could hardly be worse.

The teacher in question, Rod Denham, was a short, wide fellow wearing a brown sportcoat. He was talking with two boys and a girl, all of whom were listening intently. Mr. Denham must have felt them staring—he suddenly glanced over and, seeing Mr. Garvey, waved, an ironic smirk on his face.

"Oh, he saw us," Mr. Garvey said unhappily. "Be good for a moment, I have to say hello." Mr. Garvey got up and approached his rival with a wide smile, his arms spread in warm greeting.

Winston guessed that Mr. Garvey regretted, more than ever, not replacing all three of them with students from his math class. Well, it was too late now. He swiveled in his chair and watched more teams come in.

"You're Winston Breen!" said a voice behind him.

Winston swiveled around, and so did Mal and Jake. A boy was standing there. His hair was unbrushed and pointing every which way, and he wore an expression of wide-eyed delight. He said, "Right? You're Winston Breen! I knew you'd be here today. You *had* to be."

Winston said, "Uh."

The boy continued, glowing like a child meeting Santa Claus. "I read about you in the paper. When you found that buried treasure? Remember?"

"Uh," Winston said again. He wanted to say, "No one *forgets* finding buried treasure," but was too startled to find the words. Who was this kid?

Whoever he was, he kept talking. "I wish I could find buried treasure. But this will be just as good, don't you think? What do you suppose the puzzles will be like? Maybe they'll be really hard! I hope not. I don't like getting stuck on a puzzle. But I want them to be a little hard, because I don't want them to be too easy. You know? I hope they're just right."

Mal finally cut in, waving his hands to get the boy's attention. "Hey!" he said.

The boy, startled, turned away from Winston, as if he hadn't been aware of anyone else sitting there. The boy's big eyes blinked.

Mal, not unkindly, said, "Who are you?"

"Oh. Me? I'm Brendan. Brendan Root. I go to West Meadow. That's my team over there." He pointed to two kids, who were playing rock-paper-scissors, and their teacher, who was reading the sports section of the newspaper. "I'm not really friends with them, but they asked me because they know I like puzzles. Not as much as *you*," Brendan said suddenly, as if afraid he had offended Winston. "But I like them. What do you think the puzzles will be like today? Hard, right?"

"Maybe," said Winston. He was glad to have gotten a word into this conversation. Maybe in time he could work his way up to longer sentences.

"I hope they're not too hard," Brendan said again. "Want to see a puzzle I made up?"

"Sure," said Winston.

"I made this up myself. Are you ready?"

"Yes!" Winston had been in Brendan Root's company for perhaps sixty seconds and was already fully exasperated.

"Okay, here it is." He took a crumpled-up piece of paper out of his pocket. "I wrote this down to show people. What do these words have in common?"

BONY EACH INK LACK LIVE OLD RAY RANGE

(Answer, page 240.)

After they had solved it, Brendan said, "Did you like it? Isn't that good?"

"Pretty good," Winston agreed.

"I bet you make up twenty of those a day," said Brendan.

"More like seventeen," Winston said, trying for a joke.

And the joke was apparently achieved, because Brendan threw his head back and laughed. "Seventeen!" he said. He laughed again for several moments and then said, "I'm glad you're here. I'm looking forward to beating you at this."

Winston blinked. He could almost hear Mal and Jake, on either side of him, also blinking. But Brendan Root just continued smiling.

"You think you're going to beat Winston?" said Mal.

Brendan shrugged. "Sure. I mean, I'm going to try. Right? You don't mind, do you, Winston?"

Winston shook his head. "No. No. Try your best."

"Nobody here likes puzzles more than you and me," said Brendan. "So one of our teams is going to win. I think it might be mine." He was beaming with pride, as if he had won already. He caught himself and tried on a serious expression. "But if you win, that's okay, too."

"Thanks," Winston said dryly. He was wondering how they were supposed to get rid of this kid when Brendan was called away by his teacher. He waved to them all, smiling gleefully, and walked back to his group. The three boys watched him go with a mixture of amusement and awe.

"Am I like that?" Winston said in a low voice.

"No," said Jake.

"Not even close," said Mal.

"You let other people talk sometimes," said Jake.

"Sometimes," Mal agreed. "It's been known to happen." They watched Brendan's teacher gather his students into a team meeting.

Jake said, "He's going to be tough, don't you think?"

Winston nodded. Brendan was a little weird. But weird did not mean dumb. Often the opposite, in fact.

There were enough people in the conference room now that the noise level had risen to a steady, murmuring hum. Winston kept glancing over to the door on the stage, which would surely open at any moment. He had an alarming thought: What if the contest had already started—if the puzzle was right here in front of them and Dmitri Simon was waiting for somebody clever enough to notice it?

Winston looked around for anything that might qualify as a clue and saw nothing. There were a number of whiteboards on the wall, but these were erased and gleaming. No. Nothing tricky was going on . . . yet. He was just going to have to sit back and wait for the event to begin. He drummed his fingers on the table and tried to be patient. He wished he had brought a puzzle book with him.

"Hey, look at that," Jake said, with some concern.

Winston glanced over to where he was pointing and was amazed to see Mr. Garvey, redfaced, waving a finger at that other teacher, Rod Denham. Mr. Garvey seemed to be lecturing him. Mr. Denham wore a tight, humorless smile, and after a moment pointed at Winston and his friends, as if suggesting that Mr. Garvey go back where he came from. They traded a few more words, glaring at each other, then Mr. Garvey turned around and stormed away.

As he returned to his team, Mr. Garvey's teeth were gritted and a vein pulsed on the side of his head—he looked ready to kill a small animal. He squeezed the back of one of the chairs, as if he might pull it up and throw it against the wall, and never mind the fact that the chairs were bolted to the floor. The three boys gazed up at him, amazed and a little afraid.

"What was that about?" Mal asked.

"I shouldn't have gone over there," Mr. Garvey said.

"Did he say something to you?" Jake said. "What did he say?"

Mr. Garvey waved a hand like he wanted to forget the whole thing. He attempted a little chuckle. It wasn't very believable. The boys kept looking at him, and finally Mr. Garvey had to say, "Let it go, boys. Just let it go." He sat down, folded his hands, and tried to regain his calm.

Letting it go wasn't easy, but Mr. Garvey wasn't talking, so it wasn't like they had a choice. The traffic through the entrance petered out, but there was still no sign of Dmitri Simon. Winston counted ten teams. Was that all? He would have thought there'd be double or triple that number. He felt a vague disappointment—he liked the idea of hundreds of puzzle lovers all congregating together. Of course, the fewer teams competing, the better their chances.

He cast his eyes over the small crowd, sizing up the competition. It was impossible to predict who the tough opponents would be . . . but that didn't stop Winston from trying. Rod Denham's team from Lincoln Junior High was clearly going to be trouble, although exactly what *sort* of trouble Winston could not guess.

What about the other teams?

Brendan Root might be a serious opponent, but were his two teammates just as good? Before, the two of them had been playing rock-paper-scissors. Now they were thumb wrestling. Maybe they didn't plan on taking this seriously?

Over on the right was a team that was *definitely* taking it seriously: They were dressed in identical blue T-shirts that said BROOKVILLE BRAINS, with matching baseball caps. Did they use those shirts for other events? If they had made up these outfits in the few days since the contest was announced, that indicated a level of organization that was almost scary to consider.

Looking around, Winston counted twice as many guys as girls. Only one team was all female. The girl in the middle had her arms crossed as if this delay was a personal insult. The girl to her left was looking around with a faraway smile on her face. The third girl looked too little to be here. They didn't have matching uniforms, but their identical stillness among so much bustle and noise made them seem very serious indeed. Their teacher, a woman with a sculpted frizz of red hair, nervously jangled several bracelets on her left wrist.

Winston decided the girls would be tough. He wondered where they were from.

He didn't have time to consider the rest of the teams, because at that moment the onstage door opened and Dmitri Simon bounded into the room, followed by two other men and one woman. The crowd exploded into delighted applause. Simon was dressed in jeans and a T-shirt, and by no means looked like a multimillionaire. He looked like he might run a comic book store, perhaps playing Dungeons and Dragons or Magic: The Gathering with the kids when business was slow. Simon was overweight—indeed, he was downright fat—and his black beard was scragglier than in the picture on the potato chip bags. He was also fantastically happy.

"Hello!" he said. He all but skipped to the podium, his arms wide as if he planned on giving everybody in the room a hug.

"Whoa," said Jake.

Mal laughed and said, "That's exactly what I imagined a guy who makes potato chips for a living would look like!" Mr. Garvey glared at him and told him to shush.

Simon leaned on the podium with his considerable body weight and beamed out at his audience as the applause tapered off. "Do you kids like puzzles?" Simon shouted, which brought the cheering back to a full boil.

Simon laughed. "Me, too. All right, let me see. . . . Here's one I like. . . . What's the longest word you can think of that spells another word backward? Anybody have any guesses?"

(Answer, page 240.)

They spent some time on that, and then Simon said, "Ahh, you kids are in for a treat today. A grand adventure! Congratulations to all of you for cracking the code and making it here today, and thank you to all the great teachers who are accompanying you." Simon clapped his hands, so everybody else did, too.

The large man looked around at all of them, smiling, in no apparent rush to get the event started. "Just ten teams," he said. "You know, I sent out forty of those secret messages to schools all around the area. I thought maybe half those schools would crack the code and send a team. Shows what I know! I was off by a bunch." He laughed, as if his miscalculation was the best joke of the day. "All right," he said when his laughter had subsided. "Let's take care of the paperwork part of the festivities, shall we? And then we can get the show on the road."

Simon pulled a folded piece of paper from his back pocket and smoothed it out on the podium.

"Let's see if everybody made it," he said. "Who's from Brookville Junior High?"

Those were the Brookville Brains. Upon hearing their name, their teacher jumped from his chair and whooped as if they had already won a prize. He tried urging his three students into showing some enthusiasm but got nowhere—all three of them were embarrassed rocks.

Simon laughed and said, "All right, there's some spirit! Cross Street School? Where are you?"

These were three boys Winston had noticed earlier and dismissed as goofballs—they had spent their waiting time not chatting or strategizing but wrestling and roughhousing until their teacher had to bark at them to sit down and keep quiet. Even now, the three boys all cupped their hands to their mouths and yelled "Here!" at the top of their lungs, then collapsed into snickering. Their teacher got red-faced again and smacked the nearest one on the back of the head. Who had sent *this* group after a fifty-thousand-dollar prize?

Simon read from his list again. "Demilla Academy?"

Ah, that was probably a private school. That explained the out-fits—the two girls were each wearing a starched white blouse and a stiff blue skirt, and the boy a fancy white shirt and tie. They looked like they were on their way to cater a wedding. Their teacher, who stood up and acknowledged their presence with a grave nod, was wearing a three-piece suit.

"Where's the funeral?" Mal whispered.

"Shhh," Jake said, but he couldn't help laughing.

Simon consulted his list again. "Greater Oaks Junior High?"

That was the all-girl team. "We're here," said their frizzy-haired teacher. She started to stand, but thought better of it. Then she realized that other teachers had stood, so maybe she should, too. She stood back up. "We're here," she said again, and sat back down. She was a bundle of nervous energy. Her three students glanced at each other, and Winston could see them rolling their eyes.

Despite the fact that every other team had simply said "here" when called upon, the woman accompanying the next team insisted on introducing herself and all three team members. "I'm Mary Noone, the vice principal of Kennedy Junior High, and these are the school's three very smart representatives, John Curran, Nicole Drossakis, and Martin Oberlander."

The boy identified as John Curran said loudly, "And we're going to kick your butts!" He sat back, smiling.

There was an explosion of derisive laughter in response to this as John's teacher—or vice principal—leaned over to him, her face darkened with anger. Her reprimands did nothing to wipe the broad, confident smile from his face.

Dmitri Simon tapped the microphone in order to get everyone

focused again. When the cacophony had died down, he said, "So there's some competition for you all, I guess. Let's see . . . where's Lincoln Junior High?"

That was Rod Denham's team. He stood up, adjusted his sport-coat, and announced heartily that the "six-time champions of the local math competition league" were all present. Winston glanced at Mr. Garvey, who was wearing a sour expression.

The Marin School was next. That was another private school, al-though they were not dressed in the same formal wear as the Demilla students. "Good luck, everyone," said their teacher, a young man who might have been confused for a high school student. "We're looking forward to having fun puzzling with you all."

The next team was from New Easton, which was impressively far away. Their teacher introduced his students as "Mr. Hoffman, Miss Huang, and Mr. Hurley. And I'm Mr. Henry Horn. So I guess we're Team H." There was some good-natured laughter.

After that was Winston's own school, Walter Fredericks Junior High. Mr. Garvey stood and said, "We're here and ready to win," and sat back down. Winston tried to look as determined as his teacher, but he doubted he was very intimidating.

The last team was West Meadow Junior High, home of the eccentric Brendan Root. His team was led by the school's vice principal, a balding, genial man who introduced himself as Carl Lester.

"Okay!" said Simon. "I'm glad we're all here. I know you're anxious to get started, so let me tell you what's going to happen today. You're going to face six puzzles. The first team to send me the an-swers to all six puzzles will win fifty thousand dollars for their school." Everybody already knew what the prize was, but hearing Dmitri Simon say the number out loud added an extra degree of excitement. The room filled with the murmuring of kids wondering what their schools would do with that money. Winston could feel waves of urgency radiating off Mr. Garvey.

Simon smiled out at them. "I have a present for all of you," he said.

"Potato chips!" someone said loudly, to general laughter.

Simon chuckled. "Maybe we'll get you some potato chips, too. But right now I have something else." He gave a little signal, and Simon's assistants began walking among the audience, holding boxes. They were giving out something.

"One per team," said Simon. "Just take one."

A young man handed the "present" to Mr. Garvey. It was covered in protective bubblewrap. Mr. Garvey peeled this away and looked quizzically at what he'd uncovered. He handed it to Winston. Mal and Jake bent in to see what it was.

It was a small handheld computer—a personal digital assistant, maybe—not quite as large as a paperback book. There was a small screen and a keyboard. A stubby gray antenna poked out of the top.

"You'll need to keep this with you all day," said Simon. "This little device is going to be your best friend. It will tell you where you need to go next, and it's how you're going to send me the answers as you find them."

Winston found the power button and turned the device on. The screen came to life to the sound of a short electronic tune—*teedly-teedly-TEE!*—and then displayed the Simon's Snack Foods logo. This blinked away after a moment and was replaced with a message: "The Game Has Not Yet Begun." There was a flashing Enter button under that, so Winston hit the Enter key on the keypad. The device thought about that for a moment and then returned with the same message, almost a rebuke: "The Game Has Not Yet Begun."

All around them was the *teedly-teedly-TEE*ing of little computers starting up. Simon said over the din, "You can turn them on if you want, but you won't get very far just yet. I want to explain a few things first, and then Game Control—that's us—will send out the information you need to get going." He turned to one of the people by his side and said, "I told you the sound effects were a bad idea."

When the tweeting had died down, Simon said, "Okay. As you've all learned by now, the game has not yet begun. Here's what's going to happen. After I'm done talking, my people here will wait five or six minutes so that you can all get back to your cars. Then they'll push the button or throw the switch or whatever it is they do. . . . Anyway, they'll start the game.

"*Then* when you turn on your little devices, you'll get that very annoying start-up sound and you'll see a menu of six pages. Each page will give you information about one of the puzzles. But—aha!— you'll soon discover that only the first page is unlocked. Solve that first puzzle, type in your answer, and you'll learn the location of the second puzzle. Solve *that*, and you'll get directions to the third puzzle, and so on."

Simon looked slyly at them. "The sixth and final puzzle is a little bit different. You won't need to go anywhere to solve it. The only thing you'll find on that sixth page is a clue and the input box for sending us the answer. That's it."

Someone had turned on a computer again, and there was the now-familiar tweedling start-up sound. Everyone tittered restless laughter, and Simon rolled his eyes. "I absolutely promise, the game isn't going to start until I say so. You can turn those computers on and off all you want—but don't!" Simon said, realizing he was inviting a chorus of *teedly-teedly-tee*s.

"The first team to send us all six answers wins the loot. It's exactly that simple. We'll send out a message to all the teams when that happens, and then we can meet back here and have some hamburgers and hot dogs—and potato chips, of course—and I'll give the winning team a big, fat check."

A murmur of excitement buzzed through the room. Winston ached for Simon to dismiss them so they could get going.

Simon looked around the room. "Are there any questions?"

There are always questions, and Winston found himself clutching the tabletop in exasperation as they were asked.

"What if nobody wins?" somebody asked.

Simon shook his head with a small smile. "Somebody's going to win, believe me," he said. "We made the puzzles challenging, but not impossible. And the prize, I think, is big enough that you guys are going to give it your all, am I right?" There was general agreement and a couple of hearty "yeahs!" from around the room. Simon nodded his approval. He said, "If aliens invade and suck out your brains, well, I guess I'll come up with something. But I'm willing to bet that someone's going to win without any extra hints or clues. Anything else?"

Then somebody had to ask if you had to answer all six puzzles to win, which Winston thought was the stupidest question in the history of the world. He slumped down in his chair. He could feel Jake and Mal buzzing with anxiety as well. *Yes! You have to answer all six puzzles! Let's get going!*

But Simon answered that question patiently and a couple of other ones besides. After that, the room filled with a tense silence. There were no more questions. The game could now begin.

Simon smiled at them all, drawing out the moment. Then he said, "Okay. Get back to your cars and check your computers in about five minutes. And good luck to all of you!"

He had to shout this last bit over the explosive din of dozens of people all scrambling for the exit at the same time. There was no reason to run, but it was hard not to get swept up in the excitement. The clock was ticking down, and the game was about to begin!

"All right, stay close," said Mr. Garvey.

Office workers who had nothing to do with the contest threw themselves against the walls as a flood of kids suddenly filled the hallway. A businessman in a three-piece suit coming through the front doors was frozen in shock as the chaotic crowd rumbled toward him. He leapt to one side like a stuntman in an action movie, and gawked in amazement at the passing riot.

The kids and their teachers flooded out into the parking lot. Mr. Garvey said to Jake, who was holding the mini computer, "Turn that thing on, see if we get anything."

Winston knew that only a couple of minutes had gone by and the game would not have started yet. But he understood Mr. Garvey's impatience. Jake pressed the power button as he walked.

"*Teedly-teedly-TEE!*" said the computer.

"Nothing," said Jake. "Same message as before."

They approached Mr. Garvey's blue car. As they waited for their teacher to unlock it, Rod Denham walked by them with his students. "So these are your boys, eh, Garvey?" He had a politician's grin on his fleshy face. It was the smile you wear when you don't particularly like what you're smiling at.

Mr. Garvey, for a moment, looked like a small, tense dog, one who isn't sure whether to run or fight back. But he finally put on a similar smile and said, "Ah, logic was always your strong suit."

Mr. Denham's grin only got wider. He looked at Winston and his friends. "Good luck today, boys! You've got some serious competition out there."

"So do you," said Mal.

Mr. Denham laughed. His students didn't. They were sizing up the competition, their arms crossed, their expressions carefully neutral. The three of them looked like they had nothing in common—they were a freckle-faced girl, a tall but overweight boy, and a second boy who, with his thick glasses and oily hair, was almost a cartoon version of a math nerd. But somehow they gave off the impression that they were a team, a real team, organized and well-prepared, ready to work together as effortlessly as the gears in a clock. Winston hoped he and his friends looked half as serious.

"All right," said Mr. Denham. "Let's go, people." His team climbed into Mr. Denham's car, which was nearly as long as a motorboat. Around them in the parking lot, Winston could hear the sounds of people turning on their computers, hoping that the game had started.

Jake climbed into the passenger seat this time, so Winston and Mal got into the back.

"That man is very hard to take," said Mr. Garvey, getting into the driver's seat.

"He's used to winning," said Jake.

Mr. Garvey glanced at him, perhaps surprised by this observation. "You're right. He is. How did you know?"

Jake shrugged. "I've seen baseball coaches with that same expression. Not just confidence, but—"

"Yes," said their teacher. "Certainty. He knows he's going to win. That wouldn't be so bad, except he *does*, all the time. Drives me crazy."

"We can tell," Mal said in a low voice.

If Mr. Garvey heard that last comment, he chose to ignore it. He said, "Try that thing again, will you?"

Jake fiddled with the computer. Winston closed his eyes in an attempt to block out that opening sound effect.

"Hey! I got something new," Jake said.

Mr. Garvey's hands tightened on the steering wheel. "Read what it says. Where are we going first?"

"Hang on," Jake said, pushing buttons. "Okay. Puzzle one is at the Burstein Space Museum. Oh, hey! We get in free when we show them this computer."

"Cool," said Mal.

Mr. Garvey said, "That's right nearby. I wish it would tell us where the other puzzles will be. I'd love to skip ahead and have a puzzle entirely to ourselves."

Jake pushed buttons. "When you click the button for the second puzzle, it says you can't have it yet. Same for the others. You have to solve them in order, just like Dmitri Simon said."

Their teacher shrugged. "All right, then. Tune up those brains, gentlemen. We are on our way." He put the car into reverse and backed out of the parking spot.

Immediately there was a strange popping noise. Winston looked around but couldn't tell where it had come from. Mr. Garvey shifted gears and drove forward, and everyone became aware that something was wrong. The car was making a strange, struggling sound, and felt slightly lopsided. The teacher turned out of the parking lot, perhaps hoping the car would miraculously heal itself. But the sound didn't go away, and he decided he couldn't ignore it. He pulled over by the side of the road, just ten yards from the potato chip factory.

As other teams drove past them, leaving them behind, Mr. Garvey got out of the car. Muttering, he walked around inspecting it, and then stopped as he saw something he didn't like. Winston saw a look of unleashed horror on the math teacher's face. Jake opened the door and peered out, to see what Mr. Garvey was looking at.

"You're not going to believe this," Jake said. "We have a flat tire."

CHAPTER FIVE

THE BOYS GOT OUT of the car. Yes, it was true. The right rear tire looked like it had been in a fight and had lost. Mr. Garvey stared at it, more shocked than angry. He seemed unable to process the idea that this was happening, that things could go this wrong.

And then he processed it after all: He gave a great, unholy yell and kicked the dead tire as hard as he could. Winston took a step backward.

"Do we have a spare?" Jake asked.

Mr. Garvey stopped kicking and looked around, as if surprised to see the kids standing there. He nodded, a bit wild-eyed. "A spare," he said, like he didn't know the word. "A spare." Maybe he thought Jake was referring to bowling. Then he regained his senses and said, "Yes, of course I do." He opened the car's large rear door and began removing the supplies he had placed there. "This is going to take a few minutes," Mr. Garvey said. "This is terrible, just terrible."

"Can we help?" Winston said.

Mr. Garvey waved his hand as if the question itself was too much interference. "I know how to change a tire. Just stand back. I need fifteen minutes, that's all I need."

They watched him get set up for a minute or two, feeling useless. Then Jake elbowed Winston. "I want to go back to the parking lot for a minute. Come on." So the three boys walked back to the potato chip factory.

The visitors' parking lot had only a couple of cars left in it—all the puzzlers were long gone.

Mal looked behind him at Mr. Garvey, on his knees, removing the lug nuts. He said, "If he finishes that tire and we're not there ready to go, he is going to have a heart attack."

Jake said, "I know, but I want to see something. Where were we parked? Here, right?"

They looked around. "Seems right," Winston said. "Maybe one space over."

"Yeah. Look." Jake nudged some green shards of glass with the toe of his sneaker.

"Whoa," said Mal. "Broken glass in a parking lot! I've never seen that before!"

Jake gave him a withering look. "Do you see glass anywhere else? Look around." They glanced up and down the gray asphalt. Winston couldn't see any broken glass anywhere except where they were standing.

"So that's what gave us the flat tire," Winston said.

Jake nodded. "I think someone did it to us on purpose."

Winston blinked. "What?"

"Did you hear that popping sound right as we started moving?"

Winston thought about it. "Yeah. I heard that."

"He's got the tire off," said Mal, gesturing back to Mr. Garvey. "Let's start walking, huh?"

So they started back to Mr. Garvey's car, walking slowly. Jake kept talking. "You know Mark Mazslos? From the baseball team?"

Winston nodded. Big kid, born to play sports.

"He told me once about getting revenge on his older brother. They don't get along too well. Mark wedged a bottle under the wheel of his brother's car, nice and tight. His brother started the car, tried to back up, and blam. Instant flat tire. He says next time his brother picks on him, he's giving him *four* flat tires."

"Or maybe we drove over some broken glass and that's that," Mal said.

Jake shrugged. "Maybe. But I think that popping sound we heard was the bottle breaking."

"So who put it there?" asked Winston. "One of the kids on that math teacher's team?"

He made the mistake of saying this as they neared Mr. Garvey's car. Mr. Garvey had just gotten the spare tire into place and was screwing the lug nuts back on. He craned his head around. "What math teacher? You mean Mr. Denham?"

There was an uncomfortable pause, then Winston said, "We think someone might have given us the flat tire."

Mr. Garvey sat up a little straighter and clenched the lugwrench in his fist. His eyes widened. "Denham," he growled. "He knows I'm out to beat him. Would he do that? Would he really do that?"

"I don't know," Winston said quickly. "It could have been somebody else, too."

"We just can't figure out how they did it," Mal said.

"Come on," Jake said. "How hard is it to pop a bottle under somebody's tire?"

"We were all standing right there," Mal reminded him. "We would have noticed if somebody started crawling around under the car."

Mr. Garvey lowered the car from the jack and made sure the lug nuts were nice and tight. "Boys, get in," he said while he did this. "We'll have to worry about this later. Right now, we don't have proof that *anybody* gave us this flat tire. That means it's up to us to make up all the time we lost. This could be a real setback, but it won't be because we won't let it. Right?"

The boys stared at him.

"I said, *right*?"

Oh, that wasn't a rhetorical question. Now the boys all hastily agreed: "Right, absolutely." But Winston wondered how they could possibly catch up.

Mr. Garvey wasn't driving *recklessly*, exactly, but he was going fast enough that Winston checked his seat belt a couple of times. Winston could see the teacher's expression in the rearview mirror, and it was one of grim determination. They might not catch the other teams, but it wouldn't be because Mr. Garvey was afraid to exceed the speed limit.

After a few minutes of driving in silence, Jake turned on the mini computer. "Teedly-teedly-tee!" it said.

"Can I see that thing?" Winston said. Jake handed it to him.

Winston turned the computer around in his hands, examining it. Incredible, when you thought about it. Dmitri Simon must have spent a small fortune having these things made up. You couldn't just go into a store and buy special puzzle hunt computers.

As Jake had said, there were six numbered buttons on the screen. Right now all but the first of these was useless. A seventh button said STATUS. Winston pushed this. The device mulled it over for a few moments and then informed him, "Please check back later." Okay, then.

He called up the information about the space museum. Winston had been there a few times—on field trips with school, mostly. He wondered if the puzzle would be right where they could see it, or if they would have to hunt around for it. He wished there was *something* about that puzzle here, something they could begin thinking about. But other than the map and the instructions about how to get in free, there was nothing but the input box for when they had the answer. Glancing up at Mr. Garvey—who probably wouldn't approve of him fooling around like this—he moved the cursor into the answer box and typed in a made-up word: GLOHONKIN. He hit Enter. The device once again thought for a moment or two and then responded with, "That is not the right answer." Big surprise.

Winston turned off the computer. "I wish I'd brought a puzzle book for the travel time," he said.

"You'll have all the puzzles you can handle in just a while," Mr. Garvey said. "Don't tire out your brain."

Mal said, "Winston's brain doesn't get tired. It's scary. I don't know how he turns it off long enough to sleep."

"Well, look on the floor," Mr. Garvey said. "You might find a math book down there. I'm sure that'll have something puzzly in it."

Winston felt around under his seat and, sure enough, came up with an old workbook with various math and number games in it. He flipped through it until he came to something interesting.

You can place the digits 1 through 6 in this puzzle so that each row, each column, and every 2-by-3 box contains each digit exactly once. In addition, the digits in each shaded area must add up to the given number.

10	4	2	10		
		11		5	
3		7	7	10	
11				4	
8		10		8	6
7			3		

(Answer, page 240.)

The museum was doing brisk business now that school was out, and the parking lot was crowded. They parked and made their way inside.

Mr. Garvey took the computer from Mal and showed it to the woman at the box office. Bored, she waved them in. She was used to this by now—a whole bunch of teams had already arrived, of course.

The four of them walked through the turnstiles, continued another few paces, and stopped.

"Where are we going?" asked Jake.

"Good question," said Mr. Garvey, looking around. "Does this thing give any instructions on what to do when we get here?" He turned on the computer.

"It didn't say anything," Winston said.

Mr. Garvey pressed buttons on the computer, confirmed that Winston was correct, and made a frustrated grunting sound. They stood there, looking for anything that might be helpful. There were lots of interactive exhibits and a model of the solar system hanging from the ceiling.

"Maybe we should split up and try to find what we're looking for," Winston suggested.

Mr. Garvey shook his head. "Maybe later, if we really get stuck. I want to stay together for now. I don't want to lose any more time trying to locate lost kids."

So they wandered around. The problem was, the puzzle might be anywhere. A multimillionaire who had manufactured special handheld computers could do just about anything he wanted. Dmitri Simon might have had the museum alter one of its exhibits. Perhaps one of the interactive displays had been reprogrammed in some way? They peeked into all of them—"Fly a Rocket!" and "What Is a Moon Rock Made Of?" and "Gravity on Other Planets." Nothing jumped out at them as being particularly puzzlelike.

They had been searching fruitlessly for a good ten or fifteen minutes when Jake said, "Hey, look there!"

They whirled around just in time to see the Brookville Brains walking briskly toward the exit. They were easily the most identifiable team, with their blue baseball hats and shirts. They must have found the puzzle and solved it, and they were already moving on to the next location. Winston felt a thrum of frustration course through him. First the flat tire, and now they couldn't find the first puzzle. Yet other teams were barreling on ahead!

"Come on," said Mr. Garvey, grimly.

The four of them hustled over to where that other team had just been. The puzzle had to be around here somewhere, right? But this part of the museum looked the same as the rest. Again they stood there, bewildered and helpless, bloodhounds unable to pick up a scent.

"Where did those guys come from?" said Jake. "They came from this direction, right?"

Winston pointed generally. "Yeah. From somewhere over here."

They walked a few paces, trying to retrace the path of that other team, but it was impossible. They could have come from anywhere.

Winston turned in a slow circle, trying to figure it out. And then suddenly he was almost knocked over. He looked up to see Brendan Root and his team brushing by them.

"Hey, Winston! Fun, isn't it?" Brendan said, looking back at him as he jogged away. Winston was too stunned to reply.

Brendan's teacher looked as excited as a kid. Mr. Lester, that was his name. He jumped as he walked and pointed urgently toward the exit, as if his team wasn't already heading there. "Come on, guys. Let's go!" he said. He definitely had Mr. Garvey's competitive spirit. Brendan waved at Winston again and then sped up to join his team.

They watched them round the corner. "I told you he was going to be tough," said Jake.

"Do you know them?" said Mr. Garvey.

"We met that one kid back at the factory."

Mal looked around. "So where did they come from? Did anyone see?" No one did. "This is starting to not be funny," he said.

"Maybe we can run and ask them where the puzzle is," said Jake.

Mr. Garvey laughed. "They're not going to help us."

"Why not?"

"Would you lend a helping hand to your competition?"

Jake looked on the spot. "I wouldn't tell them the answer, but I might tell them where the puzzle could be found. I mean, if they were really stuck."

Mr. Garvey shook his head. He patted Jake on the shoulder like a game-show host consoling a foolish contestant. "That's very admirable," he said. "You stick close to me, Jake, so I can stop you from doing things like that."

Jake looked like he had something to say in response to this, but then a voice from behind them said, "Have you found it yet?"

They turned around yet again. This time, one of the Greater Oaks girls was standing there, watching them. She cocked her head. "You're part of the potato chip thing, right?" she said. "Have you found the puzzle in here?"

Winston shook his head. "No, we haven't. Have you?"

She shrugged, with an ironic little smile. "If we had, I wouldn't be asking you about it. Do you want to look together?"

All three boys looked to Mr. Garvey. Winston guessed he would have strong feelings about joining up with other teams.

The math teacher cleared his throat. To Winston's surprise, he said, "Well, I guess the more eyes, the merrier, right? Where's the rest of your team, young lady?"

She waved generally. "We split up. They're all around here somewhere. Where are you guys from?"

They began to walk, and there were introductions all around. The girl was Bethany Seymour. Winston was more than a little aware of how pretty she was, with her shining brown eyes and long, straight hair. He found himself simultaneously trying to walk next to her and *not* walk next to her, and cursed himself for his awkwardness.

Mr. Garvey said as they continued to look around the planetarium, "You're from Greater Oaks, is that right? That's rather far away."

"Yeah, it was a long drive to get here," said Bethany. "And then getting from the potato chip factory to here, Miss Norris made a wrong turn and we wound up somewhere with railroad tracks and a garbage dump. It took forever."

"Miss Norris is your teacher?"

"Yeah, my English teacher. There she is, right there."

Indeed, the nervous woman with the thick sproing of curly red hair was marching over to them. She wore a wide-eyed expression that may as well have been a sign reading, I AM FRAZZLED.

"Bethany," she said, voice shaking with agitation, "where did you go?"

"We said we were all going to split up, remember?"

"But I said to stay close by! Didn't I?"

"I'm right *here*," Bethany said, rolling her eyes.

"Where are the others?"

"I don't know. They're somewhere. They didn't leave."

Mr. Garvey jumped in. "Miss Norris, is it?" She looked at him, startled. "I'm Greg Garvey. I'm the math teacher at Walter Fredericks Junior High in Glenville. These are my boys."

Miss Norris recovered. "Nice to meet you. I don't suppose you know where the puzzle is?"

"No, I'm afraid not. But this young lady suggested we all look together, which sounds like a fine idea."

So they started moving again. "Where have you looked already?" Miss Norris said.

Jake said, "All over."

Mal said, "Those machines around the corner there . . . all that interactive stuff."

"Oh," said Miss Norris. "It didn't occur to me that the puzzle might be in there."

"That's for the best," said Mr. Garvey, "since it wasn't."

"Well, we already looked around this part," said Bethany, waving to the exhibits around them. They stood by a gigantic replica of a lunar exchange module. "Where else is there to go in this place?"

"Bethany! Miss Norris!" A voice called out, and a girl came running toward them. She was wearing a floaty pale-blue dress and sandals that flapped loudly. "We found it!"

"Giselle! Where?"

Giselle came up short when she saw Winston and his team standing there. "Uh," she said.

Miss Norris understood why she had turned mute. "It's okay, Giselle. We're all looking together. Right?"

Mr. Garvey and the boys nodded their heads and said "oh, yes" and "absolutely," a bunch of earnest bobblehead dolls.

"Okay. Come on!" Giselle shouted, gleeful. She waved at them to follow her, and they all ran a short distance to a small, black passageway. Winston could have walked by this a hundred times and not seen it—the hallway seemed to be for staff members only. There was another girl in there, looking anxious, like she was somewhere she wasn't supposed to be.

"This is it?" said Miss Norris.

"This can't be right," Mr. Garvey declared.

Giselle said, "But look!"

Sure enough, the third girl—she was introduced as Elvie—was standing by a pair of signs, each attached to a metal post. They were ads for Simon's Potato Squares. In each one, the smiling guy from the television commercial beamed out at them. Words by his mouth said, "Think square!"

They all moved into the hallway. There was barely enough room for both teams. "So where's the puzzle?" said Winston.

"I don't know," said Elvie. "I'm guessing in here." Elvie was the tiniest of the three girls—with long dark-blond hair framing her narrow face, she reminded Winston of a fairy from a fantasy movie. Elvie pointed to the wall, and Winston saw that it was really a door painted black. Like the hallway itself, it didn't seem to be part of any exhibit. Elvie jiggled the handle. "But it's locked," she said.

"This is nuts," said Mal.

"I agree," said Mr. Garvey. "Can this be right? What are we supposed to do, pick the lock? That's a fine thing to teach kids."

Jake knocked on the door. There was no answer.

"I tried that already," said Elvie.

"Maybe the answer is HALLWAY," said Giselle. She was fidgeting in the crowded space, her hands moving up and down her arms. Her brown eyes lit up as a new idea hit her. "Or SPACE! Because this is a space museum, and we're all standing in a small space, so—"

"So there's no puzzle?" her teammate Bethany demanded. "You just have to find the sign? That doesn't make sense." Bethany, it seemed, didn't tolerate suggestions she thought were foolish. Winston decided he liked her no-nonsense attitude.

"Well, the puzzle should be here somewhere . . . ," said Miss Norris, looking around the black-walled alcove.

"Maybe you have to feel the walls!" Giselle said, doing just that.

"So, what, the puzzle's in Braille?" Jake said. But he started feeling the walls, too.

Mal knocked on the door again. "It's got to have something to do with this door. That's the only thing *here*." He put his ear to it like a spy.

They were getting nowhere, and it was impossible to think in this crowded space, packed in elbow to elbow. Winston slipped back out of the hallway while the others discussed what they should do next. Mr. Garvey came out after him, and they glanced at each other, frowning.

"I don't like this," Mr. Garvey said.

Winston nodded. Would Simon send dozens of people into a tiny little hallway where the only notable feature was a locked door? Winston had created a few puzzle hunts himself, for his friends and his sister, and he understood that you couldn't leave the solvers hanging, with no idea what they were supposed to do next. Simon was either very bad at creating puzzles or something was wrong.

They saw a staff member walk by. He was wearing a lime-green T-shirt and a name badge that said VOLUNTEER. Winston rushed to catch him.

"Hey," said Winston, "can I ask you something?"

"Sure."

"You know about this potato chip contest that's happening here today?"

The guy put on a sly look. "Ah, I can't answer any questions about that. Sorry. You'll have to solve the puzzle on your own."

"But how do we unlock the door to where the puzzle is?"

The volunteer looked taken aback. "The doors are locked? To the theater?"

Mr. Garvey said, "What theater?" Winston didn't even realize Mr. Garvey had come up behind him.

The volunteer looked confused. "The planetarium. The only theater we've *got*. Are the doors locked, or aren't they?"

Mr. Garvey smiled. "I'm sure they're fine. We must have gotten ourselves all confused. Thank you very much for your help." As the volunteer strolled off, Mr. Garvey put a hand on Winston's shoulder and pulled him close. "Go to the planetarium. It's up toward the front—we passed it when we came in. I'll be along with the others in a moment."

He said that in such a conspiratorial tone, like a prisoner sharing an escape plan, that for a moment Winston only stared at him, expecting further instructions—"Start digging through the wall and watch out for guards." But instead Mr. Garvey said "Go!" again and gave him a little push to get him started.

So Winston walked back toward the entrance to the museum. He glanced behind him to see Mr. Garvey heading back to the little black hallway, and Winston heard him say, "Jake, Mal, can I speak to you for a moment?"

Winston couldn't remember seeing a movie theater in here, but as soon as he saw the doors, he realized what the volunteer was talking about. It wasn't a traditional theater, of course, but rather a planetarium where they projected an animated solar system onto a domed ceiling. You sat in a big cushy chair and felt like an astronaut looking out a rocketship's window. *A Tour of the Universe*, it was called.

He glanced back the way he had come and saw Mr. Garvey

ushering Jake and Mal, a hand on each of their backs pushing them along. "Where are we going?" he heard Mal say.

"Just walk," Mr. Garvey replied.

"Where are the girls?" Winston asked when they had caught up.

"Well," Mr. Garvey said, "I imagine they're still in the hallway." He gestured to the planetarium door. "Let's go. The puzzle's right in there."

Jake was openmouthed. "Aren't we going to tell the other team?"

Winston said, "We're all looking together, remember?"

Mr. Garvey nodded and gestured into the theater once again. "We were, and now we're not. Go in! Let's go!"

Reluctantly, Winston and his friends filed in to the pitch-black planetarium, Mr. Garvey practically stepping on their heels as they did so. They reached the center, and all eyes instinctively looked up. Projected on the theater's curved ceiling was a night sky more spectacular than any Winston had seen in real life. There were so many stars, they threatened to paint the ceiling white. There was also a series of words floating out there in the artificial universe.

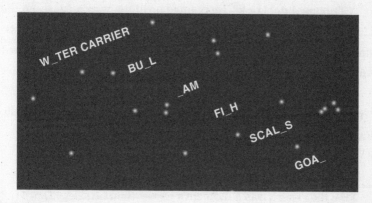

Mr. Garvey laughed when he saw the words. "All right," he said. "Finally, a stroke of luck." The boys were heading down an aisle to sit in those big comfy seats, but Mr. Garvey whispered, "No! Come back here. We won't be here long."

Winston kept glancing over at the door to the theater. He was waiting for it to open and for the girls to walk in. They had ditched them, plain and simple, after promising that they would team up. In the back of his mind, he had sort of hoped they might join forces with these girls throughout the event. Winston didn't meet many girls who liked puzzles, and that seemed like a pretty good thing to find.

He doubted Bethany or her friends would be too keen to work with them anymore.

Winston's eyes had adjusted to the dark now, and he could see silhouettes of other teams sitting in the chairs, but he couldn't tell who they were. Mr. Garvey led them into an area behind the back row—he didn't want to sit.

"If all the puzzles are this easy," whispered Mr. Garvey, "we're never going to catch up. I hope there's a real killer later on that only we can crack."

"You know the answer?" Jake said.

"Of course I do! Look!" He pointed up at the words. "Just put the missing letters back in to get one of the zodiac signs. It couldn't be simpler! Turn on that thing so we can submit the answer," Mr. Garvey said.

Jake had the computer, and he complied. *Teedly-teedly-TEE*. When Jake was ready, Mr. Garvey said, "Okay. It's Water Carrier, Bull, Ram, Fish, Scales, Goat . . . so type in A-L-R-S-E-T."

"That's not a word," Mal said.

"Just type it in."

Jake did. There was a moment's pause, then he said, "That's not the right answer."

"All right, all right," Mr. Garvey said, waving his hands as if erasing the wrong answer out of the air. "Scramble the letters. It's an anagram. How can you turn those letters into a word?" When nobody said anything, Mr. Garvey said, "Winston! This is your thing, isn't it? Mix up those letters!"

"ALTERS," Winston said after a moment of thought.

"Good! Try that," Mr. Garvey said to Jake.

Jake punched in the letters. "No."

"STALER," Winston said.

Jake pushed more buttons. "No, sorry."

"Try ALERTS," said Mr. Garvey. "It has to be one of these."

Jake shook his head. "It's not that one."

"Are you typing it in the right spot?"

Even in the dark, Winston saw Jake's eyes flash. "Of course I am." All he had to do was push the first button—the only button the computer would let him push. Did Mr. Garvey think he couldn't manage that?

Apparently so. "Let me see," Mr. Garvey said, and snatched the computer away. He glanced at the screen and then handed it back to Jake, who rolled his eyes at Winston in disbelief.

"So there's another trick to this," Mal said, looking back up at the floating words.

"A trick," said Mr. Garvey. "Yes. A trick."

They were standing fairly close to the exit, and as they watched, another team left the theater. Before the door could close, a hand opened it back up. Miss Norris peeked in and looked around. With the light flooding in from the lobby, she could see Winston and his team easily enough. She turned her head and said something, and then the girls walked in, glaring. If the four of them could blast rays of solid ice out of their eyes, Winston and his team would have been frozen forever. Bethany looked like she was on the verge of developing that power spontaneously. Winston and his friends traded embarrassed glances—they all wanted to crawl under the carpeting.

The girls and their teacher looked up at the floating words for a moment or two and then filed down into the seating area and out of sight.

Mr. Garvey watched his boys watch the girls. "All right, guys," he said. "This is a competition, let's remember that. We're in last place, and we're not going to get very far if we help other teams. Let's get back to the puzzle."

Winston may have been embarrassed at his teacher's actions, but he wasn't about to walk away from a day of puzzles. Neither were his friends. Jake looked up at the floating words. They were shimmering and golden. "I understand bull and ram and fish," said Jake, "but what is a water carrier? What's that supposed to be?"

"These are all constellations," Winston said. "Symbols of the zodiac. Water carrier is . . . um."

"Aquarius," said Mal. "That's what I am."

"Right," said Mr. Garvey. "The bull is Taurus, the ram is Aries, the fish is Pisces, the scales is Libra, and the goat is Capricorn. They're all constellations."

Winston gazed up at the floating words. The missing letters didn't spell anything—at least not anything important. Those letters had to be missing for a reason, though.

All at once he saw it. It was almost as if some unseen force had whispered the answer into his ear. "I need a pencil and paper," he said urgently. "And I need to see."

Mr. Garvey said, "You have it?"

"I might. I need to see. It's too dark in here." He marched toward the exit without even making sure the others were behind him.

When they got back out to the main exhibit hall, Winston grabbed a pencil and a scrap of paper and wrote hastily:

AQUARIUS
TAURUS
ARIES
PISCES
LIBRA
CAPRICORN

"Okay," said Mal. "Those are the signs of the zodiac."

Winston nodded. "And that's the key to the whole thing."

(Continue reading to see the answer to this puzzle.)

C
H
A
P S I X
T
E
R

WINSTON EXPLAINED THE ANSWER to his
friends: One of the phrases floating up there on the theater ceiling
had been WATER CARRIER. The sign of the water carrier is
AQUARIUS. WATER CARRIER was missing its second letter; if you
took the second letter out of the word AQUARIUS, that gave
you the letter Q.

You had to do that for each word. BULL was missing its third letter, so Winston took the third letter—U—from the word TAURUS.
And so on, until Winston had spelled the word QUASAR.

W _ TER CARRIER	AQUARIUS
BU _ L	TAU̱RUS
_ AM	A̱RIES
FI _ H	PIS̱CES
SCAL _ S	LIBRA̱
GOA _	CAPṞICORN

That was recognizably a word, but none of the boys knew exactly what it meant. Winston thought he might have heard the word on a science-fiction television show—which only made sense, seeing as the puzzle was in a planetarium. Mr. Garvey tried explaining it, eyebrows scrunching as if he wasn't all that sure himself: "It's an object in outer space," he said. "Something extremely bright and very far away. It's one of those things astronomers are always looking for with those gigantic telescopes."

Whatever else a quasar might be, it was definitely the answer to the puzzle. It had to be, but there was still a tense moment until Jake confirmed the answer with the mini computer. Then there were high fives all around, even with Mr. Garvey.

They rushed out to the parking lot. Jake glanced under each tire before getting into the car. Mr. Garvey barked at him to stop dawdling, but Winston knew he was looking for more signs of sabotage.

"What's the next stop?" said Mr. Garvey when they were all settled in.

Jake studied the computer. "Sutherland Farms."

"Sounds familiar. Where is it?"

"West Meadow. I have directions."

"All right," said Mr. Garvey. "We're off."

They drove along, and Jake read directions off the computer screen in a low and distant monotone. Winston suspected he was still upset about the trick they had played on the girls' team. It was all Mr. Garvey's doing, of course, but the girls wouldn't know that. And even if they never saw the girls again after this was over, they would return home convinced that all of them—not just Mr. Garvey but *all of them*—were underhanded and scheming, full of smiles when needing a little help but also willing to stab a friend in the back for a few seconds' worth of advantage. The girls would say to their friends, "Some of those people we met today were just awful," and they would be referring in part to Jake.

And the fact was, Jake would never cheat. Never.

If Winston was playing Monopoly with his sister Katie and had to leave the room for some reason, he would take all his money with him. If he didn't, his stack would be a little lighter when he returned. Katie was a good kid and a good sister, but the temptation to pinch a hundred dollars or slip an extra house onto Pennsylvania Avenue was, for her, too much to resist.

Jake would resist. Winston could stop the game, take a bicycle ride around the neighborhood, and come back to find the board and his bank account exactly as he'd left it. Jake was competitive—in fact, very competitive—but he was what Winston's dad called "the right kind of competitive." If he won, he wanted to know he had earned it from start to finish, fair and square.

And Mal? He might give himself five hotels on Boardwalk or rob the bank entirely so that Winston would return to see his friend sitting behind a huge pile of money and a big, fat grin. That wasn't cheating. That was just being Mal.

Winston understood why Jake was upset, but Winston wasn't entirely sure that their teacher *had* cheated. He had played a trick, certainly—offered to help another team and then snatched that help away. It was bad sportsmanship, but was it cheating? Winston couldn't quite pin that label on it . . . not when somebody else out there had given them a flat tire with a broken bottle. *That* was cheating.

And now he realized something else, something so obvious he didn't know how he'd missed it: Whoever had wedged that bottle under their tire had also moved the signs at the space museum. The signs were supposed to have been in front of the planetarium doors, guiding all the teams inside. But someone—the cheater, surely—had moved the signs to that small, dark hallway.

First the flat tire, then the disappearing signs. Someone was trying to knock them out of the race and doing a fine job of it. Was there a way to figure out who it was?

He could rule out the girls from Greater Oaks right off the bat. They wouldn't move the signs and then pretend they couldn't find the puzzle. The point of cheating is to slow down everybody else, not your own team.

That left eight other teams. Could he eliminate any others? Could he eliminate all but one?

Maybe it wasn't a cheating *team*. The cheater could be flying solo—his or her teammates might not even know what was happening. Winston could almost see it: The cheater sees the signs in front of the planetarium theater and gets the idea to move them. His team settles into the theater, looks up at the fake starry sky and those floating words. The cheater says he has to go to the bathroom and leaves. He moves the signs and then comes back to help solve the puzzle. Easy.

Well, maybe not *easy*. The cheater had to drag those signs a good fifty feet without being spotted by any of the museum staff. But somehow he had accomplished this, just in time for Winston's team to arrive and be thrown off track. The cheater sure had luck on his side.

Something in that thought shined out at him like a quarter on the sidewalk. There was a clue here to the cheater's identity. But Winston couldn't quite get a handle on it. "We were the last ones there," he muttered.

Mal had been tapping a rhythm on the car window, but now turned to look at him. "What?"

Winston didn't know he'd said anything out loud. He said, "I'm trying to figure out who's cheating."

Mal shrugged. "Sounds like a plan."

"The cheater's team got to the planetarium before we did. Right?"

Jake said, "*Everybody* got to the planetarium before we did."

"Okay," said Winston. "The cheater also arrived at the potato chip factory *after* we did." Winston expected cheers or gasps at this revelation, but instead all he got was a thoughtful and puzzled silence.

Mal finally said, "How do you figure?"

Winston sat forward. "We pulled into the parking lot and went inside. Sometime after that, the cheater's team arrived. Before they came inside, the cheater put that bottle under our tire."

Jake said, "Why did it have to be then? Why not when we were all rushing back to our cars?"

Mr. Garvey chimed in. "That would have been incredibly risky, doing it with so many people around. Winston, I think you may be right. But let me ask you this: How did the cheater know which cars were involved in the contest? Not every car in the visitor parking lot belonged to a team."

Mal said, "Maybe they pulled in just after we did. The cheater saw a grown-up and three kids. Not too hard to figure out why they were there."

Jake twisted around in his seat and said, "Who came into the conference room immediately after us? Whoever it was, that's our cheater."

"Maybe," Mr. Garvey said.

"All right, maybe," Jake said grudgingly. "But who was it? Who came in after we did?"

They all thought about it.

"Those private school kids," Mal said. "The ones dressed like waiters at a fancy restaurant."

"Are you sure?"

"Yeah. I remember thinking they were somebody official, that the game was about to start."

"How soon after did they get there?"

"I don't know. I didn't bring a stopwatch with me," Mal said.

"Who else arrived after we did?" Winston asked. Silence greeted this question. "All right. Turn it around. Who was in the conference room when we got there? We can rule out all those teams."

"Maybe," Mr. Garvey said again, more loudly this time.

"That Brendan Root kid was there," said Mal.

"The girls were there," said Winston.

"Oh, you noticed the girls, did you?" Mal teased. Winston turned crimson.

"That other math teacher was there," Jake said. "Your friend, Mr. Denham."

Mr. Garvey said, "He's not my friend."

"There were other teams there, too," said Mal, "but I can't think who they were. So I guess right now we think the cheater is on that private school team. Right?"

"Okay, that's enough," said Mr. Garvey. "You have no idea one way or the other. We're not going to accuse anybody of cheating unless we catch them in the act. I'm not a hundred percent certain that somebody is cheating *at all*. Go ahead and discuss this all you want, but I'm drawing the line at accusing anybody. Even here in the car. I don't want to hear 'I think so-and-so is the cheater.' I don't want to hear it. All right?"

The boys mumbled agreement.

"Let's just see what happens next," said Mr. Garvey.

The name Sutherland Farms meant nothing to Winston, but as soon as they pulled into the dusty parking lot, he realized he'd been here before: The farm had a petting zoo, which he'd visited back in the first or second grade, and he was pretty sure his parents had come out here to buy vegetables and fresh pies. The air was filled with a thick, earthy smell, like you could plant a seed right there in the parking lot and it would blossom before your eyes.

Winston got out of the car and looked around. The sun was really beating down now.

"Where to, do you think?" Jake asked, shielding his eyes.

"There. Look," Winston said, and pointed.

Another feature of Sutherland Farms was a maze—giant bales of hay stacked five high, creating very effective walls. Today there was a sign at the entrance: CLOSED FOR PRIVATE EVENT. Next to that stood an advertisement for Simon's Potato Squares. There was no question where the puzzle was this time around.

"That's what I like to see," said Mal. "Let's go."

They reached the maze entrance, and Winston could hear the shrieks of kids running around in there. An oldish fellow with a significant belly came over to see if they should be allowed to enter. They showed him the mini computer and the man walked away, mollified.

"A maze," said Mr. Garvey, doubtfully. "Isn't the answer supposed be a word? How is a romp through a maze going to lead to an answer word?"

Winston said, "Maybe it's hidden somewhere? Maybe they hand you the answer when you find the exit?"

"Only one way to find out," Mal said, taking a step forward. "Shall we?"

Mr. Garvey raised a hand. "Let's just think for one moment. What's the fastest way of doing this? Maybe we should all take different routes through the maze. This way one of us will definitely find the answer."

Jake said, "If Winston's waiting by the car with the answer and I'm still wandering around in there with the computer, that doesn't help us much."

Mr. Garvey nodded. "You're right. Bad idea. We stay together. Let's go. Keep your eyes sharp."

The entrance was blocked by an elaborate curtain of corn husks. They parted this, and immediately came upon a sign bearing a single handwritten letter: **T**.

"That's probably important," said Mal.

"All right," said Mr. Garvey. "Look out for more letters." He headed off in a random direction. The three boys rushed to catch up.

Hay dust floated around like snow in a snowglobe—it felt like the air itself was made out of bits of straw. It was impossible to walk around the maze without a great big sneeze welling up in the back of your head.

No one was talking about it, but everyone on the team knew this was their opportunity to catch up to the rest of the pack. If they could burn through the maze quickly, and if other teams stumbled into a lot of dead ends, then Winston's team might gain back several minutes lost to the flat tire and the time spent wandering around the planetarium.

By the time they reached their fourth dead end, however, it no longer looked like they were going to solve this thing quickly. And with each new dead end, Mr. Garvey became a little more intense. He was no longer interested in any opinions his kids might have; in fact, it was all Winston could do just to keep up with him. At one point, Mr. Garvey rounded a corner, saw it was a dead end, and wheeled around again so quickly that Jake slammed into him.

"Jake, watch where you're going," Mr. Garvey said angrily. "This is hard enough without you getting under my feet." He stormed off in a new direction. The boys glanced at each other with irritation and then ran to follow him. This was anything but fun.

There were definitely other kids in the maze—Winston could hear them—but they encountered only one team face-to-face: the kids from the Demilla Academy, who were the closest thing right now to suspects in the cheating mystery.

They ran into the Demilla team no less than three times. The first time, there were nods of acknowledgment, but no words passed between them. The second time, there was some mild laughter. "What, you again?" said the boy on their team with a friendly smirk.

The third time, nobody was laughing. Winston was fed up with the maze, but the Demilla kids looked utterly exhausted and at the end of their rope. The boy had loosened his necktie and untucked his shirt from his pants. The girls' long hair had grown limp and heavy with sweat. They looked like they would rather be anywhere else on earth.

At this point, it was clear that the two teams were heading in the same direction, so they informally joined up. Mr. Garvey, rather tired himself after going full throttle for so long, slowed down so he could talk to the Demilla teacher. The two girls fell to the back of the group where they complained to each other, hissing like peevish old cats. The boy introduced himself to Winston and his friends as Michael Scott.

Winston said, "I never heard of your school. Where is it?"

"Over in North Hendricks. It's a private school. Very exclusive." He said this last part not like he was bragging but like he was making fun of people who brag about things like that.

Mal said with some interest, "You rich?"

Michael shrugged. "Pretty much." This, too, he said as if being rich was simply a fact of life. "My dad owns a real estate company. Big bucks."

"What's with the outfits?" Jake asked.

Michael rolled his eyes. "School uniforms. We have to wear these every day, if you can believe it."

"Yeah, but you're not in school."

"Doesn't matter. As long as we're representing the school, we have to wear our uniforms. That's what Mr. Meyer says, anyway." Michael jerked his head backward, indicating his teacher.

"Your football team must be something to see," said Mal.

Michael gave a snort of laughter. "Heh. If Mr. Meyer was the football coach, they really would have to play in these business suits. The other team could tackle us by yanking our neckties."

They shared a good-natured laugh. Could this kid really be the cheater? Anything was possible, but Michael seemed all right—a genuinely good guy. He said now in a low voice, "Any other teacher would have let us wear jeans like normal kids. Mr. Meyer was not my first choice for a teacher to take us around on this today."

"I know the feeling," Winston said.

They walked in amiable silence for a couple of minutes, Winston occasionally jotting down or erasing letters as they continued through the labyrinth. None of the Demilla kids were writing anything down. Winston guessed Michael was keeping track of the letters in his head.

And then they astounded themselves by coming across the maze's exit. For a moment, none of them could believe it—Winston had grown used to the idea that they'd be wandering around in here for the rest of the day. Delighted, they stepped out into a wide field, a disorienting and wonderful feeling after so much time spent closed up by the hay-bale walls.

"Finally!" Jake said. He pumped both arms in the air like a victorious boxer.

"I'm never doing one of these things again," said one of the Demilla girls.

"Not for a million dollars," said the other.

"Unless there's another one later today," Mal said. The girls looked at him with horror.

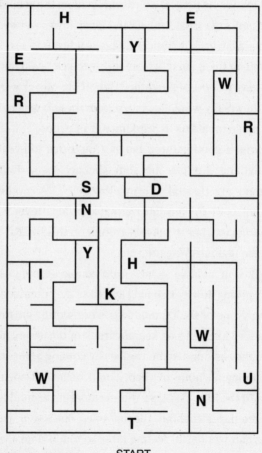

(Answer, page 241.)

START

*   *   *

Mr. Garvey said, "Okay. My boys, come over here, please."

Winston and his friends said "see you later" to Michael. Mr. Garvey escorted them a few yards away so that the Demilla team couldn't hear them.

"So," he said. "Do we all have the same answer?"

Winston said, "If you take the letters as you move from start to finish, you get the word THRESH."

Mal said, "I got that, too."

Mr. Garvey nodded. "Me too. And it makes sense, since a thresher is something you find on a farm. Jake, type it in, let's see what we've got."

Jake had already turned on the computer. He pushed buttons now, and after a moment looked up, smiling. "We got it."

Mr. Garvey gave a little fist pump. "Two down. Let's get going."

Winston looked up to see Michael walking over to them, a sheepish expression on his face. Behind him, the other members of the Demilla team watched him. None of them looked happy.

Michael tried finding a smile as he said, "Uh, hey, guys . . . what answer did you get for this?"

The answer word bubbled up in Winston's throat, but he swallowed it back down. He might not have shared Mr. Garvey's passion for take-no-prisoners competition, but even he understood that he couldn't simply give an answer to another team.

Jake understood that, too. "C'mon, we can't tell you that," he said.

Michael looked pained. "Yeah, of course not. Sorry. Can you confirm the answer? What we're typing into the computer isn't working."

"What did you get?" Winston asked.

"We got the word THUDS."

Winston shook his head. "That's not right."

Michael slumped. The Demilla team made a mistake and had come up with the wrong answer. What were they supposed to do? Michael turned back to his team and shook his head. His teacher and the two girls looked at each other, dismayed. The teacher, Mr. Meyer, came over, frowning.

"We really have the wrong answer?" he said to Michael.

"It sure looks like it."

Mr. Meyer looked at Mr. Garvey, smiling ruefully. "Perhaps you can give us a small break here. You know we went through the maze, the same as you."

Mr. Garvey, his expression carefully neutral, said, "Solving the maze was only part of it. You know that. You had to keep track of the letters you passed as you went along."

"I believe I did," Mr. Meyer said.

"You must have made a mistake. I'm sorry." They all stood there for another awkward second. Perhaps Mr. Garvey was waiting for the Demilla team to admit defeat and walk away. When that did not happen, Mr. Garvey said softly, "Come on, boys. We need to get going." He looked at Mr. Meyer and said with some sympathy, "Good luck."

Winston waved at Michael. He felt awful for them, but Mr. Garvey was right—the Demilla team had made a mistake, and they would have to figure out what to do about it. And there was only one thing they *could* do: Go through the maze again and pay more attention this time.

"Well, now we know we've pulled ahead of one other team," Mr. Garvey said as they approached his car. Winston looked behind him to see the Demilla team standing once again at the entrance to the maze. They had to go in, and they knew it . . . but none of them were willing to take those first dreadful steps.

*   *   *

Mr. Garvey was unlocking the doors to his car when Mal said, "So maybe we can run across the street and get some sandwiches at the farm shop."

Their teacher looked amazed, even appalled. He couldn't seem to think of any way to respond other than, "What?"

Mal said, "Well, it's nearly lunchtime."

Mr. Garvey waved his hands in the air like a television preacher praying for strength. "Guys!" he said. "My young teammates! Does anybody remember the flat tire that cost us twenty minutes? How about us wandering around the space museum like a bunch of lost sheep? We're slowly gaining back the time we lost, and now you want to stop for lunch?"

As if to bolster his point, a car drove by and the driver gave them a sarcastic little salute. There were three kids in the car, wearing satisfied smiles. It was Rod Denham and the Lincoln Junior High team. Mr. Denham steered out of the parking lot, leaving a cloud of dust behind them. Mr. Garvey watched them go, his teeth clenched. He then turned back to his team and spread his arms as if to say, "See?"

But Mal said, "We gotta eat sometime."

Winston expected Mr. Garvey to start yelling, but for once he maintained his temper. "We will eat in the car while we drive to the next location. I've got snacks, drinks, and beef jerky. You won't starve to death."

"Beef jerky?" Winston asked.

"Good, fast energy," Mr. Garvey said, unlocking his car's hatchback. He dug through one of the grocery sacks and came out with a pouch. "Here," he said, handing out slabs of jerky.

Winston had never had beef jerky before and wasn't about to start now. It looked like something a person could use to make a pair of shoes. Jake bit into his slab and tore off a piece, like a German shepherd with a chew toy.

"In the car, please, boys," Mr. Garvey said. "If you don't like beef jerky, I've got other things, but let's figure it out while we're moving."

Winston spied a box of cereal bars and grabbed it. A couple of those and his stomach would stop growling. Plus, there was an unexpected bonus: a puzzle on the back of the box. He had meant to take a couple of bars and put the rest back, but now he cradled the whole box in his arm as he got into the car.

Mal gave him a funny look. "Hungry?" he asked.

Winston showed him the back of the box, and Mal nodded, understanding immediately.

Each of the words in the list can be found in the grid, reading forward, backward, across, down, or diagonally. Every word contains the consecutive letters BAR, but each time those letters appear in a word, we've replaced them with a picture of a cereal bar. Can you find all the words?

Y	O	O	S	K	[BAR]	M	E	U	C
P	G	[BAR]	S	L	E	R	[BAR]	P	A
[BAR]	[BAR]	I	A	N	C	R	O	W	[BAR]
C	M	T	R	A	S	H	M	S	E
E	E	O	[BAR]	E	S	D	E	[BAR]	T
L	B	N	M	R	T	R	T	I	H
O	O	E	E	[BAR]	O	N	E	S	S
N	M	B	B	[BAR]	U	H	R	T	E
A	[BAR]	E	L	D	N	A	H	A	[BAR]
[BAR]	D	R	A	Y	N	[BAR]	K	E	R

BARBARIAN	BARKER	BARTERS	EMBARKS
BARBERSHOP	BARNYARD	BOMBARD	EMBARRASS
BARCELONA	BAROMETER	CABARET	HANDLEBAR
BARISTA	BARONESS	CROWBAR	RHUBARB
BARITONE	BARREL	EMBARGO	

(Answer, page 241.)

84

The kids settled into their seats, but before Mr. Garvey could open the driver's side door, a small SUV came speeding up. It stopped abruptly in the neighboring parking spot, almost hitting Mr. Garvey in the process. The math teacher had to jump onto the hood of his car to avoid getting creamed.

Every door in the SUV opened simultaneously, and the Brookville Brains came boiling out, determined and angry looking, like athletes sprinting onto the field before the big game.

"Watch where you're going!" Mr. Garvey yelled, arms outspread indignantly.

The Brookville teacher marched over to Mr. Garvey, his face bright red. In his T-shirt and baseball cap, he looked like a coach about to argue with the umpire. "Don't you tell me to watch anything," he said angrily. He waved a finger in Mr. Garvey's face.

Mr. Garvey looked stunned—he'd expected a mild apology, not this explosion.

"For all I know, you're the one behind all this," the teacher growled. "I know this wasn't an accident. Don't think I'm fooled! We were ahead, so you wanted to take us down!"

Mr. Garvey said, "What are you talking about?"

The Brookville teacher's fury only increased at this simple question. "I'm talking about the flat tire I just spent half an hour fixing. What else would I be talking about?"

CHAPTER SEVEN

ONE OF THE BROOKVILLE KIDS approached their teacher cautiously. "Mr. Regal, sir, we found the puzzle. We have to go through that maze over there."

Mr. Regal glanced at his teammate. Red-faced and furious, he looked like the last man in the world you'd find cavorting through a hay-bale maze. "All right. You kids get to it," he said. "I want to talk to our competition here for a moment." He laced the word *competition* with smoky anger. Winston wondered if he really thought Mr. Garvey was somehow responsible for their flat tire. More likely he was just lashing out at the world.

When the Brookville student had run off to join his teammates, Mr. Regal swung his glare around again to Mr. Garvey, who was trying to counter Mr. Regal's fury with an equal measure of calm.

Mr. Garvey said, "Someone gave us the gift of a flat tire as well."

Mr. Regal looked disbelieving, and reluctant to be anything other than angry. "Oh, really," he said. "And yet here you are, well ahead of us."

"We got ours right out of the gate, as we left the potato chip factory. Step around my car and you can see the spare tire for yourself. Believe me, we're a lot further behind than I want to be. It was a bottle—a glass bottle someone put under my tire. What about you?"

Mr. Regal slowly nodded his head. "That's what happened to us, too."

"As you left the planetarium?"

"No. We stopped at a deli for some snacks and drinks. We weren't in there more than five minutes. When we came out and backed up the car, there was a popping sound."

"I don't suppose you saw any other teams there," Mr. Garvey said.

"No. There was no one else in the store."

"Anyone else in the parking lot?"

"Don't you think I looked after I realized what had happened? There were other cars, but I don't know who they belonged to. I didn't see any other teams."

Mr. Garvey said, "We seem to have a very determined cheater in our midst."

Mr. Regal flushed again. "I should damn well say so. Obviously we were targeted because we were in the lead. We were the first ones to solve the planetarium puzzle, I'm sure of it. They can't compete with us on a level playing field, so they do these underhanded, *devious* . . ." He couldn't finish. He brought his clenched hands up in front of him as if he wished he had someone to strangle. He found his voice again and said, "I hope I catch that cheater in the act. I really do."

"I understand the feeling," Mr. Garvey said.

Mr. Regal took a deep breath in an attempt to get himself under control. "Now, if you'll excuse me," he said, "I have a puzzle to solve . . . and a contest to win." He gave Mr. Garvey a challenging stare, as if Mr. Garvey might suggest that they couldn't possibly win now. When Mr. Garvey said nothing, Mr. Regal turned his back and stormed away.

Mal said in a low voice, "All these teachers are crazy."

"Maybe they think the losers are going to be shipped to a desert island somewhere," Winston said.

Mr. Garvey watched the angry Mr. Regal for a moment and then slid into the driver's seat. Winston saw he was suppressing a smile. "What a nice guy," Mr. Garvey said as he started his car. "I wish him well."

He pulled out of the parking space. Winston took one last look at Sutherland Farms. He saw the girls from Greater Oaks—Bethany, Giselle, and Elvie—walking through the parking lot with their red-headed teacher. They must have finished the maze a few minutes ago. Winston ducked instinctively, but the girls weren't looking in his direction.

Mr. Garvey stopped at the edge of the parking lot. "Where am I going?" he said.

"Huh?" said Jake. "Oh." He began fiddling with the computer. "The next puzzle is at . . . oh, cool! Adventureland!"

"Adventureland! Awesome!" Winston and Mal grinned at each other. Adventureland was a seriously fun amusement park a couple of towns over. Winston and his family drifted over there a couple of times a year on humid summer nights.

Mr. Garvey grunted. "The first day of summer vacation that place is going to be jam-packed."

"Do we get in free there, too?" Winston asked.

"Yep. Just show them the computer."

"All summer long?" Mal asked.

Jake and Winston laughed. "Probably just today," Winston said. Mal snapped his fingers in mock disappointment.

"Okay," said Mr. Garvey. "I know where that is. Let's get going." He pulled out of the parking lot, and a few minutes later they were on a highway.

Winston gazed out the window and found himself thinking about the smile that Mr. Garvey had not entirely suppressed after speaking to the Brookville teacher. It was clear that Mr. Garvey considered the Brookville Brains' flat tire to be good news. The Brains had gotten pretty far ahead while Winston's team dealt with their own setbacks. Now they had caught up, and then some. By hurting the Brookville Brains, the cheater had inadvertently helped Winston.

He knew he shouldn't feel happy that Brookville had had such trouble, but a part of him couldn't help it. He remembered the stab of frustration he felt when he saw the Brains running out of the planetarium. He had wondered how his team would ever catch up. Well, now they had. He wondered where Brendan Root was and if his team had also had a run-in with the cheater. He hoped not . . . mostly. But he had to admit it wouldn't be entirely bad if Brendan's team was held in place for a little while.

If Winston and his team won now, would it be fair? It wasn't like *they* had cheated. Quite the opposite; they had been thrown out of the race not once but twice. If they managed to cross the finish line despite everything that had happened to them, they would darn well have earned the grand prize.

Of course, they were a long way from winning. He wouldn't count that prize money just yet.

Winston gazed out the window and soon fell into a game he played on long trips, as he watched the license plates on passing cars.

Look at the letters on the license plates you see and try to think of a word that includes those letters. The word must begin with the first letter and end with the last letter; the second letter can be anywhere in between. For instance, if you see the letters MHP, you might think of the word MISHAP or perhaps MICROCHIP.

Winston was able to think of <u>two</u> words for each three-letter set below. How many can you come up with? If you can get at least one answer for each set of letters, you're a word genius.

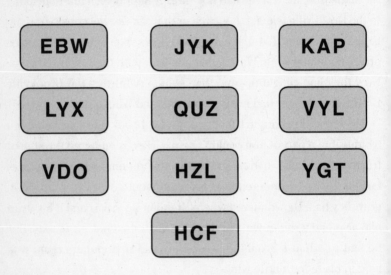

EBW	**JYK**	**KAP**
LYX	**QUZ**	**VYL**
VDO	**HZL**	**YGT**
	HCF	

(Answers, page 242.)

"Wait a second," Winston said. His dreamlike examination of passing license plates was interrupted by a random thought that had dropped from nowhere, demanding attention and pushing everything else to the side. "Wait a second," he said again, trying to lasso that thought, tie it down, figure out the words to express it.

Everybody waited, and then Mal said, "Yeeess?"

Winston said slowly, "The Brookville Brains were the first to solve the planetarium puzzle, right?"

"That's what they said," Mr. Garvey sniffed. "Doesn't make it true."

"They were one of the first, anyway. We saw them run out. And there were still a few teams in the theater when we got in there."

Mr. Garvey conceded the point with a shrug. "All right, fine," he said.

Winston felt his way along. "They had four good tires when they left the planetarium. Right? They drove to a deli, and they bought some drinks or whatever. While they were inside, someone came along and did to them what he'd already done to us."

"Gave them a back-tire wedgie," said Mal.

"Yes, he gave them a"—Winston stopped, completely derailed. He looked at Mal. "Is that really what a bottle under the tire is called?"

Mal shook his head. "I just made it up."

Winston stared at his friend for a moment and then continued. "I thought the cheater was a kid on one of the other teams, that he was cheating without anyone on his team knowing about it."

Jake said, "That's what I thought, too. That's what I *still* think."

"But it can't be," said Winston. "The entire team is cheating to-gether." He paused to give his next statement maximum impact. "In-cluding the teacher," he said.

"Wait a minute!" Mr. Garvey said. "You don't know that."

Jake turned around in his seat. "I don't get it either," he said. "How hard is it to pop a bottle under someone's tire or move a couple of signs? A kid can do that all by himself."

Winston said, "Whoever gave the Brookville team a flat tire had to follow them to the deli first. Did a kid drive the car?"

They thought about that. Mr. Garvey said, "Come on, Winston. I know there's a lot of money at stake here, but a schoolteacher isn't going to resort to cheating."

Jake gave a snort of laughter.

Mr. Garvey turned and gave him a curious look. "What's that supposed to mean?" he asked. Winston recognized a wisp of threat in that voice.

Jake must have noticed it, too. "Nothing," he said, turning to look out the window.

But Mr. Garvey persisted. "Is there something you want to say, Jake?"

For a moment, Winston thought Jake was going to keep looking out the window, saying nothing. But he said, "What you did to the girls' team was cheating. Leaving them in the wrong place."

"It was nothing of the sort," Mr. Garvey said. "It wasn't a very nice thing to do, perhaps, but it was hardly cheating. All these teams are very competitive. We're all looking for a way to get an edge on our opponents." He concentrated on the road long enough to change lanes. "Do you think if the girls' teacher had discovered the real puzzle location, while we were standing in that little hallway, that she would have come back and told us the right place to go?"

"Yes," Jake said simply. "We all said we would look for the puzzle together."

Mr. Garvey shook his head. "Don't you believe it, Jake. Don't you believe it. They would have left us there, same as we did to them."

Jake turned and looked out the window again. There was no point arguing. Jake thought Mr. Garvey was wrong, and Mr. Garvey thought Jake was wrong, and neither of them was going to convince the other.

"That said," Mr. Garvey announced, "I have a hard time believing a teacher would sink so low as to give somebody a flat tire. *That's* cheating. I still think it's one kid, not the entire team, and certainly not a teacher."

"How could a kid follow Brookville to the deli without a teacher's help?" Winston asked.

"Who said anybody *followed* them to the deli?" Mr. Garvey said. "It doesn't have to be that complicated. Another team decides to go to that same deli. The cheater is on that team. He sees Brookville's car, so he decides to give it a"—he almost said *a back-tire wedgie*, but caught himself at the last moment—"a flat tire. The rest of the team is in the deli. No one sees him do it. This kid's got a lucky streak a mile wide. But it's still just a kid playing some nasty tricks, trying to get ahead."

Mal said, "So that would put the cheater on Brendan Root's team, wouldn't it?"

"What? Why?" asked Winston.

"They left the planetarium a minute after the Brookville team. Didn't they? If anybody is going to follow Brookville to the deli, it's them."

"Yeah," said Jake. "But we already decided that Brendan's team *can't* be the cheater's team."

"We did? How did we figure that out?"

"Brendan's team was at the potato chip factory when we got there. The person who gave us the flat tire arrived *after* us."

"Oh," said Mal. He stared up at the ceiling of the car, trying to work it all out. "Then I have no idea," he said. "All I know is, this is giving me a headache."

"We're probably wrong about everything," said Winston.

"As long as we're not wrong about these puzzles," said Mr. Garvey. "That's all I care about."

Mr. Garvey had predicted that Adventureland would be jam-packed. He was wrong. It was several light-years *beyond* jam-packed. Every parking spot was taken, and a half dozen harried park employees were now waving cars to an adjoining grassy field.

Winston and his team emerged from Mr. Garvey's car and looked off to where the rides of Adventureland swirled and twirled. They were still incredibly far away.

"All right, let's hustle," said Mr. Garvey, and he began a quick jog toward the entrance. The boys followed suit.

"Nobody said anything about exercise," Mal groused. He was already falling behind.

"I'll buy you all some nice cold sodas when we get there," said Mr. Garvey. "Just keep moving."

Winston kept moving. He hoped they found this puzzle quickly—that the signs were big and that they saw them right away. Adventureland was a large park. If they had to search the whole place from front to back for a picture of Smiling Potato Chip Guy, they could be here for a long, long time.

"Hey, look there," said Jake, pointing. Brendan Root and his team were standing in the big grassy field, gazing around, looking lost and confused. Winston understood: They were searching for their car. They were *leaving* Adventureland—they had already solved the puzzle.

Winston stopped running. "Mr. Garvey, can I talk to them for a second?"

"What? Why?" Mr. Garvey said, irritated at another potential distraction.

"I want to know if they've had a flat tire."

Mr. Garvey stopped running, too. A thoughtful expression crossed his face, then he nodded. "Go ahead. Make it fast. We'll meet you right by that little shack up front where you buy the tickets."

The rest of his team continued to the park entrance. Winston veered right toward Brendan Root. He picked up the pace a little—he didn't want them to find their car just as he was getting close to them.

Brendan saw him coming and waved. "Winston!" He was happy to see his supposed rival. Delighted, in fact. His two other teammates and their teacher all looked up. None of them looked as happy about Winston's visit as Brendan.

"Hey, Brendan," Winston said, smiling. It was hard not to be caught up in Brendan's enthusiasm. He was like a puzzle-loving puppy dog. "How's the game going for you?"

"Great! This puzzle was fun, wasn't it?"

"Um, well, we're just getting here."

"Really?" Brendan looked shocked.

"Yeah, we've had a couple of problems."

Brendan's teacher said, "Where is your team, young man?" The two other kids on the team were gazing at him suspiciously. Winston guessed that Brendan's teammates were brothers. They had the same coal-black hair and thick eyebrows.

"Don't tell him anything, Brendan," said Brother One.

"Yeah, keep your mouth shut," said Brother Two.

Brendan's eyes went wide and innocent. "I won't, I won't. I thought he would have solved it already. Mr. Lester . . . this is Winston Breen!" This was said with the sweeping arm gesture of a circus ringmaster introducing the evening's top act. Winston felt himself blush.

The teacher, Mr. Lester, smiled and nodded. "Ah. Winston Breen. Brendan's told us a lot about you. How is your team doing?"

"We've solved two puzzles so far," Winston said, and saw how Brendan's teammates smiled at each other. Well, sure. They were a full puzzle ahead. "Listen," Winston continued. "A few teams think that somebody might be cheating."

"Cheating!" Mr. Lester looked amazed.

"Yeah. Have you had any unexplained problems? A couple of teams have gotten flat tires."

The members of Brendan's team all looked at each other, shrugging. Mr. Lester said, "No, I'd say we've had pretty smooth sailing. People do get flat tires now and again. I ran over some broken glass myself a couple of months ago, had to wait two hours for a tow truck. It didn't mean anybody was out to get me. I'd say it's a pretty big jump to say there's a cheater afoot."

"There's more," Winston said, and told them about how the signs in the planetarium had grown legs and walked away.

Mr. Lester looked a little more thoughtful. "Suspicious, I grant you. We'll keep our eyes open, I promise. But now we really need to find our car in this mess of a parking lot so we can move on to the next puzzle. If you'll excuse us. . . ." He smiled politely but made a shooing gesture. "We'll see you later on, back at the potato chip company." He and his boys walked slowly off, looking for their missing car.

Brendan lagged behind the others. He turned back to Winston and said, "Do you really think someone gave you a flat tire on purpose?"

Winston nodded. "Yeah."

"That stinks." Brendan really did look quietly devastated. "I wanted this thing to be you and me, going head to head. You know?"

"Well, maybe we'll catch up."

"I"—Brendan stopped. He glanced behind him. Mr. Lester and the two brothers didn't know that Brendan wasn't with them. He stepped closer to Winston and said in a low but excited voice, "I could tell you the answer to this puzzle. Then we'd be all tied up again."

Winston was alarmed. "No, don't! You'll get in trouble. We both will."

"If you didn't get that flat tire, I know we'd be neck and neck, racing toward the finish line. Two puzzle lovers! Who will come out on top?" Brendan's arms were swinging wide again.

"I . . . we can't do that. Maybe we'll catch up anyway."

Brendan paused, as if he might just blurt out the answer, consequences or no. But then he crumpled and said, "Yeah, okay." His eyes immediately glittered again. "I can give you a *hint*. . . ."

"Brendan, let's go!" Mr. Lester yelled, as if sensing that Brendan was about to give aid to the enemy.

"No hints," Winston said firmly. "I think they found the car. And I better get back to my team."

Brendan nodded. "All right." It was almost funny how morose Brendan looked, even though his team was probably winning. He slunk back over to his teacher.

Winston dashed off to rejoin his team. Mr. Garvey had allowed him to go, of course, but would probably still snap at him for taking so long.

Brendan was going to tell him the answer to this puzzle! Incredible. And incredibly stupid. If he'd allowed Brendan to spill the beans, it would have been a disaster. What would he have said to his team? "Guess what! Brendan and I cheated, so we're all set. We can move on to the next puzzle." His friends would have been shocked beyond belief.

And how would Mr. Garvey react? The math teacher had shown he was willing to bend the rules here and there. But even he would consider this to be way over the line . . . right? Winston had to admit that he wasn't sure. Either Mr. Garvey would slap Winston on the back to congratulate him, or he would yell at him until he had a seizure. Winston didn't know which possibility he found more unsettling.

All in all, Winston had to admit he'd felt a small grain of temptation to let Brendan open his mouth. It'd be nice to spring from the back of the pack into first place. Winston was enjoying the puzzles so far, but he had no confidence they could possibly win this.

"*There* you are," Mr. Garvey said as Winston approached. "I didn't know you were planning to have a picnic lunch with those guys. We watched two teams walk by while we were standing here!"

"Going in or going out?"

"Going out! They solved the puzzle! They found it and solved it, and we're just standing here. Let's go." Mr. Garvey started walking.

"Who was it?" Winston asked Mal and Jake. "Who did you guys see?"

"One of the teams had that kid on it," Jake said. "What was his name—John? You know, the one who said he was going to kick our butts."

"Oh, him. I guess he *is* kicking our butts."

Mal said, "He waved to us as he passed and said, 'Having fun?' You know the way he said it—what he really meant was 'Having fun, *losers*?' He might as well have said 'Nyahh, nyahh' and stuck out his tongue. I don't know if we're going to win this, but I sure hope we beat *him*."

"Who was the other team?" Winston asked.

"The Marin School," said Mr. Garvey. "One of the private schools. Smart kids, and they probably sent their smartest here today." He shook his head.

"Hey," said Mal. "We're smart."

"Yeah?" said Mr. Garvey. "Show me. Less talking. More walking."

They shouldered their way through the dense crowd, looking for anything that might be a puzzle. Winston was feeling particularly small and childlike, trying to make his way through groups of adults with strollers and gangs of high school kids enjoying the first day of summer break. It was uncomfortably crowded.

"Stupid," said Mr. Garvey. "Stupid to put a puzzle here on a day like this. It's just not thinking! How are we supposed to find it?"

"Other teams did," said Jake.

They found a small island of calm near some picnic tables and stopped to regroup.

"All right," said Mr. Garvey. "Where are we going?"

"I don't know," Winston said. "This place is huge."

"Does that computer give any more information?"

Jake said, "I don't think so, but I'll look." He turned on the computer, which promptly gave its opening *teedly-teedly-tee*. He poked at the buttons and said, "No. It just says Adventureland. Once we're here, we're on our own."

"Great." Mr. Garvey was disgusted.

Jake kept pushing buttons, while saying, "It would be nice if this thing told you who was in the lead." There was a moment's pause and then Jake said, "Oh my gosh! It *does!*"

"It does what?"

"It tells you who's winning the contest!"

"What? Let me see!" Winston said.

Jake handed him the computer. The Status button had brought up a simple chart, showing all their school names and which puzzles they had solved.

	Puzzle 1	Puzzle 2	Puzzle 3	Puzzle 4	Puzzle 5	Puzzle 6
Brookville JHS	●	●				
Cross Street School	●	●				
Demilla Academy	●	●				
Greater Oaks JHS	●	●				
Kennedy Junior High	●	●	●			
Lincoln JHS	●	●				
Marin School	●	●	●			
New Easton JHS	●	●				
Walter Fredericks JHS	●	●				
West Meadow JHS	●	●	●			

"There it is, all right," Winston said. "West Meadow, Kennedy, and the Marin School have all solved this. Everyone else must be here or on the way."

Mr. Garvey looked over their shoulders. "We know that Lincoln is here already," he said. "They left the farm a couple of minutes before we did."

"Lincoln," said Mal. "Which one is that?"

Jake said, "That's Mr. Garvey's archenemy."

"Cool," said Mal. "I wish I had an archenemy."

"He's not my enemy," Mr. Garvey insisted. But then he hesitated and added, "I just want to beat his pants off for once. Okay?"

Winston said, "Well, they must still be here, so maybe we can catch up."

Mr. Garvey took the computer from Winston's hands and shut it off. "We have to start moving faster. Where's that puzzle?"

They looked around. They were standing near some food carts, with long lines snaking every which way. To the right were the bumper cars—Winston could see the merry chaos of kids banging into each other. Up ahead was the park's beautiful, full-size carousel, and beyond that, the Ferris wheel. As a ride, the Ferris wheel was boring: You went up slowly, you came back down slowly. Big deal. Today, however, it caught his eye. "What's that?" Winston asked, squinting to bring it into focus.

They all turned to see. The wheel was stopped at the moment, so that people could get on or off. From here, they could only see the cars at the top. Usually, the cars were all painted bright yellow—the ride was actually called the Sun Wheel. Now there was a black painting on each car. From here, it looked like someone had painted a giant shoe on the topmost car. A shoe?

"Graffiti?" Jake said.

"I don't think so," said Mr. Garvey, hope dawning in his voice. "Let's go see."

They elbowed and shouldered their way through the crowd. Mal amused himself with an endless harangue of "excuse me, pardon me, coming through, excuse me . . ." until Mr. Garvey told him to keep quiet already.

They arrived at the Sun Wheel. Sure enough, signs had been placed all around, inviting park visitors to try Simon's new Potato Squares. This was the right place.

Each car of the wheel had been painted with a different, random icon. Was that supposed to be a rhinoceros? And an ice-cream cone? And, yes, that was a shoe painted on one of the cars.

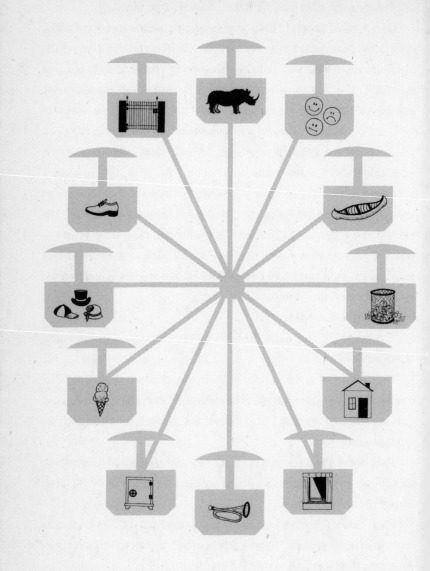

"Whatever I thought we were going to find here, it certainly wasn't *this*," Jake said.

"I'm trying to imagine the conversation Dmitri Simon had with the amusement park people," said Mal. "'I'd like to paint a bunch of pictures on your Ferris wheel.' 'I'm sorry, sir, we can't let you do that.' 'What if I gave you this big pot of money?' 'Oh, ho ho, that changes everything.'"

"So what are we supposed to do?" Mr. Garvey said.

"Dunno," said Jake.

Winston was suddenly aware of being stared at. He looked to his left and saw the team from Lincoln Junior High: Rod Denham and his three frowning kids. For a change, Mr. Denham wasn't wearing that superior smirk. Mr. Garvey and his rival made eye contact and waved to each other in a shaky display of sportsmanship. Mr. Denham then moved his team a few feet further away.

Mr. Garvey, still staring at them, said, "They were five or ten minutes ahead of us. If they're still here, they must be stuck. This is our chance to pass them by. Let's not blow it."

"Well," said Jake, "what are we supposed to do? Who has some paper? Let's write down what these things are."

Mr. Garvey had a small notebook he'd been using all day. He took out a pen and said, "Okay, toss them out to me. Start at noon."

"Start at noon?" Mal said. "It's already after twelve thirty."

Mr. Garvey stared at Mal in disbelief, then said slowly, "Pretend the Ferris wheel is a giant clock and give me the picture at the twelve-o'clock position."

"Oh."

Winston said, "That's a rhinoceros. Then there's a bunch of faces . . . a boat, or maybe that's supposed to be a canoe. Then that's a—"

"A garbage can," Jake said.

"Yeah," Winston said. "Then a house." The wheel was turning now, carrying new passengers. "After that we've got a stage or a theater or something. Then a trumpet."

"That's not a trumpet," said Mal. "A trumpet has whaddayacallem. Valves. That's a bugle."

"Okay, a bugle," said Winston. "Then a safe, an ice-cream cone—"

"Hold on," Mr. Garvey said, writing. "Okay, what else?"

"A bunch of hats. A shoe. And a fence."

"That last one is a gate," Jake said.

"Yeah, I think Jake's right. A gate."

Mr. Garvey crossed something out and then finished writing. He clicked the pen closed, looked at his boys, and announced, "I have no idea what this is."

"Me neither," said Winston.

"Do all these things have something in common?" Mal asked.

"Yeah," said Jake. "They're all made up from letters of the alphabet."

They stared at the wheel, all four of them, wide-eyed and increasingly baffled. Winston tried pairing the images up in some way. The shoe was right next to the hats, and both of those were kinds of clothing. That seemed vaguely promising . . . except why one shoe, and why three hats? Winston guessed that maybe the house and the stage could be paired up, too—they were both kinds of buildings. That didn't feel right, however. This whole line of thought seemed less than promising. Even if it was right, what then? Winston couldn't pair up any of the remaining pictures. A gate and a rhinoceros? Faces and a canoe? It was hopeless.

Mal said, "I guess the answer's going to be a twelve-letter word."

"What? Why?"

He shrugged. "I don't know. There are twelve objects . . . so maybe we have to take a letter from each one to spell out something?"

"How?" Winston asked.

"Beats me. I'm just throwing out stuff for you to use."

Winston sighed. This was the frustrating part, waiting for an idea to come from some magical place within the brain. Right now all he could think to do was stare at the Sun Wheel, rotating around.

The girls showed up a few minutes later. Bethany arrived first. She was gazing up at the Ferris wheel, unaware she had come to a stop right next to Winston, who wondered whether or not he should say something. Before he could decide, Bethany turned and saw him. She glanced up to see Mal and Jake as well. Winston might have said something at that point—though heaven knew *what*—but Bethany abruptly turned her back and stalked away. Her friends Elvie and Giselle came up right then, saw Bethany marching away, and ran to catch up.

Last to arrive was their teacher, Miss Norris. She came running up, as frazzled as ever. She was out of breath. "Girls, please," she called, between pants, "it's very crowded here, and I don't want to lose you—"

"We *said* where we were going," Bethany called back, disappearing from view around the side of the ride. Miss Norris was definitely not in charge of her team—certainly not in the same whip-cracking way that Mr. Garvey was.

Mr. Garvey caught Winston staring and gave him a light shake, as if to literally rattle Bethany and the girls out of his head. Winston, abashed, turned back to the Ferris wheel.

How could they get an answer word out of this bunch of pictures?

"Does this park have a stage?" Mal asked.

"I think it does," Winston said. "Why?"

"Well, there's a picture of a stage. Maybe it's a clue that we should go there."

"There's a picture of a rhinoceros, too," said Jake. "You think this park has one of those?"

A few minutes later, Mr. Garvey said, "A lot of teams here now. At least we're back in the thick of it." He kept looking over at Rod Denham's team to see how they were faring. Lincoln Junior High looked truly stuck, which would have been something to celebrate, except that Winston and his team weren't doing too well, either. There were several other teams gazing up at the Ferris wheel, mouths slightly agape, unable to make sense of what they were seeing. They all looked like victims of the same wizard's hypnotism spell.

"Maybe there's more to the puzzle somewhere," Mal said.

"Where?" asked their teacher.

"The other side of the wheel, maybe? There could be pictures on both sides."

Mr. Garvey looked at Mal with some surprise. "You might be right. Go and see."

"Can I go, too?" Jake asked quickly.

"And me?" Winston said. The three of them looked up at their teacher with pleading eyes. They may as well have said, "We really need to get away from you for a few minutes."

Mr. Garvey got the message and agreed. The boys tried not to appear too giddy as they left Mr. Garvey behind, but they all felt some relief as they walked away.

"I'm glad I'm only average at math," Jake said. "I'll never have him as a teacher."

"He just wants to beat that rival team," Mal said. "You should hear some of the things *you* say right before your baseball team plays Maplewood."

"That's different," Jake said.

"If you say so," Mal replied, shrugging.

Speaking of the rival team, the three of them walked past Rod Denham and the trio from Lincoln Junior High. They stopped talking as Winston and his friends drew close, and watched them pass with expressions of cool hostility, as if Winston was trying to eavesdrop or something.

"Everybody's so friendly around here," Mal said so the Lincoln kids could hear. "I am definitely inviting those guys to my birthday party."

The other side of the Ferris wheel looked no different—each picture had been painted on both sides of its car. So that was a bust; they had learned nothing new. They stopped nonetheless and looked up at the Ferris wheel from this new vantage point.

"Any idea what this is?" Mal asked.

Winston shook his head. "Not a one."

"Three teams solved it already," Jake said. "How hard could it be?"

Winston didn't reply. Every puzzle was hard when you didn't know the answer. Every puzzle was easy when you knew what to do. "Come on, let's circle back," he finally said.

They walked slowly, not saying anything. Winston stared at the pavement, the twelve pictures from the Sun Wheel spinning around in his mind. He felt like he was stumbling his way through a dark room, looking for a light switch that might not even be there. He thought of Brendan Root, who had solved this thing easily enough. "This puzzle was fun, wasn't it?" he'd said in the parking lot. What had Brendan seen in these twelve pictures that Winston was missing?

He was startled when Jake stopped his progress with a hand to his chest. "Look," he said. Winston looked up.

Twenty yards ahead was the girl's team: Bethany and her teammates, all in that same state of hypnosis, staring up at the Ferris wheel.

The three boys looked at each other, having a silent conversation about whether to continue forward or turn around like scared kittens.

"C'mon," Jake said, deciding for the lot of them.

They were only a few steps closer when Bethany glanced over and saw them. She nudged Giselle, who in turn nudged Elvie. Winston looked at his friends as if to ask, "Should we keep going?" Bethany had an expression on her face like she couldn't *wait* for the confrontation they were all about to have. But Jake never paused.

"The cheaters are here," announced Bethany. "Hide your belongings."

Winston flushed. He didn't know what to say. He knew the girls would feel tricked, but it felt awful to be accused of outright cheating.

Jake didn't like it, either. "We didn't cheat," he said.

"You left us standing in that hallway," said Giselle. "We were working together, remember? We were all looking for the puzzle together." Her pretty face was dark with disappointment.

"Our teacher did that," Jake replied in a calm voice. Winston was more than happy to let him speak for all of them. "He decided not to tell you when we found the puzzle. He's very . . . competitive. I'm sorry. We shouldn't have left you waiting there."

The girls looked at him, weighing the sincerity of this apology. The smallest girl on their team, Elvie, then said, "And what about the bathroom?" She crossed her arms while asking this, like a lawyer who knows she's about to make a defendant confess.

Winston didn't have the slightest idea what she was talking about. Neither did Mal or Jake. The boys looked at one another, each hoping somebody else knew what that question meant. Mal finally said, "I admit it. Sometimes I have to go to the bathroom."

Elvie grimaced. "The bathroom back at the farm," she said. "That was you, wasn't it?" She looked at them. "That was a mean trick."

Winston was starting to experience the detached and dizzy feeling that comes when you have no idea what is going on. "Whatever you're talking about," he said, "we had nothing to do with it."

"We're not cheaters," Jake said, a bit more adamantly. "Somebody else is cheating. They gave us a flat tire, and they moved the signs at the planetarium so that we couldn't find the puzzle. Whatever you're talking about, the cheater probably did that, too."

"I believe them," Bethany said, sounding surprised with herself.

"You do?" Giselle was shocked.

"Yeah. He's right. Someone moved those signs in the planetarium, but it wasn't these guys. They got stuck by that, same as us. They should have played fair and told us when they found the puzzle"— Bethany glanced at the boys one by one, as if daring them to argue this point—"but they didn't move the signs in the first place. Somebody's cheating, but it's not them."

"Who is it, then?" Elvie asked. Nobody could answer.

Winston asked them about this incident in a bathroom, and the girls finally told the story: Someone on the New Easton team, a girl named Krissy Huang, had gone into the ladies' restroom at Sutherland Farms. When she tried coming back out again, the door wouldn't open. The doorknob turned, but that was all—the door itself wouldn't budge an inch. She pounded on the door until Bethany heard the commotion and went to investigate. The bathroom door had been wedged shut with a small triangular block jammed tightly into the door frame.

Bethany couldn't pry it out. After calming Krissy down, Bethany ran to the young man behind the cash register for help. Soon someone came with a crowbar, and Krissy, shaken and upset, was freed.

"Who is this guy?" Jake asked angrily. "And how does he get away with so many nasty tricks?"

Nobody knew the answer to that. But as they talked about it, Winston realized something new: The cheater trapped this girl in the bathroom long after the leading teams had left for Adventureland. The cheater *couldn't* be on one of the winning teams. But why go through all this trouble, if not to steal victory from everybody else? It made no sense.

"Hey," Mal said, looking around, "where's your teacher?"

Giselle said, "Oh. Right over there." She pointed to the park bench, not that far away, where Miss Norris was sitting.

Mal said, "She's not standing over you, yelling at you to solve the puzzle faster?" He shook his head with wonder. "Would you like to trade teachers?"

The girls smiled. "No, thanks," Elvie said.

As if referring to Mr. Garvey was enough to summon him, the math teacher appeared suddenly from the other side of the Ferris wheel's enclosure. He saw his boys talking with the girls' team and called from a distance, "Excuse me. If you guys are finished chatting, I'd like to solve this puzzle before nightfall. Can we step back over here, please?"

"Sorry," Winston said, after a moment of awkwardness. "Uh, we have to go," he said to Bethany.

"I get that," she said. "See you later."

The boys and girls nodded good-bye to each other, and Winston and his friends caught back up with their teacher.

Mal said with a smile, "I think Winston is trying to win a different prize."

"How did I know you were going to say that?" Winston said. "Well, not *that*, but something close."

"They're all kinda cute, aren't they?" Jake said, looking back at them. He smirked at his friends. "Three boys, three girls. . . . You know what that means?"

"Yes," said Mr. Garvey. "We're going to lose. Can we focus, please?"

The puzzle was still here, revolving slowly in the afternoon sky. Winston still didn't have any idea where to begin.

"Well, you hoped for a harder puzzle," Jake said to Mr. Garvey as they all continued staring.

"I suppose I did. But I was hoping it would be harder for everybody else, not for us."

"Maybe we need to go on the ride," Mal said.

"What good is that going to do?" Mr. Garvey asked. "No. Just stay here."

Mal said, "What if there's something in the cars? Or maybe something on the ground that you can only see from the top of the Ferris wheel? We're not getting anywhere just standing here."

The math teacher grimaced and massaged his forehead. "All right. Maybe you're right. I don't know. But I don't want all of you going. You're on your own, Mal, all right? I want Winston and Jake to stay here and work with me on these words."

Mal nodded and sauntered off to ride the Sun Wheel by himself. Winston thought Mal had a pretty good idea: When you're stuck on a puzzle, it's good to try random stuff to see if it sparks any new inspiration. But Winston also had to admit he was doubtful that a ride in the Ferris wheel would lead anywhere.

Mal shouldered his way into the crush of people waiting to go on the ride. It was a small mob—for some reason they refused to form an orderly line.

There were other teams around the Sun Wheel, and a few of them noticed Mal getting on the ride. Rod Denham's team, off to the left, went into an urgent conference, and after a few moments, sent its own representative to go on the ride. Other teams followed suit. Bethany's team, on the other side of the Ferris wheel, must have noticed somehow, or perhaps they had the same idea on their own. In any event, here came Elvie, the smallest of the three girls. Winston wondered if she was even tall enough to go on the ride.

"All right, let's start this again," said Mr. Garvey, massaging the wrinkles in his forehead. "Pretend we just got here. Look! A whole bunch of pictures on that Ferris wheel! I'll bet this is the puzzle we're looking for!" He slapped both sides of his face in mock surprise.

Jake said, "Isn't *safehouse* a word?"

"Sure it is. Why?"

"Well, there's a safe," Jake said, pointing, "and there's a house. SAFEHOUSE."

That made a lot of sense. Winston began looking for other compound words. "Maybe that's not a trumpet or a bugle," he said. "Maybe it's a horn, and then you can make SHOEHORN."

Mr. Garvey was nodding enthusiastically. "Okay! Now we're getting somewhere. What else?"

The three of them kept staring. Winston glanced at Mal and saw him squeezing through the crowd, about to get on the ride. He wondered if they should call him back. Were they about to solve this?

Apparently not. "I hate to say this," said Jake, "but I don't see anything else. What are you supposed to do with the word *rhinoceros*?"

"RHINO HORN?" suggested Winston.

"We already used *horn* to make SHOEHORN."

"Maybe it's not a rhinoceros," Mr. Garvey said.

"Then what is it?"

"It could be . . . it could be the word *animal*." Mr. Garvey absorbed the doubtful looks from Winston and Jake. "All right, I'm just brainstorming here," he said.

Winston mentally combined the pictures and continued to get nowhere. GARBAGE HATS? RHINOCEROS FACES? After that promising start, all he could find was nonsense.

Mal was being led onto the ride now. Winston could see him hopping in to one of the cars. Elvie stepped into the same car. They seemed to be hitting it off. The Sun Wheel lurched and began to spin, and the two of them were soon swinging their way toward the top.

"I think we have to try something else," Mr. Garvey said, reluctantly.

"Me too," Winston said. "Can I see the list of words?" Mr. Garvey handed it to him.

Maybe the pictures weren't important, once you had named them all. Mr. Garvey had written the words down in a list. Winston wondered if he should write them out again, this time in a circle—maybe the pictures were in a particular order for a reason. He took the pencil from his back pocket, sat down with his back against a fence post, his knees up almost to his neck. He sketched out the words.

He looked at RHINOCEROS. Had he spelled it right? This was one of those words that always seemed to have a few extra letters in it, just for fun. "How do you spell *rhinoceros*?" he called to Mr. Garvey, but then instantly backtracked and said, "Never mind." He scratched it out and wrote RHINO instead.

And that was all it took. "Ahh!" he yelled, and threw his head backward, and hit it against the fence he'd been leaning against. He tried to jump up, but he wasn't in a position that allowed for jumping up. "Ahh!" he yelled again.

Jake asked, "Are you in pain, or do you have something?"

Winston stood up. He was nearly shaking with euphoria. "I have something."

Mr. Garvey said urgently, "You solved it?"

"I think so. Look." He held out the paper with the words written in a circle.

RHINO

GATE   FACES

SHOE   CANOE

HATS   TRASH

CONE   HOUSE

SAFE   STAGE

HORN

Winston said, "Each word is connected with the word directly opposite it."

"Connected how?" asked Mr. Garvey. "TRASH HATS? What does that mean?"

Winston shook his head. "Figuring out the connection is part of the puzzle. But I've got it."

(Continue reading to see the answer to this puzzle.)

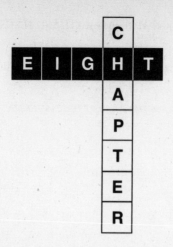

ANOTHER TEAM WALKED past. Winston thought one of the girls was Krissy Huang, who had been trapped in the ladies' room back at the farm. That would make this the New Easton team. They were staring up at the ride and trying to decide what to do next.

Winston took a few steps away to make sure they couldn't hear him. "Look," he said to his team in a low whisper, pointing at the paper. "Look at RHINO and HORN. All the letters in HORN are also in the word RHINO. If you remove all those letters, there's only one left."

"The letter I," Mr. Garvey said.

Winston continued, "You can do that with every pair of words across from each other. FACES and SAFE. Take the letters from SAFE out of the word FACES—"

"You get the letter C," said Jake. "Winston, you did it!"

Mr. Garvey said, "What word do you get when you solve every pair?"

Winston said, "ICARUS. Isn't that a word? Something out of Greek mythology, right?"

Mr. Garvey nodded in agreement. "Right, I know this one. He was the son of Daedalus. The two of them made wings out of feathers and wax so they could fly. Daedalus warned Icarus not to get too close to the sun, because the heat would melt the wax and his wings would be destroyed. But Icarus forgot what his father told him, and he flew higher and higher. And of course the sun melted his wings, and he fell into the sea."

Jake turned on the computer and began pushing buttons. "This has to be right," he said, typing in the answer. He stared tensely at the screen for a moment, and then beamed with happiness. "That's the answer."

There were high fives all around.

Mr. Garvey actually took two steps for the exit before he stopped and smacked his forehead. "Ugh! Mal is still on the Ferris wheel."

"Let's just leave him," Jake said.

"Don't tempt me." Mr. Garvey shielded his eyes, trying to find Mal on the ride. "I can't believe this. Here's our chance to pull ahead of a few more teams, and we're stuck here. Where is he?"

"Other teams have kids on the ride, too," Winston said. "If they solve the puzzle, they'll be just as stuck."

"Small consolation." He scowled at the ride, shaking his head. "Nothing to do but wait." He kept scanning the Ferris wheel, as if maybe he could climb up the outside of it and carry Mal back down.

They stood there a few moments, and then Winston said, "Can we go look at the games?" He pointed to the carnival booths a few feet away—kids lining up to throw darts at balloons and squirt water guns into the gaping mouths of clowns.

"Just stay where I can see you," Mr. Garvey said. "The second Mal steps off that ride, we are running for the gate. We are going to leave Lincoln Junior High in the dust." He kept glancing over at Rod Denham and his kids. Any minute now they might discover the solution and start cheering. Of course, Lincoln had a kid on the Ferris wheel, too—even if they solved the puzzle, they couldn't go anywhere.

Jake and Winston promised they wouldn't stray far and walked over to watch a couple of little kids try to catch plastic fish with a long pole. "Do you think we might win this?" Jake asked.

Winston shrugged. "If I was going to bet money, I'd have to put it on Brendan Root's team. They're way out in front."

"Only one puzzle ahead."

"There's only six puzzles. Being one puzzle ahead is pretty good."

A little girl caught a fat purple fish and claimed a tiny stuffed animal as her prize. She jumped with delight, and then she and her mother walked away.

"I used to love these games," said Jake. "Now they're just boring."

"My puzzle is still here, though," said Winston, gesturing to one of the other booths.

"Your puzzle? What?"

"I spotted it years ago. Come on." Winston led Jake down to a different game. A couple of teenagers were using long-barreled rifles to shoot at targets. The booth was done up like a sheriff's office in an old Western; posters on the back wall showed a bunch of villains and the reward you would theoretically get for capturing them.

Winston said, "Which three bad guys have rewards that total up to exactly a hundred dollars?"

(Answer, page 242.)

* * *

Jake was still staring at the posters when from behind them came a series of loud popping sounds. The two boys wrenched around, trying to find the source. The panicky, overdramatic part of Winston's brain insisted these were gunshots, but the rational side, less than a second later, placed the sound as mere firecrackers.

But the firecrackers had been lit among the crowd of people waiting to get on the Ferris wheel, and the result was the same as gunfire—several moments of yelling and chaos as the mob scattered like a flock of panicky birds. Winston spotted Mr. Garvey, pressed up against the fence to avoid getting trampled. The guy running the Sun Wheel had been helping people into one of the empty cars, and now he came running back to see what was happening.

Winston and Jake fought the crowd and made their way to their teacher. The staccato pops and bangs ended as suddenly as they had begun, the final explosions lingering in the summer air, along with several blossoms of gray smoke.

Winston looked around. Who had set off the firecrackers? He couldn't tell. He expected to see a couple of teenage boys, standing off to the side, laughing at the panic they had caused. But there was nobody.

People started coming back to the ride, and Mr. Garvey dismissed the event. "All right," he said. "Is Mal back yet? I'd like to get out of here already." He craned his neck, trying to figure out which car Mal was in while the ride was temporarily stopped.

At that moment, the guy running the ride said loudly, "Where's my key?" He was standing at the ride's mechanism, looking around, a bewildered expression on his face. He was in his early twenties or maybe not even that old, and had a scruff of beard and a pierced lip. "Hey!" he said. He turned to the people coming back to the ride. "Did you take my key? That's not cool, man. I need that."

Winston and Jake and Mr. Garvey watched the fellow pat his pockets and scan the ground for the missing key. Mr. Garvey's face reflected terrible understanding. He elbowed his way in and said, "What key? What did you lose?"

"The key to the ride! What do you think? The key to the Ferris wheel, man!"

Winston looked up at the ride and finally saw Mal. He was still in his car, fifty feet in the air.

The cheater. The cheater had set off the firecrackers, distracted everybody, and then snatched the key to the ride. A whole bunch of teams had people on that ride, and the cheater had bamboozled all of them in one go.

Mal, trapped on the Sun Wheel, was yelling something and pointing urgently. Winston tried to focus on what he was saying. It sounded like . . . "There! There!"

Winston and Jake whirled around, and they saw him, just for a fraction of a second: A man in a green jacket, a backpack over his shoulder, elbowing his way through the crowd, trying to get away.

Jake took off after him.

Mr. Garvey yelled, "No! Jake! Get back here!" But Jake wasn't listening. He ran at full speed—he might as well have been shot out of a cannon. Jake was one of the school's better athletes, a fact Winston sometimes forgot simply because Jake never bragged about it. Well, he was certainly reminding them now. He dodged through the crowd like an afternoon breeze, slipping sideways through tight spots, weaving around baby strollers, until Winston couldn't see him anymore.

Mr. Garvey grabbed Winston by the shoulders and shouted into his face. "Stay here! Do not move!" He took off after Jake, although at a much slower rate. Mr. Garvey didn't look like a guy used to running.

The people on the ride were beginning to realize they had a problem. Some of them were shouting "Get me down!" and "Hey! Why aren't we moving?" The guy operating the ride didn't seem to know what to do, other than pace back and forth uselessly.

"Is there another key?" Winston shouted to him.

"I don't know where the key is!" the guy shouted back, irritated.

Winston tried again. "Where's *another* key?" But the guy didn't answer, just kept looking at the ground as if the key might burrow out of its hiding place like a woodchuck.

Winston glanced up at Mal, who was clutching the bars of his skybound jail cell like a prisoner in a science-fiction movie. Beside him, Elvie was doing the same thing. At this rate, they were going to be stuck up there for a long time . . . unless somebody jumped in to solve this nasty little problem.

Knowing Mr. Garvey might actually kill him, Winston ran. *Someone* had to have another key to the ride, and Lip Ring didn't look like he was going to figure that out anytime soon.

He ran past Bethany and Giselle. "Where are you going?" Bethany yelled to him.

Not stopping, Winston yelled back, "The business office! They'll have another key!"

To Winston's surprise, Bethany burst into a run and quickly joined him. Winston heard her teacher yelling, but Bethany ignored her. She seemed to think that commands from adults—even shouted, urgent commands—were strictly optional. She was going to get into serious trouble later. Then Winston remembered that he was disobeying a direct order as well. There was going to be more than enough trouble to go around.

He headed for the heart of Adventureland. Bethany was right behind him.

The paths in the park ambled this way and that; you could hardly walk in a straight line for more than twenty feet. Winston and Bethany rounded a corner and almost crashed into a crowd of teenagers. They skirted around them gingerly, avoiding their glares and their shouts of "Hey, kid!"

"Cut through the arcade!" Bethany yelled to him and veered diagonally over to a long, low-roofed building. Winston, panting, his heart kathudding in his chest, strained to catch up. They bounded up the stoop and into the building, running past the Skee-Ball bowlers and little kids playing Whac-a-Mole.

They burst out the other side of the arcade and found themselves at the entrance to the office. The business office was a small, white house that looked like it had been blown here from a nearby neighborhood. When he was a little kid, Winston thought that some lucky family lived in that house, right in the middle of the amusement park. They ran up the three steps of the porch and through the door.

Behind a counter, an overweight woman sat pecking at a typewriter, and a casually dressed man was chatting on the telephone, leaning way back in his swivel chair.

This was not the time for politeness. "I need the key to the Ferris wheel!" Winston shouted, leaning all his weight on the counter so as not to collapse onto the floor. Beside him, Bethany was also trying to get her breath back.

The woman turned to look at him, startled. She wore a little name tag on her wildly colored blouse that identified her as Rhonda Weeks. The man on the phone ignored them—he turned away and put a finger in the ear that wasn't glued to the phone.

Winston only needed one person's attention. "The Ferris wheel is stuck," he told Rhonda Weeks. "The guy lost the key, and there are people stuck on the ride. You have an extra key, right? We need it!"

Rhonda squinted at him. "What do you mean, he lost the key?"

Waving her hands for emphasis, Bethany said, "Someone stole the key, and people are stuck on the ride."

"Ride operators are supposed to keep the key on them at all times," Rhonda said crossly.

Winston thought she was focusing on the wrong part of the problem. "Well, he lost it," he said. "Do you have an extra?"

She considered them for several long moments, and then said, "Yeah, hang on. . . ." She opened up a desk drawer and began rooting through it. Winston put a closed fist to his mouth to prevent himself from yelling at her to hurry up. He had hoped he could retrieve the key and get back to the Ferris wheel before Mr. Garvey even knew he had left. Winston felt the seconds race by while she sorted through a decade's worth of broken pencils and loose change.

"All right, here we go," she said at last. Then, to Winston's horror, she hoisted herself up from her sagging office chair. "Let's go see," she said.

Winston's plan was to run back to the Sun Wheel as quickly as they had run here. He did not get the impression that Rhonda Weeks was planning to run with them. For one thing, she was oblivious to the urgency of the situation. Also, it was clear that Rhonda Weeks had not done any running in a long, long time.

"Uh, okay," he said. He and Bethany shared a look of dismay.

Rhonda plodded to the office door, the key dangling casually in her hand. A plan materialized in Winston's brain. He knew it was a bad idea—maybe even a *very* bad idea. But he didn't see that he had a choice . . . not if he wanted to get back to the Ferris wheel during this century. There was still a chance he could get back without getting in trouble with Mr. Garvey.

Rhonda took her first slow step down the office's small porch.

Winston touched Bethany on the shoulder and whispered to her, "Get ready to run." He gestured purposefully at the key. She looked at him, at first not understanding, and then getting it all at once.

Not allowing himself to think, Winston jumped off the porch. He snatched the key out of Rhonda Weeks's fist, and ran.

"Hey!" she yelled, but Winston and Bethany were already twenty feet away. "Get back here!" she screamed. Other people glanced their way, but nobody made a move to stop them. His fevered brain tried to see into the future. Maybe this would all work out. He'd get back to the Ferris wheel, and if by some miracle Mr. Garvey was still chasing Jake and the man in the green jacket, then Winston would give the key to Mr. Lip Ring. They'd get Mal off the ride and out of the park before Rhonda Weeks caught up.

If everything went just right, there was a microscopically thin chance he might get away with this.

That thin chance vanished in the very next moment. Winston glanced behind him as he rounded the first corner and saw something he hadn't considered when he came up with this wacky idea: The guy who'd been on the telephone was no longer on the telephone. He had burst out of the office and was running straight at them. He looked very fast.

"Oh, no!" he said. Bethany looked over her shoulder and saw the problem. How could they possibly keep ahead of this guy?

"Come on," Bethany said, and ducked into the arcade again. Winston followed, trying not to panic. They had a head start, but it wouldn't last long. They had maybe ten seconds to figure something out.

Winston saw a photo booth with a curtain. A hiding spot! He started to jump in, but Bethany grabbed his arm, "No! Come with me!"

She ran down an aisle of arcade games, practically dragging Winston. She stopped abruptly and shoved Winston into the gap between two machines. There was barely enough room for him . . . but then, astonishingly, Bethany squeezed herself into the same gap, forcing Winston even further backward. He was as squashed as Santa coming down a chimney.

"Keep going," she hissed.

"There's nowhere to go," he whispered back.

"Yes, there is. Look."

Winston looked and saw that Bethany was right. The gap they had squeezed into was narrow but long, and where Winston thought it ended, it instead bent into a little L-shaped corner. Winston rounded this corner, and Bethany followed. They ended up in an even smaller space, packed as tightly as peanut butter inside a jar. But they were undoubtedly out of sight.

"That security guard would have looked in the photo machine first thing," said Bethany.

They were standing nose to nose or, more accurately, nose to chin: Bethany was about three inches taller than he was. Winston was all too aware how this would look to anybody who discovered them. He fervently hoped they were not discovered.

"How did you know about this place?" he whispered.

"My brother and I played hide-and-seek in here last year," she said. "He never found me."

"How long should we stay here?" Winston said. Bethany shrugged and shook her head.

Winston tried to listen beyond this fortress of video games, but he couldn't hear anything. The guy could be right outside their little cramped space. There was no way to know. But they couldn't stay here forever. Indeed, they couldn't stay here very long at all.

"We'll count to ten, and then we'll run," he whispered, and Bethany nodded agreement. Even a slight nod caused their heads to bonk together.

Winston forced himself to count slowly. He could feel his blood pumping in his veins; they needed to get back to the Ferris wheel. He was also a cauldron of emotions—delight, discomfort, amazement—at being so physically close to this girl who, he had to admit, he liked very much.

He reached ten, and they eased out of their hiding place. Bethany looked both ways down the aisle of arcade games.

Shaky with relief, she said, "It's okay. Let's go." They started running again. Winston still expected that guy to land on them at any second. But he was gone.

They ran down the pathway toward the final corner, euphoric at making it back to the Ferris wheel without getting caught. He felt like a spy who had successfully completed a dangerous mission.

That giddy feeling didn't last long. As they rounded the corner, Winston realized just how big a fool he was. When the security guy lost track of them, he didn't give up and go back to his office or vanish like a movie extra. He knew where Winston was going . . . and he went there first. The security guy was right there, waiting for them.

Worse yet, he seemed to have rounded up everybody involved with the puzzle contest. He was talking with Mr. Garvey, but all the other teams were gathered around, listening in. There was Rod Denham with his team, and there were Bethany's teammates. Even the Ferris wheel operator was there, Mr. Lip Ring himself. Winston groaned. The next few minutes were going to be very, very bad.

Mr. Garvey looked stonefaced, so angry he didn't know how to express it. The Ferris wheel was still not moving, which, in a way, was fine with Winston. He wouldn't have wanted to go through all this for nothing.

Everybody looked up as Winston and Bethany came into view. The man from the amusement park pointed at them as they approached. He looked like a professional wrestler, right down the furious expression on his face. "Give me that key," he said.

Winston, head down, handed the security guy the key, which he instantly turned over to Lip Ring.

"You're supposed to keep this on you at all times," the security guy said to the kid. "If this ever happens again, you can find another summer job." Lip Ring nodded his head, too afraid to speak. "Now get those people off the ride," the security guy said. Lip Ring wordlessly went to follow orders.

The security guy turned back to Winston. "And you," he said, "get out of my park."

WINSTON WAS FROZEN. He thought, Thank goodness we solved this puzzle. He couldn't imagine Mr. Garvey's reaction if they'd been kicked out without the answer they needed.

"You're still standing here. I said get out," the security guy said.

Mr. Garvey clutched Winston by the shoulder a little too tightly. To the security guy, he said, "One of my boys is on that ride. We'll wait to retrieve him, then we'll be on our way."

Miss Norris was leading Bethany away by the elbow. The security guard pointed at Bethany and said, "Her too. The lot of you. You're all out of the park."

"But we haven't solved the puzzle yet," Miss Norris said.

The security guy went goggle-eyed. "You're not solving the puzzle! You're leaving the park!"

Winston felt his stomach go sour. This was going as badly as it possibly could. Had he really thought he could run away, steal a key from a park employee, and run back here with no consequences whatsoever? Or that perhaps he would get yelled at briefly and that would be it? Well, now he knew better. He was in a ton of trouble, and what's more, it was his fault Bethany's team was getting kicked out of the park. By stealing the key, he'd ruined the contest for them—they wouldn't be able to solve this puzzle, and would never be able to win.

Should he just blurt out the answer? That would get Bethany's team back on track even if they got kicked out of the park. Mr. Garvey would be furious, of course—but then again, he already was. What's the worst that could happen to him? He wasn't sure if he wanted to find out. The answer to the puzzle—*Icarus Icarus Icarus*—bobbed in his throat, daring to be said.

Mal and Elvie joined them. The cars of the Ferris wheel are essentially metal boxes, and both of them looked like they had been in an oven set for a long, slow roast. Mal's T-shirt was soaked through with sweat.

"Whoa," said Mal when he reached them. "What happened to you?"

Winston turned to see what Mal was talking about and gasped. Wrapped in his own miseries, he never noticed that Jake had been beaten up. He had a waffle of a bruise on one cheek, his upper lip was bleeding and swollen, and he had a large black-and-blue mark under one eye. He was holding a white plastic bag, and Winston wondered where that had come from. Had it belonged to the cheater?

"Are you okay?" Winston said, appalled at himself for not noticing his friend sooner.

"I'll live," Jake said in a low voice. "I just want to get back to the car."

"That's exactly where we're going," said Mr. Garvey, steering Winston away with that hand clamped on his shoulder. Winston looked back at Bethany and her teammates. If Winston was going to shout out the answer, he'd better do it in the next five seconds.

But he couldn't. If he shouted out the word, he'd be giving it not just to Bethany's team but to four or five other teams besides. Mr. Garvey would kill him, and Jake and Mal would help. No, he couldn't just yell the answer. Bethany would have to work something out on her own. There was nothing Winston could do. He let Mr. Garvey steer them away from the Ferris wheel and the angry glare of the guard.

"So what happened?" Winston asked Jake as they walked. "That was the cheater, wasn't it?"

"Did you put him under citizen's arrest?" Mal asked.

"Citizen's arrest, yeah," Jake said, rolling his eyes. "Now I'm an honorary police officer."

"So what happened?" Winston asked again.

"It's a lucky thing we're not all driving to the hospital right now," Mr. Garvey said.

Jake put a hand up to his swollen eye. "I wanted to keep him from getting out of the park," he said. "That's all."

"Did he know you were chasing him?" Winston asked.

Jake laughed, a brief and bewildered sound. "I guess he did! The guy was like an animal that escaped from the zoo. If he couldn't go around a group of people, he'd crash right through them. The guy was *scary*."

Mal shook his head in amazement. "I would have just stopped and waved good-bye to him." He demonstrated this, waving his arm vigorously. "Good-bye, crazy, scary, cheating person! Don't come back!"

"That would have been a very good idea," Mr. Garvey said.

"Maybe I should have," Jake said. "I really thought we had to stop him. I knew I wasn't going to beat him up or anything like that, but I was hoping I could knock him down or something."

"What would that have accomplished, Jake?" Mr. Garvey asked, shaking his head.

"If I stopped him, even for thirty seconds, I thought maybe a security guard would step in and grab him."

"He was so much bigger than you," Winston said.

Jake told them his idea was to slam his body into the guy, so that they both fell to the ground. "When I caught up to him, though, I tried this football-style tackle. I got my arms around him." He demonstrated, extending his arms out wide as if to deliver a bear hug to an actual bear. Winston was amazed at Jake's nonchalant bravery. There was no way Winston could have done any of this. He would have done exactly what Mal suggested: wave good-bye.

"That's when the guy smacked me," Jake said. "I thought I was going to fall—I *did* fall, but not before our legs all got tangled up together. I tripped and hit the sidewalk. But the cheater went *flying*." Jake smiled at the memory. "His whole body was up in the air for a moment. It's too bad he was facing away from me—I would have loved to have seen his face. He landed on the ground, and he lost the bag he was carrying."

"Is this it?" Winston asked, pointing to the white plastic bag Jake was carrying. "You stole his bag?"

"No. I mean, I *wanted* to steal his bag. He had a shoulder bag, and he dropped it when he fell. I tried to grab it, but he got there first and smacked me again." He added in a low voice, "That really hurt." He put a hand up to his face. "Then he ran off," he concluded.

Mal said, "Man, if we see this guy again, I am totally going to . . . stick my tongue out at him. And then run away."

Jake told them that for a moment he could only lie there, sick with pain. "Then Mr. Garvey showed up. He helped me get on my feet."

"How long did you strangle him?" Mal asked Mr. Garvey.

Jake said, "You know, I didn't even get yelled at, now that I think about it."

"You were lying in a heap on the ground," Mr. Garvey said, a bit defensively. "Ebenezer Scrooge wouldn't have yelled at you."

"That must be the secret," Mal said. "Next time I forget to do my science homework, I'll throw myself down the stairs before I go to class. That way I won't get in trouble."

"Good plan," Winston said.

"Anyway," Jake said. "We didn't get the cheater's bag, but some stuff spilled out of it."

Winston said, "You got some of the cheater's things? Really? What did you get?"

Jake handed the plastic bag to Winston. "Take a look," he said.

They stopped walking for a moment. Winston opened the bag, and he and Mal peered in.

Winston pulled out a glass bottle. He thought at first the cheater had filled it with beads or rocks. Then he realized what he was looking at: The bottle had been filled to the neck with glass shards from other broken bottles. The world's most terrible soft drink. This was how the cheater delivered flat tires with such ease.

Mal dug around some more in the bag. He removed a small coil of twine and another string of firecrackers. Most oddly, he took out a set of mousetraps, still shrink-wrapped in their original packaging. "What was this guy going to do with a bunch of *mousetraps*?" Mal said, dumbstruck.

"There's more," Jake said. "Look at the memo pad."

"Memo pad?" Mal asked. "What was he going to do, give us all paper cuts?"

"Just look," Jake said.

Something in Jake's tone made Winston dimly alarmed. He reached into the plastic bag and found a perfectly ordinary memo pad. He flipped through the pages, many of which were crumpled and mussed. He didn't find anything exciting. "Carburetor from Mack" read one note. One page had strings of meaningless numbers, and there were doodles all over. Winston looked up at Jake questioningly.

"The last couple of pages," Jake said.

Winston turned to the last page of writing, and for a moment, he wasn't sure what he was looking at. At first all he saw was a bunch of letters and numbers. Then his glance settled on something he couldn't quite believe. Written in the cheater's memo pad was his own name: BREEN.

"What . . . ?" he said.

"That's your name!" Mal said.

"What's my name doing in here?" Winston said. "This guy *knows* me?"

Jake shook his head. "I don't know."

"What are all these letters and numbers?" Mal asked.

"License plates," said Mr. Garvey. "Your name is written next to my license plate number."

Mal said, "How does he know your license plate number?"

"I guess he saw it and he wrote it down," Mr. Garvey said. "He gave us that flat tire, after all."

There were a couple of other names in the book. Next to one license plate number was the name SEYMOUR. Next to another was SCOTT. Next to a third was DENHAM.

"Who are these other people?" Mal asked.

Jake said, "Denham is Rod Denham—that math teacher Mr. Garvey likes so much."

"Scott . . . that might be Michael Scott," said Winston, "the kid from the private school we met in the maze."

"Who's Seymour, then? A kid from another team?" Mal said. "Poor guy. Who names their kid Seymour?"

"That's Bethany's last name," Winston said. "Whoever this cheater is, he knows Bethany . . . and he knows me."

The three friends stared at each other with astonishment.

Mr. Garvey spoke up. "Okay, boys. This is what we're going to do. You guys meet me at the car. I need to go back to the Ferris wheel for a moment."

"You do?" Winston said. "Why?"

"Never mind why," Mr. Garvey said. "Just meet me by the car."

"I thought we were in a huge rush," Mal added.

"We are," said Mr. Garvey, "but there's something I have to do first. I'll be along in five minutes." He took the memo pad out of Winston's hands and the plastic bag from Jake. As he gave Jake his car keys, he looked down on the three of them and said, "Listen to me. If I get back to the car and even one of you is missing, I am going to do everything in my power to see you all get left back a grade. I'll break into the school's computer network if I have to. Maybe move all of you back to kindergarten. Do you understand?" The boys all nodded. "Then go." Mr. Garvey turned on his heel and headed back into the park.

The boys watched him go. Winston had been sure that Mr. Garvey would want to run like mad back to the car—why did he need to stay behind? Well, they had their orders. The three boys turned and trudged through the parking lot. It felt like every car in the state was parked here. They finally tracked down Mr. Garvey's car, but when they got there, nobody wanted to wait inside. Opening the doors released a hateful puff of sun-broiled air. They all said no thanks to that.

They opened the hatchback instead, and Jake dug out an ice-pack. It wasn't particularly cold anymore, but it was better than nothing, so he wrapped it in some paper towels and held it against his swollen lip.

"What do you think Mr. Garvey's doing?" Mal said.

"Telling the other teams what happened," Winston guessed. "Warning them about the cheater."

"That makes sense," Jake said. "I wonder why he didn't just say that."

Winston kept thinking about that bottle filled with broken glass. What an ugly trick. He imagined the cheater breaking a bunch of glasses and jars, then carefully pouring the shards into empty bottles to make his booby traps. Who would think of doing something like that? And why was he doing it at all?

"Who is this guy?" he said out loud.

"The cheater?" Mal said. "He has to be working for somebody."

"Who?" said Jake. "A rival potato chip company?"

Mal said, "I was thinking more like one of the other teams." He stood up from where he'd been sitting on the car's tailgate. "We all thought the cheater was somebody playing in the puzzle hunt. That's still true. But instead of doing all the cheating himself, he's working with somebody else. The kid on the team solves the puzzles, while his . . ."

"Older brother?" Winston suggested.

"Maybe," said Mal. "While his older brother—or whoever—runs around tripping everybody up."

They thought about that.

"Jeez," said Winston. "Someone really wants to win this thing. And it doesn't make sense. All the prize money goes to the school. It's not like the kid gets anything."

"He gets to say he won," said Jake.

"That's still a lot of trouble to go through," Winston said.

They fell into silence, the three of them now sitting in the grass beside the hot car. They were too hot and tired and confused to try to figure out the mystery of the cheater and how Winston's name wound up in his memo pad. Mal dug out some food, and Jake took a bottle of water. Winston found himself staring up at the big

ADVENTURELAND sign in the distance, and within a few minutes he was jotting down an idea for a puzzle.

All the words in this crisscross can be made from the letters in ADVENTURELAND. One word has been placed to get you started. Can you fit the rest into the grid?

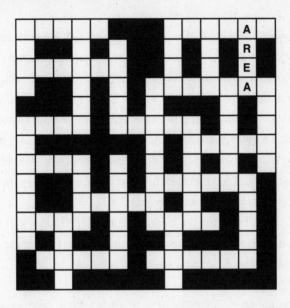

Four Letters	**Five Letters**	**Six Letters**	**Seven Letters**
AREA	DATED	ANTLER	ETERNAL
AUNT	ELUDE	AVENUE	LANTERN
DENT	EVENT	ELATED	
DUEL	LATER	NATURE	**Eight Letters**
EARN	LEARN	NEATER	EVALUATE
EVER	LEAVE	NEVADA	
LAND	NAVEL	RENTAL	
NEAR	RATED	UNDEAD	
NERD			
RANT			
REEL			

(Answer, page 242.)

After a while the car was aired out well enough, so the kids sat inside with the doors open. They were still mulling over everything that had happened in the park. "It's ridiculous that you got into trouble for getting that key, Winston. You got us out of there! You're a hero!"

"What about me?" Jake said.

"Who, you?" Mal said. "The cheater got away!" He gave an exaggerated snort of digust. "Getting yourself beat up isn't heroic."

Jake laughed and took a playful roundhouse swing at him.

Winston didn't feel much like a hero. He'd retrieved the key, sure, but he felt bad about getting Bethany's team kicked out of the park. If only that security guard had helped Jake catch the cheater instead of chasing Winston for stealing a key! Then everything would be fine, and nobody would have gotten into trouble except the man in the green jacket, the one guy who deserved it.

He looked off toward the park entrance. Mr. Garvey still wasn't coming, but he saw Bethany and her team heading in their direction. "Guys, look," he said.

"More happy kids enjoying a fun-filled day of puzzles," Mal said. He was being sarcastic, of course. Bethany, Elvie, and Giselle all looked miserable. For once they were trailing behind their teacher, who was storming ahead, presumably to her car.

Winston watched them for a moment, then said to his friends, "Come on." The three of them got out and walked over to the girls.

"Did they let you solve the puzzle before kicking you out?" he asked, a false cheerfulness on his face.

"It doesn't matter," said Bethany, not stopping. "We're quitting the game."

Winston was astonished. "You're what? Why? Because we got in trouble for stealing the key?"

Bethany shook her head. "Because of what that cheater had. Your teacher said my name was in his assignment pad." She stopped now and faced him. "Is that true?"

"Mr. Garvey told you that?" Winston asked. Well, duh—of course he had.

"Is it true?" Bethany said again.

Winston could only nod agreement. "Yeah, it's true. My name was in there, too."

"It was?" Bethany looked surprised. "Your teacher didn't say that."

Giselle was looking at Jake's face. "Are you okay?"

"I'll live."

"Did the cheater hit you?"

Jake tried a smile. "Not as hard as the sidewalk did."

"Wait a minute," Bethany said. She pointed at Winston. "Your name was in that book, but you guys aren't quitting?" She looked at all of them, her eyes shining with accusation.

"Uh, no," said Mal. "I don't think we are."

"But that's not fair!" Giselle said, spinning around to face Miss Norris. "We shouldn't quit, either!"

Miss Norris once again hadn't realized that her girls had gotten away from her—in this case, they had stopped while Miss Norris marched onward to her car. Now she came back, looking frustrated. Her red hair was frizzier than ever—it looked like she had recently received a moderate electric shock.

"Girls, I'm done talking about this. Stay with me. Don't you understand what's happening? I'm taking you home right now."

"We're quitting for no good reason," said Bethany.

"There's some strange man out there who means us harm," said Miss Norris, as firmly as Winston had ever heard her speak. "I wouldn't call that no reason."

Bethany groused, "I don't understand how my name could be in his stupid book. I wasn't even supposed to be here today. I was supposed to go to a wedding. But we couldn't go because my father got sick. So I came to this instead. Now my whole team has to quit because I'm here."

"Wait a minute," Winston said. "When did your plans change?"

"Yesterday. After dinner."

"So you didn't know you were going to be here until last night?"

Bethany nodded. "Pretty much."

Miss Norris began leading her girls away again. Winston was processing a whole new line of thought. He wished he could stop time for a little while—just hit the pause button and sit here on the ground, thinking about what Bethany had told him. She wasn't supposed to be here, yet her name was in the cheater's memo pad. What did that mean?

He had to ask some questions before the girls were taken away forever. He chased after them. "Miss Norris," he called. "Were you the one to break the code? The invitation to the puzzle contest?"

Miss Norris looked at him. "Our vice principal did it, mainly. I was there. We didn't know what it was. A bunch of teachers helped out in the staff room."

"Did you call the phone number?"

"No, the vice principal did."

"But you heard him do it," Winston persisted.

Miss Norris took a deep, annoyed breath, unsure where this was going or why she was allowing herself to be interrogated by a twelve-year-old. But she said, "Yes, I heard him make the phone call."

"At that point, you didn't know who was going to be on the puzzle-solving team, right? The vice principal didn't give any names out."

"No. He just said the name of our school into the answering machine. We didn't figure out who was going to be on the team until later. May I ask why you're asking?"

Winston said, "I'm trying to figure out how the cheater knew who would be here today. Bethany says that *she* didn't know she was going to be here until last night. But the cheater had her name. It doesn't make sense."

Miss Norris nodded, as if agreeing. But she said, "It also doesn't matter. This has gotten a little too dangerous, and I have a responsibility to these girls."

"We're not afraid," said Bethany. "Are we, Elvie?"

"I'm a little afraid," Elvie said in a quiet, serious voice. "It's creepy that there's this guy out there doing all these things, and it's terrible what he did to Jake."

Jake's hand went up to his black eye at the mention of his name.

"You see?" said Miss Norris.

"But I still don't think we should quit," Elvie concluded. "That's what the cheater *wants*, you know. He wants us to quit. So I don't think we should."

Miss Norris was quiet for a moment, as if she couldn't immediately find a response to Elvie's logic. Then she shook her head and said, "It doesn't matter. We've been kicked out of the park, and we never solved this puzzle. So we can't win anyway. Let's go."

Winston again considered giving them the answer to the Ferris wheel puzzle. Somehow, he didn't think Miss Norris would appreciate that.

But then he said, "Wait! You can still solve this puzzle!" The girls and their teacher turned and looked at him. He couldn't believe he hadn't thought of this sooner: Winston dug a piece of paper out of his pocket. Yes. All the words from the Ferris wheel, written in a circle.

It was everything they needed. He extended the paper to Miss Norris. "Look. You don't need the Ferris wheel at all. All the words are written right here. I can't tell you the answer because I guess that would be cheating. But you can still solve the puzzle."

Miss Norris looked at Winston's extended arm, then took the piece of paper from his hand.

Sensing a crack in her teacher's resolve, Bethany said, "It's my name in that book, and I don't want to quit. The boys aren't quitting, and neither should we! And if we can solve this puzzle after all. . . . Miss Norris, please! Let's keep playing!"

Miss Norris looked at the paper. She glanced up at Winston, her expression somewhere between suspicious and hopeful. "You're giving this to us?"

"It's my fault you got kicked out of the park," Winston said.

"It's Bethany's fault," Miss Norris said. "She followed you."

"I'm sorry," said Bethany. "I shouldn't have run away. But please don't make us quit. We'll listen to you from now on. We'll be good." Elvie and Giselle nodded in fervent agreement.

Miss Norris did a poor job suppressing a smile, and Winston knew the girls had won. "Get in the car," their teacher said. "If we all stay together from now on, we'll keep playing. If you run away from me again, that's it. We're going home. Also, you have to solve this puzzle, of course," she added, waving Winston's piece of paper.

The girls jumped up and down. Giselle said, "We will! Let's go!" They all danced their way through the parking lot. Bethany looked over her shoulder and beamed at Winston. That was thank you enough.

As the girls walked down a row of cars to Miss Norris's sedan, Jake said, "Oh man. She totally likes you, Winston."

Winston didn't know what to say to that and was almost relieved when a voice behind them said, "I thought I told you boys to wait by the car!" Mr. Garvey was suddenly marching toward them. He looked beside himself with exasperation. Winston and his friends flinched. Mr. Garvey said, "I thought I threatened dire, drastic consequences if you boys were not by the car when I arrived."

"The car's right there," Mal said, pointing.

"Yes. And you're *here*. Thank you for making my point for me. Let's go. We have a lot of work to do yet." He marched back to his car, the boys following.

"What were you doing back there?" Jake asked.

Not turning around, Mr. Garvey announced, "I thought I had a responsibility to tell the other teams about the cheater."

"You sure scared Bethany's teacher," Winston said. "They almost quit."

Mr. Garvey stopped. "Almost?" he said. "She said she was taking her girls home."

"They changed their minds," Mal said.

They all saw it, right then. Mr. Garvey knocked his fist against his leg and shook his head—an expression of frustration. Winston and his friends traded a few charged looks.

Winston said to Mr. Garvey, "Did you *want* them to quit?"

Mr. Garvey tried on a smile. "I didn't try to talk them out of it, if that's what you mean." He looked at his car. "You boys left all four doors wide open, *and* the trunk. That's just great."

Mal said, "We were airing it out."

Mr. Garvey shook his head and got into the driver's seat. Winston took the passenger seat next to him. "Did anybody else quit?"

"Hmm?" said their teacher, starting the car, not looking around.

"Did any of the other teams quit when you told them about the cheater?"

Mr. Garvey said carefully, "Two other teams decided this fellow maybe made things a little riskier than they preferred. Mal, Jake, get in the car already!" Mal and Jake slid in, troubled looks on their faces.

"Who else quit?" Winston asked.

Mr. Garvey backed up, and the car bounced in the grassy field. He said, "That private school that dresses so fancy, what's their name? The ones we met in the maze."

"The Demilla Academy?"

"That's right," said Mr. Garvey. "Their teacher agreed that his students' safety had to be considered. So they bowed out. So did another school, New Easton Junior High. A girl on that team apparently had her own run-in with our friend. Frightened her quite badly." That, Winston knew, would be Krissy Huang, who'd been locked in the bathroom.

Jake asked, "Did you show them that stuff to warn them about the cheater, or to get rid of the competition?" There was a sharp tone in his voice.

There was a brief snarl of traffic at the exit. Mr. Garvey used the opportunity to look at Jake in the backseat. "I did the responsible thing. I told them about the cheater and that he had some of our names and license plate numbers. That's all. Now, let's move on to the next puzzle, and let's win this contest. Shall we?" He turned around in the driver's seat and zoomed out of the amusement park, as if hoping to leave this conversation back in the parking lot.

The boys got the message, and a strange, tense silence filled the car. Winston watched the road go by. Mr. Garvey was right . . . sort of. They had to tell the others about the cheater and the notes he'd taken. But he had the vague idea that Mr. Garvey did more than that. Winston could easily see him presenting the memo pad in such a way as to convince teams to quit the race. Three teams out of ten had given up after Mr. Garvey spoke to them. Bethany and the other girls had changed their minds soon after, but still. Mr. Garvey sure had a talent for getting teams to drop of out of the game.

He wants us to quit, you know. That's what Elvie had said, regarding the cheater. And she was right. Who would be happiest about seeing teams drop out of the race? The cheater . . . and whoever the cheater was working with.

Was there a chance that Mr. Garvey was working with the man in the green jacket?

No. No. Stop it, Winston told himself. For heaven's sake—their team had been the very first hit by the cheater, when they were given the back-tire wedgie. Mr. Garvey wasn't working with the cheater. That was insane.

But Winston was sure that his teacher tried to frighten other teams into dropping out of the contest. And that meant, for at least a few minutes, his goals and the goals of the man in the green jacket had been the same. Winston glanced at his teacher and decided that bringing up this observation wasn't a very good idea.

"Where are we going now?" Mr. Garvey asked. "Where's the next puzzle?"

"Oh, right. I've got it, hang on." Mal had the computer and busied himself pushing buttons. "Now we're supposed to go to a police station! A precinct back in Glenville." He recited the address.

"A police station?" Mr. Garvey mused. "What on earth kind of puzzle could Simon put there?"

"Maybe they'll put us in jail," said Mal, "and we'll have to break out."

"How far behind are we now?" Mr. Garvey asked. "What does that computer say about who's winning?"

Mal pushed more buttons and let out an excited gasp. "We're coming up on puzzle number four, right?" he said. "Listen to this! Nobody has solved it yet."

The air in the car filled with a new urgency. They could catch up. They were, in fact, catching up.

"It must be really hard," said Winston.

Jake said, "Brendan Root and those guys . . . they must have been there for half an hour or more by now."

"They must be stuck," said Mr. Garvey, his voice as hopeful as a child opening his birthday presents. "If they're stuck, and we get there and figure it out quickly, we're still in the game." His eyes were gleaming. "We're still in the game," he said again, as if to say it repeatedly was to make it true.

Winston asked to see the computer, and Mal handed it to him.

	Puzzle 1	Puzzle 2	Puzzle 3	Puzzle 4	Puzzle 5	Puzzle 6
Brookville JHS	●	●	●			
Cross Street School	●	●	●			
Demilla Academy	●	●	●			
Greater Oaks JHS	●	●				
Kennedy Junior High	●	●	●			
Lincoln JHS	●	●	●			
Marin School	●	●	●			
New Easton JHS	●	●				
Walter Fredericks JHS	●	●	●			
West Meadow JHS	●	●	●			

"Everybody has solved the Ferris wheel puzzle now, except for New Easton Junior High and Bethany's team," Winston said.

"New Easton dropped out," Mr. Garvey reminded them. "And I'm afraid the girls were kicked out of the park, so I'm not sure what they're going to do." He didn't sound sorry at all, of course.

There was an awkward silence in response to that. "Huh, yeah," said Mal. "Well, they'll figure out something, I'm sure."

Winston resumed looking out the window, so that Mr. Garvey wouldn't see him smiling.

After a minute, Winston asked, "Did you show the memo pad to Mr. Denham?"

"I did," said Mr. Garvey.

Of course he had, Winston thought—Mr. Garvey wanted to scare his rival team into quitting.

The math teacher continued, "And they were on the verge of solving the Ferris wheel puzzle, by the way. We're ahead of them now, but only barely."

"Did Mr. Denham have any idea why his name was on the cheater's list?"

Mr. Garvey shook his head. "He saw the cheater for a quick moment, right before he ran away. He didn't get a great look, but he swears he's never seen the guy before in his life. He couldn't imagine how the cheater would know his name. Are you concerned that your name was on his list, Winston?"

"I guess I am a little."

"Well, you stay close to me. I'm not going to let anything happen to you. Just because we're not running away like scared rabbits doesn't mean I'm not taking this person seriously. How do you think he knows about you?"

Winston had been wondering about that himself. Suddenly, he

realized there might be a way to figure out the answer. Maybe. He sat up a little straighter in his seat, and thought about it. Yes. A really wonderful idea was sprouting in the middle of Winston's brain like a whole flower garden.

If he got very lucky, he could find out who was cheating.

"Winston?" said his teacher. "Hello?"

"Mr. Garvey," he said, "can I borrow your cell phone?"

THE VOICE ON THE other end of the phone was gruff and impatient. "Who's this?" it said, all but accusing Winston of interrupting something important.

Winston felt himself losing his nerve. The man he'd called, Ray Marietta, was an ex-policeman who had been an important part of Winston's last treasure hunt. Winston hadn't spoken to him in months, and he'd had the idea that maybe Ray would be happy to hear from him. That idea went right out of his head the moment he heard Ray's voice.

"Uh, Ray, hi. . . . It's Winston. Winston Breen."

"Winston?" Ray sounded surprised. "What can I do for you?" Ray made this friendly question seem very unfriendly, as if he could not imagine what Winston might ask that Ray would be willing to do.

Winston wasn't sure where to begin. His realization was this: The cheater had called him at home the same day they had cracked the code. Who else could have made that strange, suspicious phone call? It had to be the man in the green jacket, or whoever was working with him. That's how the cheater knew Winston would be here. He was willing to bet that the other people on the cheater's list had received similar calls.

"Can you trace a phone call?" Winston asked.

There was a startled silence from Ray Marietta, followed by loud, raucous laughter. Winston had never heard Ray laugh before. He sounded like a washing machine with too large a load in it. *HUH HUH HUH HUH HUH!* Winston got the feeling his brilliant plan was going to die right here at the first step.

"You want me to *what*?" Ray said when he could speak again. "Why do you need a phone call traced?"

Winston explained as succinctly as he could: that they were playing in a puzzle contest sponsored by Simon's Snack Foods, but someone was running around sabotaging other teams, and this cheater, whoever he was, had beaten up his friend Jake.

"Is that the short kid with the big mouth?" Ray asked.

"No, that's Mal," Winston said. During that last treasure hunt, Ray had met both his friends, and he'd found Mal to be more annoying than a cloud of mosquitoes. Ray gave a little grunt, like he was sorry it hadn't been Mal who'd been smacked around. Winston finished his recap of the events by talking about the cheater's list and how Winston's name had been on it.

"Are you saying this guy is after you specifically?"

"It looks that way. Me and a bunch of others."

"Why didn't you call the police?"

"I thought I was."

"You know what I mean," Ray said. "The police who are actually police. I'm retired, you know that."

"That didn't occur to me," Winston said. "I just thought of you."

Ray grunted again. "All right. What do you want? To trace a phone call? I can't do that. Besides, how would that even help you?"

Winston said, "The cheater called me. Or somebody working with the cheater. I want to know who made that phone call."

Ray was silent for a moment or two before saying, "Well, first of all, you can't trace a phone call without a court order, and I can't get a court order because I'm not on the job anymore. Second of all, you can only trace a phone call that's happening at that moment. This phone call happened when? Last week?"

"A few days ago," Winston said, his heart sinking.

"Yeah," said Ray. "You can't trace that call."

"So there's nothing you can do," Winston said.

"Oh, now," Ray said. "I didn't say *that*. This guy, whoever he is, really beat up a kid?"

"And he gave at least two teams flat tires," Winston said, "and he sabotaged the Ferris wheel over at Adventureland. We have to find out who he is."

There was a silence as Ray thought for a moment. "All right," he said. "What's your phone number?"

"My home number or the cell phone I'm on now?"

"Both."

Winston said his home number, and then had to ask Mr. Garvey for his cell phone number, which he relayed to Ray. "What are you going to do?" he asked.

"I know a guy," Ray said. "He might be able to do something. I'll call you back." And before Winston could ask another question, Ray hung up.

"Is he going to help?" Jake asked when Winston closed Mr. Garvey's phone.

"I think so," he said.

"How is our old pal Ray?" Mal said.

Winston thought of that small grunt Ray made after he'd asked if Mal had been beaten up. "He says hi," Winston said.

As they approached the police station, there was some conversation about whether or not the puzzle would be difficult to find. It was not. In fact, it was quite a spectacle and had attracted a crowd.

Winston pressed his nose against the car window, trying to comprehend what he was seeing. On the police station's neatly manicured front lawn, a platform had been built with six makeshift jail cells. Each one held a prisoner. The prisoners were dressed like they had been brought here from a 1920s-era silent movie: They wore old-fashioned convict uniforms with wide, black-and-white horizontal stripes, and little black-and-white caps. The prisoners paced in their small cells, sometimes stopping to grasp the bars and stare out at the gathering audience.

At various points around the platform were advertisements for Simon's Square Potato Chips. The onlookers must have been perplexed about the connection between potato chips and this mock outdoor prison.

Mr. Garvey parked. In his excitement, he went a little too fast and had to slam on the brakes—all the kids in the car lurched. They got out of the car. The weird homemade prison looked very far away.

"Come on, let's run!" Jake said, and started doing just that.

"Wait, wait, *wait!*" Mr. Garvey shouted, and they all stopped abruptly. Winston nearly ran into Jake's back. Then Mr. Garvey said, "Why am I telling you to wait? Go! Run! I'll catch up."

So they all ran again. "But stay together!" Mr. Garvey shouted after them.

It was hot out, but it was good to run, and great to feel like they were still in the game. Winston looked around for Brendan Root but didn't see him anywhere. Maybe they had solved the puzzle in the last few minutes. Still, they were definitely catching up.

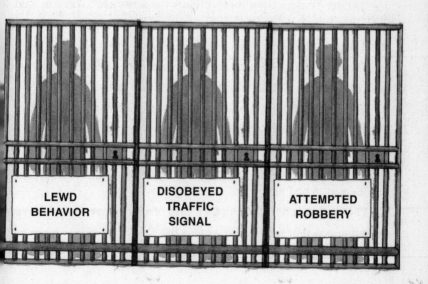

He saw a couple of other teams staring at the prison from a distance, or studying something they had written down.

They drew closer to the pretend prison, and now Winston saw another element of the puzzle: In front of each cell was a sign, supposedly showing what each prisoner had done to earn this humiliation.

A photographer stood to their right, taking pictures of this crazy scene. A label on his shoulder bag identified him as working for the local newspaper. The photographer called out, "Hey, Tommy!"

The man in the Lewd Behavior cell looked around, wondering who had called his name. He spotted the photographer, who sang out, "I knew they'd catch you one day!" He cackled, and Tommy, in the cell, nodded wearily, like he'd heard this joke several times already.

Jake said, "So what is this?"

Winston said, "I have no idea."

"Stole friend's *chickens*?" Mal said. "What kind of crime is that?"

"Dmitri Simon chose these crimes for a reason," Winston said, trying to think of some ideas. Or even one idea. Right now he had nothing.

They all thought about it for a few moments. "Do they really put you in jail if you disobey a traffic signal?" Jake asked.

"My sister would be in jail a dozen times by now," Mal replied. "She thinks stop signs are suggestions."

Mr. Garvey had caught up, panting a bit. He looked around, his face a mix of wonder and bafflement. "This is a puzzle?" he said.

"Seems to be," Mal said.

The math teacher took another gasp of air. "I guess Dmitri Simon isn't interested in sudoku. So what is this?"

"We don't know yet. We were just looking at those signs."

Mr. Garvey nodded. "Attempted robbery," he said. "Counterfeiting. . . . Yes, these certainly look important. How many letters are on each sign?"

That was a pretty good thought, so they counted. There were twenty letters in the first sign . . . and also in the second sign. The third sign had fourteen letters. Winston thought maybe they could apply the familiar 1 = A, 2 = B, 3 = C alphabet code, but that gave them a word beginning with TTN. Not very promising.

The prisoners continued to pace. They all looked sorry they'd gotten involved with this event. Perhaps they hadn't considered just how long they would be in these closed-in little cells with nothing to do but walk back and forth. At least real prisoners get a cot to lie down on. These guys didn't even have that.

The signs, the signs, the signs. That had to be the important part of the puzzle. Did those crimes have something in common? Winston couldn't see that they did.

There was a shout from his right. Winston looked and saw the team from Lincoln Junior High. Rod Denham, sweating profusely, held a piece of paper, and his three students stood close around him, studying it. Intensity radiated off them like sunlight. They had just come up with an idea. As Winston watched, one of the kids nodded excitedly to another, who took the small computer out of his backpack and turned it on. Winston could hear the *teedly-teedly-tee* start-up sound. The teammate began pushing buttons and, after a moment, gave a huge fist-pump in the air. The team traded high fives, and the kids from Team Lincoln ran off to the next puzzle. Rod Denham followed behind them a bit more slowly.

Mr. Denham glanced over at Mr. Garvey. That smug smile was back on his face. "You were ahead of us for a moment there, Garvey," he said as he passed. "Good for you!" He chuckled as he walked away.

Mr. Garvey turned scarlet. He couldn't find any way to respond—he just stood there looking furious. His competition with Mr. Denham was like a virus in his bloodstream.

Jake said, "He just says those things to throw you off your game."

Mal added, "It's psychology! He's messing with your brain." He twittered some fingers through his hair as if giving his own brains a stir.

Mr. Garvey whirled on them. "I know that. Obviously I know that." He took a deep breath as his kids watched him. He pointed at the prisoners and barked, "Would the three of you focus more on the puzzle and less on me, please? I want to hear some ideas. Now!"

So they turned around and stared some more at the jail. After a while, Mal said, "Let's move closer." That was something to do, anyway, so they bobbed their way through the small crowd of on-lookers—shoppers and restaurant-goers who had to stop and gaze at this spectacle.

Jake said, "Hey, look at that."

They looked at the prisoners. They looked at the signs. "What am I looking at?" Mal said.

"The numbers. That's probably important, isn't it?"

Winston didn't see any numbers, but then all of a sudden he did. Each of the uniforms bore a white patch embossed with a black number. The man who had supposedly Cheated Your Neighbors (and why "your" neighbors? why not "his" neighbors?) was prisoner #238.

"Might be a red herring," Mr. Garvey said. "Might just be part of their costumes."

"Can we write them down anyway?" Winston asked. So Mr. Garvey got out his pad and pen again. He made a little chart.

#238 Cheated your neighbors	#159 Stole friend's chickens	#136 Counterfeiting	#236 Lewd behavior	#678 Disobeyed traffic signal	#348 Attempted robbery

"Yes!" came a cry to their left. They all spun their heads. It was Bethany and her team. They had approached the cells, too, and now they were jumping up and down—all four of them, including Miss Norris. After this short celebration, they all ran back to the parking lot.

"Whoa," said Jake.

"They came closer to the prison, just like we did," said Winston. "Maybe these prisoner numbers are important after all. Maybe that's the key."

(Continue reading to see the answer to this puzzle.)

Mal saw it first. It was almost as if the answer had snuck up from behind and grabbed him. His arms flailed out in different directions and he yelled with astonishment: "Hey! HEY!"

"Hey, what?"

"Wait a second, wait a second," Mal said. He seized the notebook out of Jake's hands and stared at it with widening eyes. "Ah!" he yelled after a moment. "See! See? See!"

Winston was amused. "Either he has the answer," he said, "or his brain has exploded."

Mal finally calmed down enough to explain what he'd discovered. The prisoner number *was* important. The first number was #238. If you took the second, third, and eighth letter out of that prisoner's crime, you got the word HEY. You needed to take the first, fifth, and ninth letter out of the second crime, which gave you the word SEE.

They quickly counted out the rest of the letters they needed. This gave them six three-letter words.

HEY   SEE   CUE   EWE   EYE   TEE

"That's not a coincidence," Winston said.

"It's not an answer, either," Mr. Garvey noted. "What are we supposed to type into the computer?"

"All six words?" Mal suggested.

"Yuck," said Winston.

But they agreed it was worth a shot, so Winston turned on the computer and navigated his way to the proper place. He typed in the six words and, not surprisingly, was told, "That is not the right answer."

"No dice," he said.

"We've got it," said Mr. Garvey. "We just don't know it yet. How can we turn these words into the answer we need?"

(Continue reading to see the answer to this puzzle.)

Jake got it this time. Winston felt a pang of jealousy. He hadn't contributed a single thing to this puzzle. Well, he'd solved other things today. You couldn't solve them all.

It was so obvious Winston felt ashamed for not seeing it immediately. The six words all sounded like letters. HEY didn't sound *exactly* like the letter A, but the other five words undoubtedly clued the letters C, Q, U, I, and T. Put them all together and they spelled ACQUIT. That had to be the answer, and it was. Winston, fingers shaking with excitement, typed it into the proper space, and received a congratulations in return.

"That was some fast solving, boys," said Mr. Garvey. "That's exactly the break we needed. Come on! We can do this!"

Back in the parking lot, Mr. Garvey fumbled with his keys as he tried unlocking his car. A couple of cars away stood another team, engaged in some sort of high drama. Winston recognized one of the boys: John Curran, the obnoxious kid who said he was going to kick everybody's butt. So this was the team from Kennedy Junior High. John was yelling—screaming, really—at one of his teammates, a girl who was sitting on the tailgate of her teacher's car, her hands up to cover her face. Winston heard John shout, "How could you do that? How could you be so stupid?" John's teacher had a hand on his shoulder. She was trying to pull him away. The third teammate was just standing there, arms crossed, staring at the ground, a picture of defeat.

Winston knew what this was. He looked at the rest of his team, and they'd all figured it out, too. The smart money was that the cheater had pulled another stunt.

Mr. Garvey walked over. "What happened here? Are you okay?" he said.

The teacher looked up. "You're part of the contest, right?" the Kennedy teacher asked. Mr. Garvey nodded. "Well, we're having a little problem here. It seems this young lady lost the computer we were given."

"I didn't! I'm sorry!" the girl cried. "I think someone stole it. I think someone picked my pocket!"

"Ridiculous," said John Curran. His arms were crossed indignantly. "Who would steal it? *How* would they steal it? You think one of these other kids is a professional pickpocket? You lost it! You ruined this whole contest!"

"Actually," Mr. Garvey said sadly, "it might not be as ridiculous as you think." He explained about the cheater and the other things he had done.

Beyond that, however, there was nothing they could do to help the Kennedy team. The girl, Nicole, had kept the mini computer in a pocket of her backpack. After they'd solved the prison puzzle, Nicole had reached for the computer so they could submit their answer . . . and discovered the pocket unzipped and empty. They had looked all around them and then they ran back to the car to see if maybe it had dropped out there. Nothing. It was gone, and the Kennedy team, which had been fighting for the lead, was ruined.

"This cheater stole something while standing in front of a police station," Mr. Garvey said as they pulled out of the parking lot. "This guy doesn't give up."

CHAPTER ELEVEN

IT WAS GOOD TO BE HOME. The Glenville town green, a quick bicycle ride away from Winston's house, was the site of the fifth puzzle. It was a large expanse of lawn with the town hall on one end and the library at the other. Park benches, the rich green grass, and a nearby row of small shops attracted people on every sunny day, and today was no exception.

Dmitri Simon had trained them by now to expect the unexpected—after the Ferris wheel and that crazy prison, Winston would not have been surprised to see a parade of camels and elephants on the town green. So they were brought up short when they didn't immediately see anything that resembled a puzzle—no grand spectacle, no chaotic and strange element dropped onto the green for passersby to gawk at. There were a lot of people walking, enjoying the day, and that was it.

Mr. Garvey kept looking around. "Is this the right place?" he said. "Are you sure?"

"The computer said the town green in Glenville," said Jake.

"This is Glenville," Mal declared. "This is the town green."

"Look," Jake said. "There's the Lincoln team."

It was true. Lincoln Junior High was walking along the green as a group. Where were they going? As Winston watched, they approached a girl wearing a bright yellow T-shirt. They talked with her for a minute, and then the girl handed them something. The Lincoln kids looked at it and fell into an intense discussion while the girl wandered away.

"Hmm," said Mr. Garvey.

Now that Winston looked around a little more closely, he saw a lot of people on the green wearing brightly colored T-shirts. There were a dozen or more of them, in a vibrant rainbow of colors. A young man wearing a loud purple shirt walked in their direction—and as he got closer, Winston saw the words "Simon's Snack Foods." Aha.

The young man, wandering aimlessly, pivoted on one heel and sauntered back in the other direction. On the back of his shirt was a picture. Winston strained his eyes to make it out. It was . . .

"An egg?" he said. "That guy has an egg on the back of his shirt."

"You'd think it would be a potato," said Mal.

"Why a potato?" Winston asked.

"He works for a potato chip company. Duh."

"Look over there," said Jake, pointing elsewhere. They watched as a girl in a green T-shirt walked by. On the back of her shirt was a picture of a pair of shoes.

They observed the scene for a few moments more, and then Mr. Garvey said. "All right, guys. Believe it or not, we're going to split up."

"We are?" Mal said.

"Look around," their teacher said. "These kids in the shirts are everywhere. If we have to go up to every one of them, it's going to take forever." He began pointing around the green. "Jake, you take that area. Mal, you go over there. Winston, head in that direction. I'll go over here. Approach these people, get whatever they're giving out, and then we'll meet back here in ten minutes. All right? Go!"

They went off in all directions.

Winston looked around as he walked and saw more teams—there was one sitting on a bench, there was another running to catch up to a guy in a red T-shirt. He glanced toward the street just as a car parked—all the doors opened and another team flew out, ready for anything. They stopped short when they discovered they didn't know where to go or what to do. Well, they would discover the people in the T-shirts soon enough.

He wondered where Brendan Root was. How close were they to winning?

Winston also wondered if the cheater was around here somewhere. What was that guy planning to do next? And to whom? A cold shudder shook him—suddenly, being off by himself didn't seem like such a hot idea. Ray Marietta had asked, "He's after you specifically?" That was the typically blunt way Ray put things, but it was true. The man in the green jacket was after him, and a bunch of other kids, too. He was somewhere nearby—Winston was sure of it. He was watching, waiting to make his next move.

Stop it, he told himself. He was frightening himself like a little kid reading ghost stories. Winston was out in the open, in a familiar, public place, in full view of fifty or a hundred people. There wasn't much the cheater could do here. Still, better to get the job done and rejoin his team.

Up ahead was a girl in a green T-shirt with a picture of a snail on the back. How strange. Winston ran up to her.

"Uh, hi!" he said to her. "You're . . . you're giving away something?"

"Do you have an answer for me?" she said.

Winston didn't know what that meant. "An answer? To what?"

"To my riddle: If you beat me, I will yell. What am I?" She looked at him expectantly.

"That's a riddle?" Winston asked.

"It is. Do you know the answer?"

He didn't. The girl saw the blankness on his face and nodded with sympathy. She said, "You can come back and tell me the answer whenever you have it. Bye, now." She wandered off.

Could the answer be a snail—the picture on the back of her shirt? No, that didn't make much sense, funny as it might be to imagine hitting a snail and having it yell at you, angrily waving its slimy little antennae.

All at once he had a blast of realization—the right answer was going to be on one of these shirts. He just had to find the right person. And one of these other people had a riddle, the answer to which would be a snail.

Winston was suddenly whipping his head around, trying to see everywhere at once. The town green never seemed larger, and the college kids in the colored T-shirts were all over the place. He ran to the next closest person and looked at his back. This guy's picture was a can of paint. That wasn't the answer to the girl's riddle, either.

The guy noticed Winston and turned to face him. He was frowning and spread his arms out like he was about to sing opera. "I have a riddle for you," he intoned gravely. "Tell me the answer if you can." This guy was definitely taking his role seriously. Maybe too seriously.

"Okay," Winston said.

The guy cleared his throat theatrically and said, "I get shorter the longer I stand. What am I?"

Winston sighed. He didn't know the answer to this one, either.

The guy saw that Winston didn't know and shook his head, clucking with pity. "If you cannot answer, I cannot help you. Good day to you." He swept himself around as if he thought he was wearing a great royal robe instead of a purple T-shirt.

Had it been ten minutes yet? Winston had only spoken with two people. Maybe they shouldn't have split up in the first place. He looked around for Mal and Jake and didn't see either of them. Winston could swear the town green was lengthening before his eyes, as if two giants had grabbed it from either end and were stretching it out.

He heard someone call his name and spun around. He was glad to see it was Brendan Root, who was practically skipping toward him. Winston grinned. He'd have to figure out a way to get in touch with Brendan when this was all over. They would have a lot to talk about, if Winston was able to get a word in edgewise.

"Winston!" Brendan said again. "You caught up!"

"Have you guys finished?" Winston asked, dreading the answer.

He was relieved when Brendan only shook his head. "I think we're almost done with this puzzle. I'm looking for a"—he gave Winston a look like a kid caught stealing cookies. "I can't tell you what I'm looking for, can I?"

"Probably you shouldn't."

Brendan rubbed his hands together hard, as if not blurting things out required a real and true effort on his part. "Are you almost there, too?" he asked.

"We just got here a few minutes ago, so it looks like you guys are still pretty far ahead."

Brendan couldn't hide his satisfaction. "I thought maybe we weren't winning anymore," Brendan said. "We got hung up at the police station. We lost a lot of time there."

"Oh?" Winston thought of the cheater. Had he struck again? "What happened?"

Brendan said, "We spent forever staring at those signs, and we didn't think to move closer to examine the prison or the prisoners. So we didn't see the numbers on those uniforms for a long, long time. Man, were we stuck. Mr. Lester was going crazy."

Winston nodded in understanding. "My teacher has had some crazy moments today, too."

As if responding to his cue, Winston heard his name bellowed from across the park. Winston saw Mr. Garvey, back where they were supposed to meet, waving his hands in the universal gesture of *Come on, already!*

"I gotta go," he told Brendan.

"All right. I'll see you back at the potato chip factory! Good luck!" He was standing less than two feet away, but he waved happily. This was someone having a mighty good time.

When Winston arrived back at the park bench, Mr. Garvey was frowning and tapping his foot impatiently. Mal and Jake had already returned. "Let's have the report. These people had riddles for you, right?"

"Yeah," said Winston. "Although nothing I could answer."

"Me neither," Mal said. "I kept waiting for 'Why did the man throw the clock out the window?' but it never came up."

Jake said, "I think I know what's going on, though."

"Me, too," Winston said.

"It's clear what's going on," Mr. Garvey said curtly. His state of agitation was on the rise again. "The answers to the riddles are on the backs of these shirts. We need to collect all the riddles and write down all these pictures. Then we can sit quietly and match them up. That's the cleanest, most straightforward way of attacking this problem." He withdrew his memo pad and a pen. "Okay, give me the riddles you've heard so far."

Winston recited the two riddles he had heard.

"Only two?" Mr. Garvey said.

"That's all I had time for before you called me back."

Mr. Garvey grunted and turned to Mal. "All right, go ahead."

Mal recited three riddles in his most serious tone. He saw that Mr. Garvey was in no mood for fooling around.

"Jake?"

"Uh . . . I can only remember two," Jake said. He recited his two riddles.

Mr. Garvey said, "We need them all, Jake. What were the others?"

Jake looked off in the distance as if hoping the riddles had been written on the side of the town hall. He tapped his forehead, looking frustrated.

Mr. Garvey sighed. "Too many knocks in the head playing football, I'd imagine," he said.

Jake was offended. "I don't play football. I play baseball."

Mr. Garvey rolled his eyes as if the distinction between various sports was so small that it was hardly worth arguing about. "Baseball, football. It doesn't matter." He tapped his memo pad with his pen. "This is unacceptable. We need the rest of those riddles, and we need them now. We're *close*, gentlemen. We're close! Winston, I saw you talking to that young man again. What did he say about their progress?"

"He said they were almost done with this puzzle."

Mr. Garvey looked like he'd bitten into a lemon. He tore pages out of his memo pad and handed them to the three boys. "Okay. We're separating again. Go back to the same area you covered before. *Run* and write down every riddle these people have to say. Don't worry about answering them. Don't even *think*. Just write down the riddles. And write down what each person has on their back. Write it all down and get back here *fast*. Do you hear me? Fast!" He looked at them, trying to drill his intensity into them with his stare. Winston, for one, got the message. "Do you each have a pen?" They all did. "Then go!"

It took a while, and toward the end, Winston could feel Mr. Garvey's agitation like radio waves from across the green. But the college kids in the colored T-shirts kept walking around, and it was hard to keep track of which ones he had spoken to and which ones he had not. He went up to the same bland-faced, sandy-haired kid three times in ten minutes.

Mr. Garvey was again the first back at the park bench they were using as a home base. When Winston returned, he was slumped over, frowning deeply and looking at the mini computer. "West Meadow has solved this," Mr. Garvey said. "That's your friend, isn't it?"

"Yeah. Brendan Root's team."

"They're almost done. All they need now is the sixth answer." Mr. Garvey looked up. He looked like he had aged ten years since this morning. "We're running out of time," he said. "We could have won this whole thing if hadn't been for the cheater. We caught up, but it wasn't enough." He shook his head, too tired to be angry.

Mal and Jake got back within thirty seconds of each other. "Did you get all the riddles?" Mr. Garvey asked. "And all the pictures on the back of their shirts?"

"I think so," Mal said.

"Let's see."

They sat together on the bench and compared notes. Winston could see that Jake was still sore about Mr. Garvey's sports comment—their teacher had practically called him a dumb jock. But he was willing to put aside his disgust for the sake of the team. He wondered if Mr. Garvey noticed that.

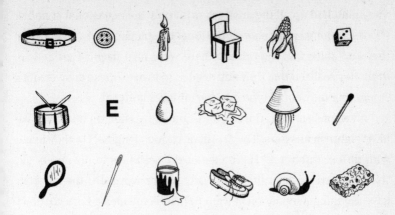

- *I have one eye and a sharp toe. What am I?*
- *Sometimes I have two eyes, and sometimes I have four, and my life often hangs by a thread. What am I?*
- *Most people put me out at night yet do not lock me out. What am I?*
- *My coat is very thin indeed, but you wear me around the house. What am I?*
- *I get shorter the longer I stand. What am I?*
- *You must break me before you can use me. What am I?*
- *My legs are strong, but I will not run and play. You sit upon my lap for hours every day. What am I?*
- *Scratch my head and it's no longer red. What am I?*
- *I'm round in the daytime and long at night. What am I?*
- *If you beat me, I will yell. What am I?*
- *I will not burn in a fire, and I will not drown in the water. What am I?*
- *Sometimes you can't make a move without me. What am I?*
- *I'm the end of time and space. In fact, I'm the end of everyplace. What am I?*
- *If you turn me around, I can no longer see. What am I?*
- *Throw away the outside, cook the inside. Then eat the outside and throw away the inside. What am I?*
- *I'm full all day but empty at night. What am I?*
- *I may be small, but I fill my house from top to bottom. What am I?*
- *I am full of holes, but I can still hold water. What am I?*

(*Answer, page 243.*)

They matched up all the answers, with only the occasional stumble. ("Does a sponge grow shorter the longer it stands?" Mal asked.) After they had solved all the riddles, there were high fives all around . . . until they realized that they still needed to turn all these answers into something they could type into the mini computer.

"All right," said Mr. Garvey, a distant expression on his face. "We have eighteen answers. They're all of various lengths. Do they begin with different letters?" He looked at the scribbles in his notebook. "No. We have to turn these into an answer word. Do the answers have anything in common? I want to hear some ideas! Let's go, don't make me do this by myself."

Jake said, "I think we need to give each answer to the person who asked the riddle. Remember? They were giving something away when you told them the right answer."

Mr. Garvey looked startled for a moment, then smiled sheepishly. "Of course. That's clearly what we need to do. I should have thought of that myself."

Jake nodded with mock sympathy. "Too many blows to the head," Jake said, tapping the side of his own head. "Affects the thinking."

Winston looked at his friend and then quickly over to Mr. Garvey, who by his expression was trying to figure out how to accept this obvious jab. For a moment, Mr. Garvey looked like he was going to begin a long discussion with Jake about the things you are and are not allowed to say to one's teachers—that teachers are allowed to rib you, but you had better watch your step if you wanted to rib *back*. But they didn't have time for that. Mr. Garvey decided only to put on a weak smile and say, "Touché, Jake. Now, let's go."

They ran up to the closest person, who grinned broadly when he saw them coming. "I will not burn in a fire, and I will not drown in the water. What am I?" he asked.

"Ice!" said Winston.

"Well done!" said the guy. He reached into this pocket and pulled out a small piece of plastic. "For you."

It was a letter tile, perhaps from a board game. It was cherry red, with a white letter engraved into it: **R.** The three boys and their teacher huddled around this small tile, staring at it like it contained the wisdom of the ages.

Mal finally looked up. "That's it? That's all we get?"

"Yep." The guy walked away.

"All right," said Mr. Garvey. "We need to answer every single one of these riddles and get all their letters." He shook his head and looked around at the many colored T-shirts. "This is going to take forever."

"Wait a minute," Winston said. He'd had an idea—not a bright lightbulb but a quick little firefly wink. He looked at the **R** in his hands. "We're going to get a letter from every single person here, don't you think?"

"I don't know," said Jake. "Probably."

"What are we going to do with them?"

"Scramble the letters into an answer," Mr. Garvey said. "Why are we talking about this? Let's go!"

"Wait!" Winston said. The firefly was growing. "There are eighteen riddles. If that means we're going to wind up with eighteen different letters, that's going to be a problem."

"Why?"

"Because scrambling that many letters into an answer is really, really hard. That's a *lot* of letters."

They dwelled on that for a moment. Even Mr. Garvey could see that Winston was right. It was easy to envision sitting on the ground, shifting around letter tiles until the sun went down.

"So what are we supposed to do?" said Mal.

Winston said, "I think there's something more to this puzzle. I think the pictures on the back of these shirts are important."

"Well, yeah," Jake said. "I wouldn't have gotten half these riddles if I didn't have the answers in front of me."

Winston shook his head. "The answer to this guy's riddle was ice. I think we need to find the volunteer who has the picture of an ice cube on the back of his shirt."

"Yes!" said Mal, seeing the whole thing now. "That has to be it. It's a connect the dots!"

"It is?" Mr. Garvey said doubtfully. "A connect the dots?"

"Well, no," said Mal, correcting himself. "It's a connect the riddles! Where's the guy with the ice cube?"

They looked around. Were there really only eighteen college kids? The way their bright T-shirts blended in with the innocent bystanders walking around, it looked like there were a hundred of them. How were they supposed to find a particular T-shirt in all this?

They spread out, walking slowly away from each other, four pairs of eyes scanning the green, trying to find a single moving detail in all this chaos. Winston saw other teams running around. There was Bethany and her team, chasing after a girl in a red shirt. There were the Brookville Brains, making things more confusing with their own bright blue T-shirts. The Brains had suffered through their own flat tire, but it looked like they had caught up again. And there was Brendan Root's team, sitting on a park bench, studying something on a piece of paper. So they were still hard at work, trying to figure out that sixth answer. Was anybody nearly as close to winning as they were? Surely not. Winston almost felt like giving up—they could just go to the nearby pizza parlor for an Italian ice while they waited for Brendan Root and his team to win. It could happen at any moment.

"There!" Jake shouted. He pointed to a purple shirt and began running. Winston and the others tried to keep up, but that was impossible when Jake was going full tilt, as he was now.

By the time the rest of them had caught up, Jake had already been asked the riddle, answered it, and been handed another letter tile: **E**.

Mr. Garvey was the last to arrive at this second checkpoint. He put his hands on his knees and bent over, trying to catch his breath. He looked like he wanted to lie down on the ground for a while.

"Should we not run?" Jake asked him, a little too sweetly.

"No, no," Mr. Garvey gasped, waving a hand. "It's fine. I'm just . . . I'm just"—he took a deep breath and tried straightening up—"I'm just old. And it's been a long day."

Mal said, "So where are we going now? What riddle did we just answer?"

Jake said, "If you turn me around, I can no longer see. The answer was a mirror."

"Oh! We just passed that one!" Winston said, spinning around, trying to find it again. "I saw it! I know I did."

"If I have to run to sixteen more places," said Mr. Garvey, "the one after that is going to be a hospital. You guys go ahead and finish this. I'm going back to our bench. Go fast! Maybe there's still time." He glanced over to where Brendan Root's team sat. He was keeping an eye on them, too, waiting for the moment when they would all start leaping around in victory.

So as Mr. Garvey walked slowly back to their bench, Winston and his friends ran, arms swinging and legs pumping, for the next colored T-shirt.

This was a tall, rail-thin guy in a yellow shirt. "You must break me before you can use me. What am I?" he asked.

They had to consult their notes before answering, "An egg!"

The thin guy was pleased. "Yes!" he said to them. He dug into this pocket. Winston expected another letter tile, and he was not disappointed. This time it was a U.

"R-E-U?" Mal said as they ducked into the shade provided by a tree.

"Is that going to spell anything?" Jake asked.

"Reunion?" Winston suggested. "But the thing is," he added, "if we're spelling something, we might not have started with the first letter. We could have started somewhere in the middle of the message. Let's just keep going and see what happens."

This turned out to be good advice. They went to the next three people in order and collected an N, an S, and another U. The last riddle sent them in search of a picture of a belt.

They searched all over and for a few minutes thought maybe this guy had wandered away from the town green entirely. They finally spotted him off in a corner. As they ran up to him, Winston frowned. He looked familiar. Hadn't they already spoken to him?

Yes, they had, as they discovered when he asked his riddle: I will not burn in a fire, and I will not drown in the water.

"Wait a minute," Jake said. "We already answered that, didn't we?"

"Hey, yeah," Mal said. "Ice. This was first person we spoke to. He's steering us back to the guy with the ice cube on his shirt, and then we can keep going around and around in a little circle. Fun!"

Winston groaned. "You're right. I must have made a mistake. Mr. Garvey's going to kill me."

"What letters do we have now?" Jake asked.

Mal had been collecting them. He opened up his palm to reveal a half dozen sweat-damp letter tiles. "R-E-U-N-S-U," he read out loud. "Roonsoo!"

"That's not a word," Jake said.

"All right," Winston said, "but look." He plucked the first two letters out of Mal's hand and placed them at the end. "If we start with the first U, we get the word UNSURE."

"Do you think that's the answer?" Jake said anxiously.

"I think it's worth trying."

Jake didn't need to be told twice. Mr. Garvey had given him the mini computer, and now he turned it on. There was the initial *teedly-teedly-tee* that Winston was going to hear in his dreams tonight and then Jake got busy pushing buttons.

"Three teams have solved this puzzle," Jake said.

"Did anybody solve the sixth puzzle?" Mal asked.

Jake shook his head. "Not yet."

"Plug in our answer already," Winston told him.

"All right . . . hold on . . . " Jake pushed more buttons. He looked up, startled. "*Four* teams have solved this puzzle!"

Mal said, "Who's the fourth?"

"We are, dummy! That was it! UNSURE is the answer." Jake danced around, pumping his arms in the air.

Winston felt like he'd been whapped over the head with a huge, soft pillow. "Are you sure?" he said.

"No, I'm *unsure*!" Jake said happily. "Come on!" He started running back to Mr. Garvey.

Winston worked out the rest of it while he ran. It was simple enough, when he thought it through: He'd been right all along that each riddle led to a picture on a different shirt. Winston assumed that they'd have to follow a trail made up of all eighteen people, running from one to the next. But they had the answer after solving only six riddles. Winston guessed that this puzzle consisted of three different riddle trails, each made up of six riddles. You didn't have to solve every single riddle to get the answer, and part of the puzzle was simply realizing that. Tricky stuff.

Mr. Garvey was happily stunned when they told him they'd figured out the answer and already plugged it in. He stood up and looked around, as if expecting someone to hand them an award. "We did it," he said. "We really did it."

"Not yet," Mal said. "One more puzzle to go."

"Right," said the teacher. He looked sharply over to Brendan Root's team. They were still on their park bench on the other side of the green. Winston smiled in recognition when he saw that Brendan was pacing, staring at the ground. He was deep in thought, waiting for a lightning bolt of inspiration to strike. Brendan's teammates were slumped on either end of the bench like broken bookends. Winston recognized that, too: They were out of ideas and giving in to hopelessness. Brendan's teacher was sitting on the bench, waving his arms with emotion. All in all, they looked pretty stuck. Winston felt a small blossoming of hope.

"All right," said Mr. Garvey. "We can do it. I know we can. We can come from behind and win it all, cheater or no cheater." He took out a fresh piece of paper and wrote down all the answer words.

QUASAR

THRESH

ICARUS

ACQUIT

UNSURE

"That's it," said Mr. Garvey. "That's all we get."

"There was a clue in the computer," said Winston. "Wasn't there?"

"Oh, yeah!" Mal said. "What does it say?"

Jake pressed more buttons on the computer. Then he groaned. "Oh, no," he said. "That's the clue?"

"What? What is it?" Winston peeked over Jake's shoulder, saw the computer screen, and smacked himself in the forehead.

The clue to the sixth puzzle was the same sign they'd seen all day long—the guy with the shiny teeth, holding up a bag of square potato chips. "Think square!" the man was eternally saying.

"That's all we get?" Mal said. "Think square? What does that mean?"

Silence descended on the team. Winston didn't know how to "think square," and nobody else had any ideas, either.

Mr. Garvey's phone rang, a shrill jangling tweet. He answered it, listened for a moment, and then handed it to Winston. "It's for you," he said.

"For me?" Winston said, and then he remembered: Ray Marietta! Could the ex-cop really have figured something out? He took the phone from his teacher. "Ray?" he said.

"All right," Ray said brusquely. "I had someone look into your little problem."

Winston was puzzled. "Really? Who?"

"I do a little private detective work once in a while," Ray said. "It's brought me in touch with some colorful characters. I know a guy, he knows everything there is to know about the phone system. If anyone on earth could get the phone number of somebody who called you, this is the guy."

"You hired a computer hacker?" Winston was astounded.

There was a small silence on the line, and then Ray said, "Well, that would be illegal. So, no, I'm not going to say he's a hacker. He's more like a magician. A telephone magician."

"Okay," said Winston, but he thought, He's a hacker. Winston was amused and a little amazed at the idea of Ray Marietta, big and no-nonsense, calling up a computer hacker on his behalf. "What did this magician say?" Winston asked.

Ray said, "I gave him a brief rundown on everything you told me. I gave him your phone number, and he just called me back. He was able to get a list of the people who called your house that day. You say this guy, the cheater, called you in the afternoon? Somewhere around four o'clock?"

"Yes." Winston held his breath. Was he really about to learn the identity of the cheater?

"You got one phone call at that time," Ray said. "It came from a residence in West Meadow. Someone with the last name of Root. Do you know anyone with that name?"

WINSTON HAD HOPED Ray Marietta could help them out, providing answers to a few mysterious questions. Now, hanging up the phone, he found that the questions had only multiplied.

Jake and Mal were staring at him. "What did he say?" Jake asked.

"Brendan Root called me," Winston said quietly. He looked up at his friends. "That mysterious phone call a few days back? It was Brendan Root."

"That kid?" Mal said. They all looked over to where Brendan was still pacing.

Winston couldn't wrap his head around it. "But he can't be the cheater," he said. "And he can't be working with the cheater. That makes no sense!"

"Why not?" said Mr. Garvey. He was also gazing over at Brendan Root and his team. "They haven't been hit by the cheater. Isn't that what you told me? No flat tires. No sabotage of any kind. Isn't that suspicious? The man in the green jacket is working with one of these teams. Why not them?"

"But," Winston said, wondering what he was about to say.

"And your name was in the cheater's papers," Mr. Garvey reminded him. "How did the cheater know you would be here? Simple." He pointed across the town green at Brendan. "That young man called you and asked you directly."

Winston stared at the trees and the sky. Mr. Garvey was right—he had to be. Brendan called him hoping to find out if Winston would be at the puzzle event. Told the answer was yes, Brendan had spread the news—he'd told the man in the green jacket, who put Winston on the list of kids to watch out for. How else could Winston's name have found its way onto the cheater's list?

But it still felt wrong, somehow. Winston thought back to the conversations he'd had with Brendan Root. That first meeting back at the potato chip factory—Brendan seemed *thrilled* to meet Winston and acted like someone who couldn't wait to start a one-on-one, do-or-die puzzle competition. Heck, Brendan didn't have to come over to introduce himself at all, but he did.

And then, in the parking lot of the amusement park, Brendan wanted to cheat to *help* Winston. Brendan would have given Winston the answer to the Ferris wheel puzzle if Winston had agreed. He was sure of it.

"So what do you want to do?" Mal said. "Walk over there and accuse him?"

"Of course not," Mr. Garvey said airily. "Don't be silly. They haven't won yet. If they do, then we'll discuss how to make use of this interesting new information." Mr. Garvey smiled for maybe the first time all day. He looked as satisfied as a cat with a new toy. He continued, "Until then, we have a puzzle to solve ourselves, don't we? We should get back to that." He shook the list of words for emphasis.

Yes, true. They still needed to solve the sixth puzzle. Winston tried to distance himself from thoughts of Brendan Root. It wasn't easy. It was too incredible, the idea of Brendan tracking him down and calling him. And it was even more incredible to imagine Brendan passing that information on to that crazy and dangerous man who had fought with Jake.

Why had Winston said yes to the mysterious caller's questions? Why did Winston tell a total stranger—and one trying to disguise his voice!—that he planned to be at the puzzle contest? He should have just hung up and then Winston's name wouldn't have been on that list and then maybe they would have won this whole thing by now.

"Winston!" said Mr. Garvey. Winston looked up at his teacher, who shook the list of words yet again.

Right. The puzzle. They still had work to do. Reluctantly, Winston stood up and looked again at the five answer words.

QUASAR

THRESH

ICARUS

ACQUIT

UNSURE

"Let's hear some suggestions," Mr. Garvey said.

Mal said slowly, "Maybe these words are all clues."

"To what?"

"To the sixth word."

Winston looked at the word list. "You're saying that *quasar*, *thresh*, and *Icarus* are all clues to the same answer? What answer could that be?"

"I don't know," Mal said. "Some word I've never heard of, would be my guess. Is there a mythological farmer who lives in outer space?"

No, there wasn't, of course. That was a dead end, so they all tried to think of new ideas. The four of them paced, and stared at the words, waiting and hoping for something to jump out at them. "There are two Q's," Jake said after a while.

"So?" said Mr. Garvey.

"There are two H's," Jake continued. "There are two C's. There are two I's. . . . Isn't that strange? There's two of just about everything."

"There are four U's," Mal said. "There are four A's."

Jake counted and saw Mal was right. "That's still an even number," he said.

"But what does it mean?" Mal asked.

Jake didn't know. He shook his head and went back to staring at the words.

Silence fell on the group once again. Winston looked back over to Brendan Root, still pacing over there on the other side of the green. His team had a pretty big jump on the sixth puzzle, but so far they hadn't gotten anywhere. That momentary spark of hope Winston had felt was dying out. How could they catch up when Brendan and his team had been thinking about this for so much longer?

Jake was poking at the mini computer again. "Five teams have solved everything but the final puzzle. It's anybody's ball game."

There was shouting to their right. They looked over to see the Lincoln kids on the next bench down, maybe twenty yards away. They were jumping around and slapping each other happily.

Mal said, "Make that *six* teams have solved everything but the final puzzle."

Mr. Garvey stood up as if to make a pronouncement. He was pretending to ignore the team from Lincoln, but Winston could see he was fueled with a new urgency. "These are all six-letter words," he declared.

"Do you think the final answer is going to be six letters, too?" Winston asked.

"I think that's likely," the math teacher said.

"There's the library," Mal said. "Let's go get a dictionary. We'll plug every six-letter word into the computer, one at a time."

"Brilliant, Mal," said Jake. "We'll have the right answer in fifty or a hundred years."

"Better than never," Mal said. "The first word is probably . . . AAAAAA!" He pronounced this by emitting a weird and strangled yell.

Jake and Winston laughed. "I don't think that's a word," Jake said.

"Sure it is," Mal said. "Along with YAAARGH and BLAAAGH and all those comic-book screams."

Mr. Garvey was suddenly standing over Mal, glaring down at him. "If you can't take this seriously," he said, "then go wait in the car."

Mal shrank as if Mr. Garvey was about to stomp on him. "I'm taking this seriously!" he squeaked.

"You're making jokes," said Mr. Garvey. "Not even funny jokes. If you don't have something useful to add, then keep your mouth shut."

Mal slowly crawled backward a few feet, like a wounded crab, to get away from the teacher.

Mr. Garvey wasn't done. He had anger and frustration to spare. "You too, Jake," he said. "If you don't want to solve this last puzzle, then take Mal back to the car."

Jake was nonplussed. "What'd I say? I didn't do anything."

"You're not solving the puzzle!" Mr. Garvey said. "You're laughing with your friends and picking at the grass!"

"I'm thinking," Jake yelled back, though he tossed aside the blades of grass in his hands. "We're all thinking. I had an idea. It just didn't work. What do you want from me?"

The math teacher was now pacing. He was angry beyond reason, his frustration boiling over after a long and hectic day. "This is what I meant, Winston. We could have had this last answer! We might have won by now! We might have beaten everybody!"

"If what?" Winston said, and then realized the answer as the question left his mouth.

Mr. Garvey seemed to realize he was on the verge of going too far—indeed, may have already crossed that line. He didn't answer Winston's question but sat down on the bench, shaking his head.

Mal repeated, "If what?" He looked at Winston.

"Nothing," Winston said, looking away.

Jake smelled blood. "No. What is he talking about?"

Winston looked at his friend. He hated this, but what was he supposed to do? Winston said reluctantly, "Mr. Garvey didn't want you or Mal to be on the team. He wanted to replace you with kids from his math class."

They all looked at Mr. Garvey, who absorbed their stares and finally tossed his arms in the air. "I wanted the best possible team," he said. "Is that so wrong? I wanted kids that I knew would take this seriously."

"We're taking this seriously," Mal said.

"Not seriously enough," Mr. Garvey said.

Winston felt his stomach twist and untwist. He said in a small voice, "Mal and Jake have both solved puzzles today. They got the prison puzzle before I did." Mr. Garvey said nothing. "They're both good at puzzles," Winston persisted.

"Fine," said Mr. Garvey. He looked stiffly down at Mal and Jake. "I apologize for implying otherwise."

Jake said to Winston, "How did you talk him into keeping us?"

Winston was a little embarrassed. He twisted a fistful of grass for a moment and then admitted, "I said I wouldn't do it without you guys."

Mal and Jake gaped at each other with real surprise. Then Jake fell backward, laughing at the sky.

"Aren't you the bestest buddy!" Mal said.

"Quit it," Winston said. It was one thing to stand up for your friends. It was another thing to be caught doing it. He didn't want to feel like the hero of a bad television show.

They were all quiet for a minute or two. Mr. Garvey seemed to understand that he had forfeited the right to yell at them . . . at least for a while. Mal and Jake didn't want to rag on Winston any further. And Winston was rolling the five words around in his mind, looking for the sixth.

It looked like every park bench had been taken over by a team. Winston could still see kids running around, talking to the people in the brightly colored shirts. Did those kids know what they were doing yet? Had they figured out the secret behind this puzzle, or were they just collecting riddles at random and waiting for a brilliant idea to strike?

Directly across the town green, Winston saw Bethany and her friends sitting together. If none of them were out chasing down riddles, that meant they had the answer to this puzzle and were looking for the sixth and final word, just like them.

Winston watched his math teacher's head swivel back and forth, watching Brendan Root's team on the one hand and the Lincoln team on the other. Someone was going to get that final word soon. Winston shared Mr. Garvey's sense of helplessness, that it probably wasn't going to be them. None of them had any ideas.

"Maybe the answer is QUAINT," Mr. Garvey suddenly said.

"What?" Jake said.

"Quaint," he repeated.

Mal squinted and said, "I thought you didn't want to try random words."

Mr. Garvey flushed and stood up from the bench. "Look at the answers," he said. "They begin with the letters Q, T, I, A, and U. If you add the letter N and scramble them all up, you get the word QUAINT. Who has the computer?"

Jake said, "I do."

"Give it to me."

Jake stood up. "That's not the answer. It doesn't make any sense."

Mr. Garvey held out his hand. "Jake, give me the computer."

"If I'd suggested that answer," Jake said, "you'd make fun of me for being a dumb baseball player. Or football player. Or whatever it is I play."

Winston and Mal shared a panicked glance. Mr. Garvey advanced on Jake, his eyes glaring. "I'm not going to argue with you, Jake. Just give me the computer!" He grabbed it away from Jake's loose hands.

Maybe Mr. Garvey had expected Jake to argue further. Maybe he expected to have to wrestle Jake for possession of the computer, like two little kids fighting over a toy. But Jake didn't resist one iota when Mr. Garvey snatched the computer away.

Mr. Garvey used too much force. It was like lifting something that you think will be very heavy . . . but is instead surprisingly light. Mr. Garvey snatched the computer from Jake's hands only to throw it backward over his own head. For a frozen moment, they all watched it fly through the air. Winston's heart stopped as if it had predicted what was going to happen next.

The mini computer hit the back of the park bench. There was a sharp cracking sound. The computer then dropped to the seat of the bench, teetered there for a moment, and fell to the grass.

Mr. Garvey made an inarticulate cry and ran to pick it up. He inspected it for damage and then pressed the power button. There was no *teedly-teedly-tee*. He pressed the button again. Nothing. Mr. Garvey shook the computer lightly, and Winston could hear a slight rattling sound. Something in there had become disconnected. The computer was dead.

It felt like an hour or two had passed with Mr. Garvey standing there cradling the dead computer in both hands like a beloved pet and the three boys stunned and not daring to move an inch for fear of somehow making things worse. Although how things could get worse than *this*, Winston could not imagine.

But it wasn't an hour. Only a few seconds passed before Winston heard muffled laughter. Winston looked over to see the team from Lincoln Junior High sitting on the next bench down. They had seen what had happened. Even their teacher, Rod Denham, had his hand over his mouth to hide his amusement. His eyes were shiny with pleasure.

Mr. Garvey saw that, too. His face was painted with fury and humiliation. He said to Jake in a low voice, "What did you do? You've ruined us."

Jake looked terrified, but he nonetheless said, "If you hadn't grabbed it out of my hand, it wouldn't be broken!"

"If you had given it to me when I asked for it, I wouldn't have had to take it from you! Now what do you want to do? Hmm?" The math teacher looked at all of them. "What should we do now? Even if we solve the puzzle, we have no way to submit our solution. It's like you boys don't *want* to win."

"I want to win," said Mal. "But I wasn't planning on having a heart attack if we didn't. It's not the end of the world to lose."

Mr. Garvey waved a finger at him. "That's the attitude you've been giving me all day. Acting like a kid on a picnic." He repeated Mal's words as if he'd never heard such a concept uttered before. "It's not the end of the world to lose!"

"Well, it's not!"

"If that's what you think, Mal, then you're *going* to lose. To win, you have to care. You have to focus on it. You have to be driven."

"So if Brendan Root wins," Jake said, "I guess you'll be the first to congratulate him? He was so driven that he actually cheated."

Mr. Garvey rolled his eyes. "I'm not in favor of cheating, Jake. I never said I was."

But Jake persisted. The fear was already out of his voice. "Did you tell those other teams about the memo pad to warn them or because you wanted them to get scared and quit?"

The math teacher gave a little laugh. He looked around as if trying to find somebody to share his disbelief. "What, this again?" he said.

"I'm just asking," said Jake.

"We're not talking about that," said Mr. Garvey. "We're talking about the computer that *you broke*." He waved it in Jake's face.

"I didn't break it! I didn't grab it out of your hands and fling it into the nearest hard surface!"

Winston said, "Uh, guys."

Mr. Garvey was red-faced. "Jake, go home," he said. "We're close enough to where you live, aren't we? Just leave. Whatever is going to happen here can happen without you. We don't need you here."

Winston had never seen a grown-up this angry.

"You're kicking him off the team?" Mal said.

Mr. Garvey turned on him. "You want to go, too?"

"Uh, guys," Winston said again.

"What is it, Winston?" asked the teacher. "You want to leave, too?

Fine. What does it matter now? We're disbanded. Is everybody happy?"

"I solved the sixth puzzle," Winston said.

Mr. Garvey blinked at him. So did Mal and Jake. It was like Winston had reached into all of them and switched them off. Mr. Garvey's mouth opened and closed a few times and then he said, "You did what?"

"I solved it. I solved the last puzzle." He showed them what he had scribbled on the paper in his hand. "Think square. That was the only clue Simon gave us, and I finally realized what it meant."

"You solved the puzzle?" Mr. Garvey was still catching up to this new development.

Winston said, "It's a puzzle I've seen in one of my magazines. You guys know what a word square is?"

"It's the same as a crossword puzzle, isn't it?" Mal said.

"Sort of. Not really. It's a square, and each word in the square is written twice—once reading across and once reading down."

"So all of these words can fit into a word square?"

"These five words . . . and a sixth. And that final word is the answer we're looking for."

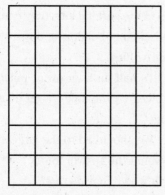

QUASAR

THRESH

ICARUS

ACQUIT

UNSURE

(Continue reading to see the answer to this puzzle.)

*　　*　　*

Mr. Garvey's delight was short-lived. Without thinking, he pushed the On button again and was quickly reminded that the thing was broken, its screen now gray and lifeless. Winston had had the vague and silly notion that solving the sixth puzzle would cause the computer to magically heal itself. But no.

A lot of good having the final answer would do them when they had no way to send it to Dmitri Simon back at the potato chip factory. They just couldn't win.

Mr. Garvey kept pushing the power button as if something different might happen. He mashed the other keys on the keyboard. He smacked it on the back like a father burping a baby. Finally, he gave up and sat on the park bench, his arms dangling at his sides, a man who has reached the end of the road. He wasn't happy about finding the sixth answer, nor was he angry at the boys anymore. In a way, Mr. Garvey looked a bit broken himself.

"There must be something we can do," said Winston.

"Drive to the factory?" Mal suggested. "Real, real fast?"

Mr. Garvey looked up, considering that. Winston envisioned him zigzagging through traffic like a madman, refusing to hit the brake for any reason. They might not even stop in the parking lot—they could crash through the front door of the building, bulldozing down the narrow hallway and into Dmitri Simon's office.

But Mr. Garvey shook his head. "It's half an hour away, maybe more," he said in his new, defeated voice. "By the time we get there, someone else will have figured this out."

"I have an idea," Jake said softly. "We should go to the girls and tell them what happened. They can submit the answer for us."

Mal was bewildered. "Why on earth would they do that?"

"Because we'll split the prize money with them."

If Jake had said that even five minutes ago, Winston guessed that Mr. Garvey's head would have simply exploded. But now the math teacher looked thoughtful. Then he frowned and slumped back on his bench. "No. They wouldn't help us after what we did at the space museum."

"What *we* did?" Mal said, making *we* sound like the most unbelievable two-letter word in the English language.

Mr. Garvey sighed. "What I did. Okay? What I did. I double-crossed them, and there's no way they're going to help us now."

"They might," Jake said. "Yeah, you played that trick on them, and that wasn't very nice. But Winston helped them back in the amusement park. They might not want to help *you*, but they might help *him*."

"Winston helped them?" Mr. Garvey said. "How?"

Jake filled him in. Winston was astonished that Jake was telling Mr. Garvey this. He wanted to back slowly away, give himself a head start for when the math teacher lunged from the bench to try to kill him. A team had been about to quit . . . and Winston not only convinced them not to, but *helped them* on a puzzle? In Mr. Garvey's world, such a thing was unthinkable.

But Jake had a funny look on this face while he laid this all out, and when he was done, there were a few seconds or a minute where Mr. Garvey didn't react at all, as if he couldn't figure out *how* to react.

He finally looked at Winston and said, "You gave them help on the amusement park thing?"

Winston nodded his head. He was still ready to leap backward if he had to.

But Mr. Garvey said, "Then Jake's right. They might help us back.

We need to ask them. Come on. We're running out of time." And then he was up and walking briskly across the width of the town green, heading for the girls sitting on their own park bench.

The boys trailed slightly behind. Winston said to Jake, "I can't believe you told him that."

Jake grinned. "What could he do?" he asked, talking low so that their teacher couldn't hear. "Is he going to get angry? How dumb would that be? If you hadn't helped the girls, there would be nobody we could turn to. Now we might be able to get some help of our own. He should get down on his knees and thank you."

"I'd like to see that," said Mal.

They were getting close to where the girls were sitting, and Winston could see Mr. Garvey slow down a tad. What was he going to say to them? Winston might have lent them some assistance, but Mr. Garvey was still the guy who left them standing stupidly in a dark hallway.

The frosty look on Miss Norris's face as they approached the bench was further indication that this wasn't going to be easy. Winston cast a glance over to Brendan Root's team. Brendan was no longer pacing. The whole team was sitting on the park bench, huddled over the same piece of paper. Did that mean they were on the brink of solving the sixth puzzle? He fought the urge to run over there and ask.

Mr. Garvey cleared his throat. "Miss Norris," he said. "We have a little problem and perhaps you could"—the words got stuck somewhere as he looked at the chilly expression on Miss Norris's face. He backed up and tried again. "Perhaps you might find it in your heart to help us."

"Help you," Miss Norris repeated tonelessly.

Mr. Garvey held up the dead computer and explained what had

happened. The boys sent embarrassed glances toward the girls—it made them all look stupid as dirt that they had allowed the computer to break—and Bethany and her friends sent smirky, amused glances right back.

"So what can we do?" said Miss Norris. "Even if I was inclined to help."

That didn't sound good, but Mr. Garvey pressed on. "You wouldn't just be helping me," he said. "You'd be helping yourself. How close are you to solving the sixth puzzle?"

Miss Norris looked at Mr. Garvey suspiciously, not sure she should answer. But she finally decided to see where this was going and said, "We're still looking for a breakthrough."

Giselle piped up. "We thought maybe there's a message spelled out in these words."

"But we can't find it," said Elvie.

Mr. Garvey clapped his hands together, a salesman looking to close the deal. "Well, I'll tell you what," he said. "We have that last puzzle solved. We know the answer. Winston here came through in a big way." Winston smiled sheepishly as Mr. Garvey slapped him on the shoulder. "But we can't submit the answer with our dead computer. Meanwhile, that team over there"—he pointed to Brendan Root and company—"has been working on the final answer for a long time and are surely minutes away from getting it." He took a deep breath and said it: "If you submit the sixth answer for us . . . we'll split the prize money with you."

There was a stunned pause. The first to recover was Bethany. "You want to tell us the last answer?" she said.

Mr. Garvey completely misread the tone of her voice. "Of course!" he said, a big smile emerging on his face.

"No!" she countered, and Mr. Garvey's smile quickly disintegrated.

Bethany jumped to her feet. "Sure I want to win," she said, "but I don't want someone to tell me the answer to the puzzles. I want to figure them out myself." The other girls on the team nodded in agreement.

"It's just one puzzle," Mr. Garvey said. He kept glancing over to Brendan Root's team. Winston understood his nervousness—it felt like there was a large digital countdown timer somewhere, and it was quickly approaching zero.

"I want to figure it out myself," Bethany insisted.

"I guess that's a no, Mr. Garvey," said Miss Norris, not looking sorry in the least.

"What if I gave you a hint?" Winston said. "Got you on the right track. You guys can still figure it out. Then you'll submit the answer, and we'll split the prize."

The girls and Miss Norris looked at each other. Mal said, "Come on. You'll get a hint for the final puzzle. And you can take home twenty-five thousand dollars to your school."

That was the right move. Hearing that large sum of money said out loud melted them all. Soon the girls were nodding at each other, and Bethany said to Winston, "All right. What's the hint?"

Winston said, "Do you know what a word square is?"

"Yeah . . . ?" Bethany said, waiting for more, but Giselle's eyes immediately lit up. "Think square!" she shouted.

"Of course!" said Elvie, and soon the three of them and their teacher were writing things on a piece of paper and whispering to each other. There was nothing Winston or his teammates could do but stand there and wait. Mr. Garvey couldn't figure out what to do with his hands—he combed them through his hair, he put them on his hips, he massaged his wide forehead. He looked like he was trying not to scream at them to *solve faster*.

The girls looked to be on the brink of success. Giselle said, "Ooh, so this goes here!" and Bethany said, "And that means this has to go here!" and then there was a final, eternal pause as the girls looked at what they had created. Then Elvie said, "That has to be it! We did it!"

They showed what they had written to Winston.

A	C	Q	U	I	T
C	R	U	N	C	H
Q	U	A	S	A	R
U	N	S	U	R	E
I	C	A	R	U	S
T	H	R	E	S	H

"So the last answer is CRUNCH?" Bethany said.

"Yes!" Mr. Garvey all but exploded. "Type it in! Put it in the computer!"

Miss Norris glared at Mr. Garvey but removed the mini computer from her small purse. It instantly began to *teedly-teedly-tee*. She gave it a confused look. "I didn't turn it on yet!" she said.

"Is our computer broken, too?" Giselle said.

Winston had a terrible feeling. He turned toward Brendan Root's team. They were no longer sitting on their park bench. He glanced all around the town green, but they were nowhere to be found. His stomach began to sink down to the middle of the earth.

Miss Norris hit a button on the computer. The screen plinked on, and even standing ten feet away, Winston could see that something was different. Instead of the usual start-up screen, there was some kind of message, written in big, black letters.

"Uh-oh," said Miss Norris.

"What does it say?" Jake asked.

She looked up, surprise and dread mixed together on her face. "It says, 'Please return to Simon's Snack Foods. The contest is over. We have a winner!'"

CHAPTER THIRTEEN

IT WAS SILENT IN the car. Now that it was over, now that Winston didn't have any puzzles to think about or look forward to, he was miserably aware of just how hot and sticky and tired he was. His hair was plastered to his head, and his T-shirt was clinging to him as if it had been coated with glue. Mal didn't look much better—he was slumped over and might have been on the edge of sleep. Jake's hair had a tendency to curl on humid days—he looked like someone had given him a haircut with an eggbeater. Mr. Garvey looked weariest of all and had giant splotches of sweat under each arm. They all looked gross.

Their depressed expressions weren't helping. They'd been so close to winning! If the girls had just gotten the answer a little faster . . . or better yet, if they had allowed Mr. Garvey to tell them the answer. Winston understood Bethany's desire to solve the puzzle herself, but he couldn't get around the fact that it had cost both teams twenty-five thousand dollars.

And the cheater had won. Maybe they should have told the girls they knew who the cheater was. Maybe that would have made them more interested in winning *immediately*.

Their teacher had tried calling the potato chip factory, hoping to speak with Dmitri Simon, but he was never able to get a human being on the line. Winston wanted to ask Mr. Garvey what they were going to do now. They didn't know for a fact that West Meadow had won, but it seemed a good bet. When Brendan and his teammates were called up as the winners, was Mr. Garvey going to stand up and yell, "Not so fast!" That would be an ugly scene.

"At least your rival didn't win," Mal, in the passenger seat, said to Mr. Garvey. It was the first thing anybody had said in a good ten minutes.

Mr. Garvey grunted.

That seemed to be all the reply Mal was going to get. He turned and looked back out the window.

Jake and Winston exchanged a sad glance and then looked out their own windows. Nothing much else to do. Mr. Garvey was not about to be consoled. Yes, if the girls had acted differently, they would have won. But even before that, if Mr. Garvey hadn't thrown the computer into a hard wooden bench, they would have taken the prize money themselves, with no need to split it. That was going to eat at Mr. Garvey for a long, long time.

Winston kept thinking about Brendan Root. It was hard to believe that kid had been the cheater all along—or, no, was *working* with the cheater. What was Brendan's relationship to the man in the green jacket? How could that wacky seventh-grader possibly know that vicious and mean grown-up?

He kept hearing Brendan's tunefully happy voice in his head. His excitement about meeting Winston, back at the start of all this. His remorse, in the Adventureland parking lot, that Winston had fallen behind. And most jarringly of all, the fact that Brendan had offered to help him—had offered to give him an answer.

That's not what people do when they're trying to cheat to win. They don't offer to cheat to help the competition.

Winston was slowly becoming more and more sure that Brendan wasn't the cheater. Maybe Brendan had called him, but there had to be some other explanation as to how Winston's name had gotten into that memo pad. Somebody else was behind all this, not that enthusiastic, puzzle-happy kid.

It sure looked bad, though. Why else had Brendan called him—disguising his voice, no less!—if not to scope out the competition? Why did the man in the green jacket hit every team except for West Meadow? Their teacher didn't even believe there *was* a cheater. Of course, that was before the man in the green jacket had made his dramatic entrance, complete with fireworks. Brendan's teacher would certainly believe him *now*, after Winston pointed at Jake's face, which was a rainbow of black-and-blue bruises.

"When we get there," Mr. Garvey now said, "let me do all the talking."

"What are you going to say?" Jake asked.

"I don't want to make a public spectacle of this thing. I'll try to reach Dmitri Simon and take him aside for a few minutes. If I'm able to do that, I'll tell him about the cheater and how we have proof that it's this boy on the West Meadow team." Mr. Garvey tapped the steering wheel thoughtfully and continued, "I don't know what Dmitri Simon will do at that point. Maybe he'll divide the prize money among the rest of the teams. Maybe he'll ask if anybody else had the final answer and give prize money only to those teams. All I know is, we're not letting West Meadow and that kid get away with this."

"I feel bad for the other kids on that team," Mal said.

"For all we know, all the kids were in on it," said Mr. Garvey. "Don't feel sorry for anybody."

They fell back into silence. Winston wished he had never thought to call Ray Marietta. Who knew that path would lead to Brendan Root? Winston was certain Mr. Garvey was going to accuse the wrong person of cheating, but there was nothing he could do to stop it. He thought ahead to the expression of disbelief and betrayal that would surely flood Brendan's face when Dmitri Simon refused to hand over the prize money . . . and told them the reason why.

"Do we still have the cheater's things?" Winston asked.

"They're in the back," Mr. Garvey said. "Why?"

"I don't know. I just want to see them." Winston reached behind him, difficult with the seat belt on, and grabbed the plastic bag with the cheater's stuff in it. A coil of strong twine. A string of firecrackers. A set of mousetraps.

And here was the bottle filled with broken glass, its neck stuffed with aluminum foil to keep the shards in. Winston thought of the man in the green jacket, sitting in his garage, smashing glass with a hammer and carefully pouring the broken bits into a bottle, a satisfied smile on his face. Who was he? Could he really be Brendan's older brother or some other relative? Who else would do something so extreme for a kid Winston's age?

Looking at the bottle, Winston found his thoughts moving in a new direction. If it wasn't Brendan Root who started all this, then who had? If the man in the green jacket was working with someone, who could it be? Winston had a hard time believing it was *any* kid, not just Brendan. So was it one of the grown-ups? One of the teachers? Would a teacher go so far as to hire someone to sabotage all the other teams?

Winston glanced at the back of Mr. Garvey's head. It didn't seem so outrageous at all, did it? All it took was a desire to win, multiplied by a billion. Mr. Garvey was halfway there himself, and a few of the other teachers were right there with him. Mr. Garvey wanted to show up his rival teacher from another school. Maybe another teacher needed that prize money for a special project. Maybe a third teacher simply never wanted to lose.

He was holding the bottle up to the sunlight, revolving it slowly back and forth, watching the rays bounce off the shards. Something was nibbling away at the back of his mind. Something to do with this bottle.

"Would you get a flat tire just because you drove over some broken glass?" he asked. "Not a booby trap like this, but just some broken glass lying on the road?"

"Maybe," said Mr. Garvey. "I guess it's possible."

"That's happened on my bicycle a few times," Jake said.

"Yeah," Winston said. He was thinking of Brendan Root's teacher, who had dismissed the notion of a cheater so readily. Anybody could get a flat tire, he said. He'd recently had one himself. At that point, Winston didn't know how to argue with him.

And just like that, all the puzzle pieces slammed together in his mind. If Winston had been standing, he would have fallen down. He put his hands up to his head, to keep it from popping off his neck entirely.

"What's wrong with you?" Jake asked.

"Brendan isn't the cheater!"

"He's not?"

Winston shook his head. "It's his *teacher!*"

"What?" Mr. Garvey said. "How can you know that?"

"It's the broken glass," Winston explained. "Brendan's teacher refused to believe that someone was cheating. I told him about the flat tires, and he still didn't believe me. Do you know what he said?"

"What?" Mal asked.

"He said, 'I ran over some broken glass myself a couple of months ago. I had to wait two hours for a tow truck.'"

"All right," said Mr. Garvey. "So what?"

Winston sat forward. "I never told him the flat tires had been caused by broken glass."

They all thought about that for a few moments. Mr. Garvey said slowly, "Did he say, 'I ran over some broken glass *also*'?"

"He said it in such a way," Winston insisted, "that he knew the flat tires had been caused by broken glass. How could he have known that?"

Mr. Garvey was shaking his head. "Even if you're right, Winston, that is not a lot to hang your hat on. It's certainly not proof."

"We might be able to prove it," Winston said. "Maybe."

"How?"

"First of all, what was that teacher's name? Does anybody remember?"

"I do," said Mr. Garvey. "I've seen him around before. He's not a teacher, he's an administrator or a vice principal or something. . . . Lester something. No, wait. Lester is his last name. Carl Lester."

"Good," said Winston. "Can I borrow your phone again?"

Mr. Garvey looked at Winston in the rearview mirror, surprise in his eyes. "Who are you calling? Your policeman friend again? You can't call the police on this guy when you don't have any proof."

"I'm not calling anybody. Mal is."

Mal sat up straight at the mention of his name. "I am? Who am I calling?"

"Carl Lester's wife."

They were getting close to the potato chip factory. Winston was a bundle of jittery nerves. A whole lot of things had to work out in the next few minutes. For one thing, he didn't know if Carl Lester was married. For another, would his telephone number be in the phone book? Would the wife, if she existed, be home? After a day when luck had turned against them at every opportunity, it seemed like Winston was now asking for an awful lot to go right.

The first part worked out: They called information and got the number of the only Carl Lester in the phone book.

"Do you know what to do?" Winston said to Mal.

"I got it," Mal said. "No problem." He had Mr. Garvey's cell phone.

"I don't know why I'm agreeing to this," said Mr. Garvey.

"Do you want to make the call yourself?" Winston asked.

Mr. Garvey said loudly, "I don't think we should be calling this woman *at all*."

"Too late," said Mal. "I'm dialing."

Mr. Garvey pulled into the parking lot of Simon's Snack Foods and navigated around to the visitors' area. He pulled into a spot and shut off the engine. Winston looked at the modern building connected to the old-fashioned factory. It felt like a year since they had been here last.

Mal finished dialing the number. Everyone in the car was watching him. He cleared his throat like an actor about to take the stage, which is exactly what he was.

"Are you sure he can do this?" Mr. Garvey asked.

"I'm sure," said Winston. "Shhhh." He'd never shushed a teacher before.

Someone must have picked up the line, because Mal suddenly said, "Ah, hello, is this Mrs. Lester?" The voice that came out of his twelve-year-old body was, all of a sudden, surprisingly mature and adult. Mr. Garvey's jaw dropped a few inches. Brendan Root wasn't the only kid who could disguise his voice on the phone.

Mal continued, "Good afternoon, Mrs. Lester. I'm Malcolm, I'm calling from Bronco Towing. I believe it was your husband—Carl Lester, is that right? Yes. I believe it was your husband who had a flat tire a couple of months ago and required our services, and we like to call our customers and see if they were satisfied. Is he there?" Mal listened for a moment. "No? Well, do you know if he was pleased with his towing experience?" He listened again. "This was for a flat tire he had. About two months ago. Drove over some broken glass as I recall . . . ?" He looked up at them, his eyes shining as he continued the conversation. "No? There was no flat tire? Are you sure?" He nodded again. The woman was sure. "Well, maybe I have the wrong Carl Lester. What does your husband do for a living?" Now Mal gave a euphoric fist pump, punching the roof of the car. "He's an educator. No, I think my Carl Lester did something else, I must have the wrong number, you have a good day anyway. Thank you very much. Goodbye." He hung up, smiling broadly.

Winston and Jake applauded with gusto. Mr. Garvey shook his head in wonder. "I was told you worked *backstage* in the drama club," he said.

"I'll get onstage yet," Mal said happily.

"I believe you will."

"So they didn't get a flat tire," Mal said. "Not two months ago, not as long as she can remember. Carl Lester lied! That proves it!"

Mr. Garvey held up a hand. "It doesn't prove anything. It's a very interesting piece of information, but it's a long way from proof."

"What else can we do?" Jake said.

Winston looked out the back window. More cars were pulling in—more teams coming back to see who had won. And here, right on time, was the team from West Meadow. Carl Lester, at the driver's wheel, looked jubilant. Brendan was in the passenger seat, and the two other teammates were in the back. One of them was pounding his fists on the ceiling and howling with glee.

"We can't let them get away with it. What are we going to do?" Jake asked again.

Nobody knew the answer to that. After some silence, Mr. Garvey undid his seat belt and opened his door. "Well, whatever's going to happen, we better get inside for it. Come on."

More cars had pulled into the parking lot by now, and there was a slow, ragged parade back into the offices of Simon's Snacks. Everybody looked pretty much like Winston felt—hot, tired, fed up. They found themselves walking side by side with the team from Lincoln Junior High, and even though the competition was over, Winston *still* felt a few glares being sent in their direction from Mr. Garvey's Mathlete rivals. Winston glanced at Mal, and they both shook their heads. Who knew competitive math was such a blood sport?

His stomach rumbled. Didn't Dmitri Simon say something about having a barbecue? Yes, Winston thought he did. Good—all Winston had eaten today were those cereal bars, a small bag of potato chips, and a few sips of water.

They filed through the lobby and back toward the conference room. The teams had blown out of there hours earlier like a stampede of bulls, but on the return trip, they were a much more subdued group—exhausted, muscles sore from all the walking and running, voices hoarse from yelling. It had been a great day, and even when you figured in the cheater and his own single-minded math teacher, Winston had to admit he'd had a fun time. Thank goodness his friends had been here.

All the teams automatically sat in the seats they had occupied this morning, as if doing otherwise would have violated some unwritten law. At each place was a small booklet. "WANT MORE PUZZLES?" it said. Winston flipped through it. It looked, indeed, like a bunch more puzzles by Dmitri Simon. Excellent. Winston put it in his back pocket for later.

Everyone could tell who had won—the West Meadow team was the only one wearing broad smiles. They accepted some congratulations from the team sitting next to them, and Carl Lester pumped the other teacher's hand like he'd just been elected mayor.

With everyone back in their original seats, it was clear that some teams had not returned. The Demilla Academy was gone, as Mr. Garvey had said—they had taken their fancy clothes back home. The New Easton team was also gone. The girl on their team had been locked into the bathroom. That must have thrown a little scare into them, even before the cheater and his memo pad had been revealed. And the Kennedy team, their computer lost or stolen, had not come back to see how things turned out.

The missing teams stood out like gaps in a smile, and Winston felt a pang of shame that it was his teacher who had talked two of them into dropping out.

Dmitri Simon and his associates came in through the stage door, and there was a small round of applause—less wild and raucous than at the start of the event. Winston looked around and saw that some teams weren't clapping at all. Mr. Regal, the coach of the Brookville Brains, had his arms crossed and a scowl on his face, and a few other people around the room wore similar expressions.

Simon seemed pleased, though, as he took his place behind the podium. "Welcome back, everybody! Well, almost everybody. You all look hot and tired, but I hope you had a good time. And I hope you're hungry, because we have about a thousand pounds of food in the picnic area behind the factory."

There were some cheers in response to this. Jake said to Mr. Garvey, "I don't think you're going to get a chance to speak to him before he awards the winner."

Mr. Garvey rubbed his forehead. "I'm thinking, I'm thinking," he said.

"We seem to have lost a couple of teams," said Simon, looking around the room. "That's too bad. More food for the rest of us, I guess!" He patted his protruding belly with a grin.

Mr. Regal, arms still crossed tightly, yelled out, "What are you going to do about the cheater who was running around? Huh?"

Dmitri Simon looked startled. He wasn't even sure who had yelled that, or why. "The cheater? What do you mean?"

And then suddenly everybody was yelling. It was impossible to hear anybody's individual words, but from the look on Simon's face, he was getting the general gist: Something had gone wrong with his carefully planned event. He waved his hands, trying to get things under control. "All right," he said loudly. "All right, settle down, everybody!" Quiet slowly descended over the room again. Simon let the silence drag on for a little bit while he thought of what he was going to say next. Winston glanced over to Carl Lester and the West Meadow team. Mr. Lester looked the smallest bit nervous—or maybe that was Winston's imagination.

"This is the first I'm hearing about this," said Dmitri Simon. "Someone cheated? Really?" He chuckled in disbelief. "I don't see how. Did somebody steal the answers from another team? Did someone steal the answers from *me*?"

"He gave us a flat tire!" yelled the coach of the Brains.

"He broke the Ferris wheel!" yelled Rod Denham of Lincoln Junior High. Oh, right, they'd had a kid stuck on the ride, too—Winston had forgotten that part.

Dmitri Simon was astounded. "He broke the Ferris wheel?" he repeated. "How do you break a Ferris wheel?"

"He locked a girl in the bathroom back at the farm!" This was Bethany doing the yelling this time. Simon looked over at her, more and more disturbed.

There was some more shouting, and people were starting to overlap each other again. Simon once again called for quiet, and the yelling petered out. Simon looked to his associates, who looked neutral and calm. They shrugged back at their boss.

"All right," said Simon. "Why didn't someone call me? Tell me about this sooner?"

"Your phone system is like another puzzle," the Brookville Brains coach yelled out. "A really hard one."

Simon frowned. "Oh," he said, thrown off balance. "Well. We're going to look into this, I promise. We're not going to have a whole discussion about it right now. If you have any information about this cheater, please come up to me or one of my partners here. If we determine that the event was compromised in any way, we will make amends. I swear to that. I'll make a donation to every single school if I have to." One of the partners looked alarmed, and Simon said, "Oh, calm down, Robert. I'll do it from my personal account." Robert, rebuked, took a step backward and regained his calm expression.

"For now, however, we're going to proceed," Simon continued. "We do have a winner, and I want to use this time to congratulate them. It was very exciting, sitting here at headquarters watching the answers come in. We thought for a while that nobody was going to solve that prison puzzle—you guys really had us nervous. But finally one team managed to break through and get all the way to the end. So let's have a round of applause for the kids from West Meadow Junior High and their vice principal, Carl Lester!"

There was applause, dampened by the specter of the cheating scandal. Winston looked at Mr. Garvey, who was not applauding and was in fact frowning deeply. They had hoped to tell Simon what they knew before West Meadow had been officially declared the champs. This wasn't working out very well at all.

Carl Lester led his boys down to the stage. One of Simon's assistants floated off stage for a moment, and returned with a six-foot novelty check, with FIFTY THOUSAND DOLLARS written on it in huge type. The assistant wasn't sure how to hold his giant thing and stumbled and fumbled it to center stage.

Winston found himself getting to his feet.

As the applause died down, and before Dmitri Simon could begin his congratulatory speech, Winston called out, "Brendan! Hey, Brendan!"

Everybody on the stage looked up to see who was shouting.

Mr. Garvey gave Winston an incredulous look. "What are you doing?" he said softly.

"I have an idea," Winston said, and he called out to the group on the stage, "Brendan! Did your teacher tell you to call me?"

Brendan Root blinked rapidly. "What?" he said.

"You called me a few days ago. You tried disguising your voice, and you wouldn't tell me your name, but I know it was you. Did your teacher tell you to do that, or did you do it on your own?"

Several dozen heads turned back and forth between Winston and Brendan. They were all aimed at Brendan now.

Dmitri Simon interrupted this long-range conversation. "Excuse me, my friend," he called back to Winston, "I think this can wait, don't you?"

"I'm afraid it can't," said Mr. Garvey, getting to his feet as well. "If you'll just give my student the benefit of the doubt for a moment, I think you'll see this question is very important."

Throughout this, Winston kept his eyes on Brendan, who loved puzzles as much as him and maybe more. He thought Brendan was on the brink of solving one more puzzle . . . one he didn't necessarily *want* to solve. Looking very small on the stage, Brendan turned to look at his teacher, who was watching him warily. Brendan then peered back up at Winston, disappointment and maybe even grief on his boyish, round face.

Yes, Brendan had figured it out. People from other teams were complaining about a cheater . . . but Brendan's team hadn't been affected in the least. And now here was Winston asking this very unusual question.

"Yes," Brendan said. "My teacher asked us to find out who would be on other teams. That's why I called you."

One of Brendan's teammates said, "Shut up!"

There was an explosion of muttering from the others in the room. Carl Lester, smiling, put a hand on Brendan's shoulder as if to lead him offstage.

Winston called out again, "Mr. Lester! Do you know why I asked Brendan that question?"

Dmitri Simon was no longer trying to hush Winston. In fact, he looked pretty interested in what Winston was saying.

Mr. Lester didn't know where to go or what to do. He looked up at Winston. "I'm not really sure what you're talking about, young man," he said.

"Well, we recovered some stuff from the man in the green jacket. That's the cheater everyone's so upset about. He had a list of license plate numbers, and he also had a bunch of our names. I was on that list, for instance. So how did the cheater know I was going to be here?"

"How . . . how would I know that?" Mr. Lester said.

"You told your students to ask around. You told them to find out who was going to be here. You and your friend made up a list of people to watch out for. Kids you had to knock out of the way if you were going to win."

"I did no such thing!" Mr. Lester said. "How dare you!"

"Yes, you did," said a new voice. It wasn't Brendan. It was one of his teammates. One of the two brothers. The other brother turned and gasped at this betrayal, but the boy continued. "It's just like he said. You told us to guess who might be at this event. I told you her name." The boy was pointing at Bethany. "I remembered her from the science fair this year."

"I was on that list, too," said Bethany. "Bethany Seymour."

"Who else was on this list?" Dmitri Simon asked.

Brendan's teammate, continuing despite his brother's outrage, said, "My brother learned that a kid named Michael Scott was going to be here. And my teacher told us he thought a particular teacher, Mr. Denham, would be here."

"I *am* here," said Rod Denham, looking somehow affronted that he wasn't recognized.

"Where is this list now?" Simon asked.

Winston and his teammates looked at each other. Then Winston fished the memo pad out of the plastic bag. All eyes turned to him as the bag crinkled and crackled. Carl Lester's eyes were filled with a growing panic; everyone else watched with fascination. Winston walked down the aisle to the stage and handed the memo pad to Dmitri Simon. "The last couple of pages," Winston said.

Simon flipped to the right spot and stared. After a moment he said, "Breen. Seymour. Scott. Denham. It's all right here." He looked up and said to his men, "Escort this man to the small conference room and keep an eye on him. And call the police."

"Wait!" said Carl Lester, putting up his hands to keep grasping arms away from him. "Wait! This is crazy! Get away from me!" Simon's men were not security guards; they didn't know how to restrain someone who didn't want to be restrained. Carl Lester didn't get away from them with the expertise of a secret agent—he fought back more like a child who doesn't want to take a bath. But he escaped their grasp and made a break for the upstage door. One of the other men grabbed for him and missed. There was chaos up on the stage now. Winston and Brendan jumped away as the men ran around the stage. Lester stormed by them, out the door, and was gone.

"Oh, for crying out loud," said Dmitri Simon. "Go get him! Can't the three of you stop one guy from leaving a room? I don't want that guy running around my building! You go that way and you go *that* way," he yelled at his men as they stumbled their way out of every possible exit. "Watch the parking lot! Don't let him get back to his car!"

Winston walked shakily back up to his team. Mal said to him, "It doesn't matter. Even if he gets back to his car, he's not going anywhere."

"What?" Winston said. "Why not?"

"Maybe you'll notice that last bottle is no longer in the plastic bag." Jake gasped. "You didn't!"

"Oh, yes." Mal grinned. "I gave him a back-tire wedgie."

CHAPTER FOURTEEN

EVERYONE COULD TELL Dmitri Simon was angry—not just at the people who screwed up his game by cheating, but at himself for allowing it to happen. He regained his smile just a little after Carl Lester was recovered in the parking lot, but he was no longer the boisterous Santa Claus they had all met at the start of the day.

He announced that everyone should go enjoy the picnic, but that he and his men would be speaking to each team in an effort to figure out what had happened . . . and who, if anybody, should be awarded the prize money.

The teams were led to a large field behind the factory. Winston accepted some congratulations and claps on the back from kids on other teams. Mal tried to get everyone to lift Winston up on their shoulders, as if he had just caught the winning pass in the Super Bowl, but there were no takers, least of all Winston.

The employees of Simon's Snack Foods were already behind the factory, sitting at picnic tables and eating hamburgers. Music was playing, and several large barrels contained bags of potato chips and pretzels. Winston wondered if Simon's workers were sick to death of eating salty snacks.

The boys and their teacher claimed a picnic table and sat.

"What's going to happen now?" Jake asked.

"Now I am going to have about seventeen hamburgers," said Mal. "I've had enough cereal bars to last a lifetime."

"You had two cereal bars," Mr. Garvey said. "Two. And having that food handy saved us valuable time. We wouldn't have won if we'd stopped off for lunch somewhere."

"We didn't win," Jake said. "Not until Simon says we did."

"We'll see about that," Mr. Garvey said. "Go get your food. I'll watch the table."

So the boys got in the long line for food. Dmitri Simon had, as usual, pulled out all the stops. There were three grills serving up all kinds of picnic fare, but before you even got there, there were two tables stocked with salads and side dishes. The mood wasn't as celebratory as Simon surely had hoped, but everything looked delicious.

They waited patiently in line, paper plates and plastic utensils in hand. As they approached the grills, Jake said, "Look over there."

Across the field, Brendan Root had a picnic table to himself. He was slouched over, head in hands. His teacher was gone, and his teammates, the two brothers, were sticking to themselves. Winston wondered how Brendan was even going to get home.

"Let me get a hot dog, too, please," Winston said to the man serving the food.

A few minutes later, bearing an extra plate and a can of soda, Winston said to Brendan, "I brought you some food."

Brendan looked up. His eyes were red—he'd been crying. He had stopped now, but his great and happy enthusiasm was a long way off. "Thanks," he said dimly. "I'm not really hungry."

"Maybe you will be later," Winston said as he sat down. Jake and Mal had gone back to Mr. Garvey.

Brendan watched Winston work on his burger for a few moments and pushed the food around on his own plate. "People think I cheated," he said.

"No, they don't," Winston said. "I know you didn't. It was your teacher."

"He asked us to guess who might be on other teams. 'It's always good to be prepared,' he said. I didn't know what he meant by that. Anyway, I knew you were going to be here—I mean, it's a giant puzzle event!—but I called you just to make sure. I told my teacher your name, and he wrote it down."

"It's okay," Winston said.

"The next day I saw a picture of you on his desk," Brendan continued.

"A picture?" Now this was a surprise.

"The one from the newspaper," Brendan said. "After you found that last treasure."

"Oh. That," Winston said. That made sense. The local newspaper wrote a story about the previous treasure hunt and included a picture of Winston and his friends. Carl Lester must have tracked that down and given it to the cheater so he would know what they looked like. How very creepy.

"Even when I saw your picture on his desk," Brendan said, "I never guessed what he was going to do. Why did he do it?"

Winston could only shake his head. "I don't know," he said. "I guess he really wanted to win."

"So did I," Brendan said sadly.

Winston didn't know how to make Brendan feel any better. He wasn't sure if that was even possible right now, so soon after the grand prize had slipped away. At least Brendan took a bite of his hot dog. Winston looked around for Brendan's teammates, but they were nowhere in sight. Then he started looking at the picnic tables. His eyes jumped from table to table, his mind calculating. Brendan was temporarily forgotten.

"What are you looking at?" Brendan asked.

Winston laughed. "I think I found a puzzle."

Brendan looked around. "You did? Where?"

"The picnic tables. Look! Starting from where we're sitting, we can walk in a straight line to another table, and from there to *another* table. You can trace a path that hits every picnic table by walking in a straight line horizontally or vertically. When you hit a table, you can turn or keep going straight. If you do it right, you'll hit each table exactly once."

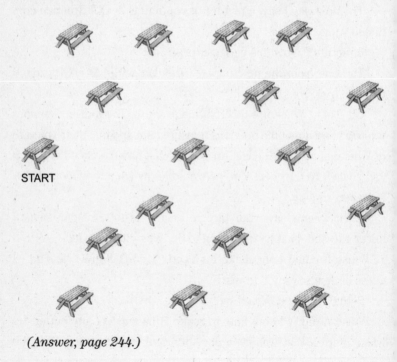

START

(Answer, page 244.)

Brendan looked a little better after solving the puzzle, so Winston invited him back over to his picnic table. Brendan thought about it and shook his head. "Everyone probably thinks I'm as much a cheater as my teacher." He looked startled for a moment and said, "Hey, those two words are anagrams of each other!"

"What?"

"*Teacher* and *cheater*. You can scramble the letters of one to get the other."

Winston was amused when Brendan laughed his old happy laugh. He'd been trying to think how to make Brendan feel better, and all it took was some scrambled letters. When Winston again invited him to sit with Mal and Jake, Brendan came along, carrying his plate of food.

His friends instinctively understood that Brendan needed a lot of cheering up. They greeted him like a long-lost relative. "Hey, Brendan!" Mal said with an over-the-top happiness. Jake stood up and clapped Brendan on the shoulder, welcoming him to their picnic table like it was a secret society for only the very coolest people. Brendan soon looked more like his old self.

"Where's Mr. Garvey?" Winston asked.

Jake gestured with his chin, and Winston turned around. Mr. Garvey was talking with Dmitri Simon and three of Simon's men.

"They called him over?" Winston said. "I thought they were going to speak to all of us."

"No," Mal said. "He went over by himself. He said they had to be told that another team had solved the final puzzle."

They watched Mr. Garvey, who was talking as much with his hands as with his mouth, passionately trying to convince Dmitri Simon that there was another winning team ready to claim the grand prize. Simon's expression was unreadable from this distance.

"Your team solved the final puzzle, too?" Brendan said.

"Yeah," Winston said. "Took us a while. Think square . . . I had no idea what that meant."

"Well, if somebody else wins, I hope it's you guys," Brendan said seriously.

"We might," Mal said. "Maybe they'll let us have it just to stop Mr. Garvey from talking to them anymore." He imitated a desperate potato chip executive: "Yes! Please! Take our money! Take whatever you want! Just go away!"

They all snickered at that.

Jake said, "Do you think he's telling the full story?"

"What do you mean?"

Jake leaned in and spoke softly. "We're supposed to split the prize money with the girls. Do you think he's telling them that? We never got to submit the answer with the computer, so there's no proof we made that deal with Bethany's team."

They thought about that as they watched Mr. Garvey talking to the other men.

"You think he's trying to claim the entire prize?" Mal said. "You think he's cutting the girls out?"

"I don't think he's arguing to give them *more* money."

"What's your teacher doing?" said a new voice, and Winston spun around to see Bethany standing there, arms crossed, glaring down at him. Giselle and Elvie stood behind her like backup singers.

"I don't know. We were just talking about that."

Bethany pointed sharply at Winston, as if Mr. Garvey was Winston's misbehaving pet dog. "Dmitri Simon already interviewed my team. We told him exactly what happened—that we were going to split the money," she said. "If he's over there saying something different, they might decide we're *all* lying. They might not award the prize to anybody!"

They continued to watch the men talking. Winston said, "I'm sure he wouldn't do that." He didn't believe the words coming from his own mouth.

Nobody else did, either. Bethany snorted.

Jake snorted, too. "He would totally do that," he said.

"But what can he tell them?" Winston asked. "What can he say to make them think we deserve the prize money all by ourselves?"

Bethany made an exasperated sound. "It's easy. It's totally easy. All he has to do is say your computer broke after it beeped and said another team won. Then you gave us a hint to solve the last puzzle because it was all over anyway."

"Is that what happened?" Brendan asked.

"What?" Bethany said. "No! That's what I'm saying!"

"Sorry. I just got here," Brendan said.

"That's the bunch of lies their teacher is telling Dmitri Simon right now," Bethany said.

They all looked over to Mr. Garvey, who was still at it, giving his complicated version of events to Simon and his men. Now, as they watched, Mr. Garvey pointed back to the picnic table. Dmitri Simon turned to look at Winston and his friends. Simon said something else and then turned and began to walk toward them. Mr. Garvey tried to follow, but one of Simon's men put a hand up and stopped him. What was that about?

Dmitri Simon reached their table. He was all smiles. "Hello again, girls," he said to Bethany's team. "I'd like to talk with these fellas for a few minutes."

"What did that teacher say to you?" Bethany asked. "Because if he said anything about—"

Dmitri Simon raised a hand, and Bethany quieted down. "I just need to speak to these boys for a minute. Please."

Bethany bit her lower lip as if to keep a lock on the many things she wanted to say. She finally muttered, "Sure. Okay." She gave Winston one of her patented glares as she led Giselle and Elvie away.

Brendan stood up, too. "I guess I'll go get another hot dog. Okay?"

"Sounds great, Brendan," said Simon. "I'm sorry again for everything you've been through today. It's not fair that your teacher did this. I mean, it's not fair to *you*."

"I still had fun," Brendan said. "You know. Up until—"

"I know," Simon said, patting Brendan on the shoulder. Brendan left to get his second helping.

Simon took a deep breath and sat down. The bench groaned with displeasure at the sudden extra weight. "What a day, huh?" Simon said to the three boys. He shook his head with something like amusement. "I figured once a team had gotten that sixth answer, there was no need to continue the game. I had the computers programmed to summon everybody back to the factory after somebody won. It didn't occur to me that the winning team might self-destruct so spectacularly." He looked more carefully at Jake's bruised face. "I guess you're the one who made direct contact with the cheater."

"I made direct contact, all right," Jake said ruefully.

"Are you okay?" Simon asked.

"It still hurts a little. Not too bad."

Winston said, "Did you talk to Carl Lester? Did he tell you why he did all this?"

Simon gave a snort of laughter. "Yeah. The guy was so nervous about getting caught, he told us the whole thing before he even knew what he was saying. Apparently, our friend Mr. Lester likes to gamble. He owed a bunch of people a lot of money. He thought if he won my contest, he could use his power as vice principal to funnel that money to himself. He was going to steal it all."

Jake said, "And who was the other guy?"

"A buddy from one his card games," Simon said. "Mr. Lester was going to give him a cut. We've got his name, and the police are going to his house right now. Personally, I can't wait to meet him."

Mr. Garvey was still standing at a distance, staring at them, held back by one of Simon's partners. Simon gestured over there and said, "So. Your teacher tells me you figured out the sixth and final answer." Simon looked at the three boys. "Is that true?"

This was apparently the big moment. "Yes," said Winston.

"Tell me about it. Tell me how you solved the puzzle." Simon sat back, ready to hear the story, that friendly smile remaining on his face.

Winston glanced at his friends and then started to talk. It was clear what was happening: Dmitri Simon wanted to verify what Mr. Garvey had said.

And what *had* their teacher said? Had Mr. Garvey tried to cut the girls out of their half of the prize money? Winston had to admit it was possible. Sure. Mr. Garvey might have decided it wasn't fair that the girls should get so much money just because they hadn't broken their computer. It's not like the girls would be able to prove he'd promised them anything. And it would mean twenty-five thousand extra dollars for the school.

But that would only work if Winston didn't tell the whole truth, right now.

He couldn't do that.

He started to speak . . . and stopped. If his story contradicted what Mr. Garvey told them, Dmitri Simon might not give the prize money to them *or* the girls. Simon might decide everybody was stretching the truth, that he couldn't figure out what really happened, and he would simply give the money away to charity or something.

Everybody was looking at him, and Winston realized he had gotten halfway through his first sentence and then stopped like his brain had winked off. He gave a little cough and started again, telling the story just as it happened: The broken computer. Winston figuring out the word square. Going to the girls for help and giving them a hint so they could solve the final puzzle, too. He told Simon they had promised to split the money with them if they won.

Dmitri Simon turned to Mal and Jake. "Is that what happened?"

Winston's friends glanced at each other, then nodded hesitantly.

Simon gazed at them for a few more eternal moments and then smiled. "Okay. I'm satisfied." He clapped Winston on the shoulder and stood up. "Good for you. You guys did real good."

"We did?" Mal said.

"What just happened?" Jake asked.

"Well," said Simon, looking amused, "you win. You've won the contest."

They were all thunderstruck. Winston had convinced himself he was telling a different story from his teacher. "We did? We really did?"

"You really did," Simon said. "You confirmed exactly what your teacher told us, and since nobody else solved the final puzzle, the prize money is yours. We'll make the announcement in a few minutes. No giant check for you guys, because we only had one and it has the other team's name on it. Sorry about that. But you'll get a *real* check, for your half of the prize. I'm sure you'll agree that's a lot better."

"Yeah!" Jake said, still looking more startled than pleased.

"Congratulations to all of you. I'll also send all of you a case of potato chips. What do you like? Oil and vinegar? Barbecue?"

"I want to try those square chips," Mal said.

"You got it," said Simon. He nodded over to his assistant, who finally let Mr. Garvey pass. He all but ran back to the picnic table, as if to undo whatever damage Winston had caused.

"What happened?" he asked breathlessly as he arrived.

"All is well," Dmitri Simon assured him. "Your boys confirmed exactly what you said. Congratulations." Simon shook hands with Mr. Garvey, who looked weak with relief. As Dmitri Simon walked away to tell his men the news, Mr. Garvey all but collapsed against the picnic table, a hand over his heart.

"I can't have another day like this for a while," he said.

"We won," Winston said. He was still getting used to it. After everything that had happened, they'd looked down and discovered they had crossed the finish line. Incredible!

"We won *half*," Jake reminded them.

Mr. Garvey laughed and groaned at the same time. The laughing finally edged out the groaning, but he also looked a little green around the edges—as if he was thinking, Did we have to offer the girls quite so much?

Winston was ready to fall asleep right there in the grassy field. He was exhausted from all the running around and the drama that had followed, and now on top of that, he was full of hamburgers and potato salad. Yes, he would be sleeping well tonight.

A couple more kids congratulated Winston as they walked by. The full story was out now. The people from the potato chip company had set up a microphone, and Dmitri Simon introduced Winston's team as the winners of the contest and called the girls up, too, as he related the strange story of how the two teams came to split the prize. He also decided to give ten thousand dollars to each of the other schools—even Brendan Root's school. "I made a few mistakes today," Simon said. "I should have given you a way to get in touch with me so we could have taken care of this cheater business. Failing that, I should have at least allowed those computers to accept the last answer from more than one team. Yeah, I screwed up, but at least I can make amends to all of you. What do you think of that?"

Everyone in the crowd thought that was just fine. Even the teams with the sourest expressions were now delighted. The only person who looked at all unhappy was Dmitri Simon's accountant, but Simon ignored him.

Bethany no longer glared at Winston. Right before she left, they traded e-mail addresses, and then they didn't know whether to hug or shake hands or what. They settled on waving. Jake and Mal would have normally spent several minutes poking fun at him for that, but they had their own awkward and clunky good-byes with Giselle and Elvie, so nobody made fun of anybody—unless you counted Mr. Garvey, whose sideways smile told them he was deeply amused by all of this.

Finally the picnic was over, and everyone meandered back to the parking lot. Jake and Mal were up ahead somewhere, so Winston found himself walking along with Mr. Garvey.

"A good day," the teacher said, tired but satisfied. "A lot of ups and downs but, all in all, a very good day. Wouldn't you say?" He mussed Winston's hair.

"I was worried when Dmitri Simon came over that maybe what we said wouldn't match what you told him," Winston said.

Mr. Garvey nodded ruefully. "You thought I left out the part about asking for help from the girls."

Winston didn't say anything. It sounded bad to have it said aloud.

"I won't say I didn't think about it," Mr. Garvey said. "All I had to do was say we solved the final puzzle all by ourselves—which is *true*—and we'd have fifty thousand dollars instead of twenty-five." He cleared his throat. "That's a lot of money."

Winston said, "But you thought they'd ask me those same questions, and our stories wouldn't match?"

"Actually, that never crossed my mind. To be honest, I thought they would take my word for it, whatever I said." He stopped walking. Up ahead, Jake punched Mal in the arm for some reason. Mr. Garvey said, "I made a bad impression on you kids."

"What do you mean?" Winston said, although he thought he knew.

The teacher shook his head. "I see the way the kids look at me sometimes. In the classroom, in the hallway. They think I'm a bad teacher. I give homework on Fridays. I don't let students off the hook when it's clear they don't know something. My tests are hard. Yes, some of my students . . . they think I'm a bad teacher." He looked down at Winston and said, "I'm not used to being looked at like I'm a bad *person*. And I think I earned some of those looks you and Mal and Jake were giving me."

Winston didn't know what to say to that, but Mr. Garvey wasn't done talking anyway. He said, "When I went back into the amusement park, I had the specific idea of trying to scare Rod Denham and his team out of the race. I acted all worried, like I was considering quitting myself— although, of course, I meant to do no such thing. I wanted *him* to get scared and quit. He didn't. And in fact, I think he saw right through me. Two other teams bought my act, and they quit the race." He took a deep breath. "Jake was right. I did the cheater's work for him. I couldn't have done a better job if I'd been working with him from the beginning. When I thought about it later on, I didn't like myself very much.

"So when I went to talk to Dmitri Simon, I decided to tell the truth for a change. I told how the girls had helped us, and the promise we had made to them in return."

Winston said, "You looked so nervous when he came over to talk to us."

"Sure!" said Mr. Garvey. "I thought *you* were going to leave out the bit about the girls, because you might have thought that's what *I* did. That would have been a damn foolish comedy of errors." He chuckled. "I should have known you would tell the truth. You're a good kid."

He started walking again, and Winston followed.

Winston found himself dwelling on one small detail of the teacher's speech. He said as they walked to the parking lot, "So, uh, you give homework on Fridays?"

Mr. Garvey laughed. "You'll find out in September."

CHAPTER FIFTEEN

THE TWO KIDS sat in the living room. The coffee table held the remains of an explosion of puzzle magazines, snacks, and drinks. The television screen displayed a dingy castle dungeon. Two armor-clad knights advanced on each other, waving their swords.

"Okay," Brendan Root said, fiddling with the joystick. "How do I play?"

WANT
MORE
PUZZLES?

CARE FOR SOME DESSERT?
Six more puzzles by Dmitri Simon

I've got six puzzling desserts for you! The first five puzzles have a word as their answer. The sixth, "Make Your Own Sundae," will tell you how to combine all those answers. The result will be a very sweet treat—exactly what you deserve!

Apple Pie

What's as American as apple pie? This puzzle, that's what. Each of the clues below leads to a word or phrase that contains the letters USA, in that order. The shaded letters, reading down, will spell out a clue to a six-letter word.

1. _ U S _ ■ A _   Play or movie where people sing and dance
2. _ U ■ S A _   An extremely powerful and distant object in outer space—or the answer to the planetarium puzzle
3. _ _ U S _ _ _ A ■   Pest control you bait with cheese
4. ■ U _ S _ A _   A day of the week
5. _ U S _ _ A _ _ ■   Country that is home to many kangaroos
6. _ _ U _ S ■ A _ _   Home of New Orleans
7. _ U S _ A ■ _   Wife's mate
8. _ U S _ A _ ■ _   Facial hair over the upper lip
9. _ _ U S _ _ ■ A _   How some people live on the water
10. _ U S _ ■ _ _ A _   Janitor
11. _ U _ _ ■ S A _ _   Deep, soft, muddy goo that will slowly swallow whatever stands on it
12. U _ S A ■ _   Hazardous
13. _ _ ■ U S A _ _   10 x 10 x 10
14. ■ U S _ _ A   Moscow's country
15. ■ _ _ U S A _ _ _   Song that features the line "I come from Alabama with a banjo on my knee" (2 words)
16. U ■ _ _ _ S A _   Patriotic fictional "relative" (2 words)
17. _ _ U S A _ ■   Seasoned meat stuffed into casings, like a hot dog

___ ___ ___ ___ ___ ___ ___   ___ ___ ___ ___   ___ ___ ___   ___ ___ ___

1 2 3 4 5 6 7   8 9 10 11   12 13 14   15 16 17

Fruit Plate

Sure, cakes and cookies are yummy, but don't pass by the fruit plate! You can find seventeen kinds of fruit in the grid below, reading up, down, left, right, or diagonally. After you've found them all, the leftover letters, taken row by row, will spell out a clue to a six-letter word.

```
M U L P A P A Y A C
R T E O B A N A N A
B A P R I C O T K P
R N S L D G M U E P
A G S P N T M E C L
B E R A B Q I G H E
U R M A U E S N E M
H I S A P E R A R O
R N T A S E E R R N
M E L O N O P O Y N
```

APPLE   LEMON   PERSIMMON
APRICOT   MANGO   PLUM
BANANA   MELON   RASPBERRY
CHERRY   ORANGE   RHUBARB
GRAPE   PAPAYA   TANGERINE
KUMQUAT   PEAR

Jelly Roll

This jelly roll is filled with a bunch of yummy letters. Answers go in two directions—in and out. The starting and ending numbers for each answer are given to you. If you get stuck on the In clues, try the Out clues. By working back and forth, you should be able to fill the entire jelly roll. When you're done, the circled letters, following the inward path, will spell out a word.

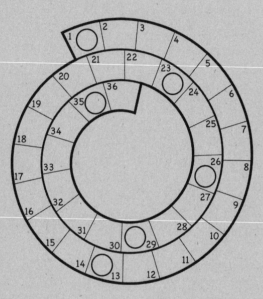

In		Out	
1–10	Rocketship or UFO, for instance	36–33	Run away
11–13	Music with a heavy beat	32–30	Vehicle that travels underwater, for short
14–17	Resident of the Garden of Eden	29–25	Informed
18–21	Fairy tale monster	24–20	Apple drink
22–25	Cubes that come with many games	19–15	Become insane (2 words)
26–28	Uncooked	14–10	Not together
29–33	Treat terribly	9–5	Wild comedy
34–36	Santa's toymaking helper	4–1	Ballplayers' headgear

Candy Sampler

There's a wide variety of candy in this box. Each piece contains a word, and each word (except for one) is the answer to one of the questions listed below. Answer each question, and cross off its answer—the last word remaining is the one you need.

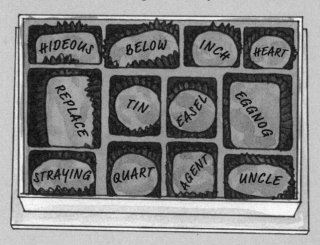

1. Which word becomes a kind of sea creature when you take the last three letters and move them into the middle of the word?
2. Which word becomes a new word if you change the last letter to the next letter in the alphabet?
3. Which word becomes a new word when you put the letters FI at the start?
4. Which word becomes a new word when you put the letters ICY somewhere inside it?
5. Which word becomes a new word when you tack a Z at the end?
6. Which word becomes a part of the body if you move the first letter into the third position?
7. Which word becomes an animal when you put a W at the front?
8. Which word becomes a color if you add a letter to the front and the back?
9. Which word becomes a country if you add an A and scramble all the letters?
10. Which word becomes the name of a planet if you scramble its letters?
11. Which word is hiding a musical instrument backward inside it?

Chocolate-Chip Cookie

Instead of chocolate chips, this cookie is packed with letters. Before the cookie fell and broke into pieces, the letters spelled out all the months in the year but one. Can you figure out which month is missing?

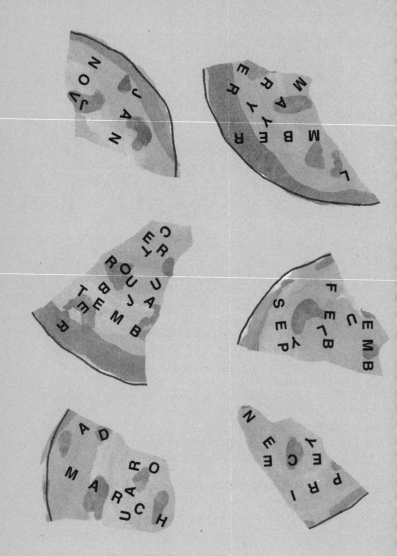

Make Your Own Sundae

Now you have five words, one from each of the previous puzzles. Carefully follow the directions below, and if you do your job right, I'll give you something really sweet.

1. Alphabetize the words and number them 1 to 5.
2. Write the words out, all in a row, in this order: 2nd, 3rd, 1st, and 5th.
3. Oh wait. I forgot to tell you: The 1st word in that row of words should be spelled backward.
4. Remove the last letter. In fact, remove this letter wherever it appears.
5. Double the 12th letter.
6. Remember the 4th word? We haven't used that yet. Delete all these letters, as many times as each appears, in your letter string.
7. Switch the 1st and 2nd letters. Switch the 8th and 9th letters. Switch the 11th and 12th letters.
8. Cross off every other letter, starting with the 2nd letter. Read what remains!

CARE FOR SOME DESSERT?

Answers

Apple Pie

MUSI**C**AL
QU**A**SAR
MOUSETRA**P**
TUESDAY
AUSTRALI**A**
LOU**I**SIANA
HUSBA**N**D
MUSTAC**H**E
HOUSEB**O**AT
CUST**O**DIAN
QUIC**K**SAND
UNSA**F**E
TH**O**USAND
RUSSIA
OHSUSANNA
U**N**CLESAM
SAUSAG**E**

Captain Hook, for one, is a PIRATE.

Fruit Plate

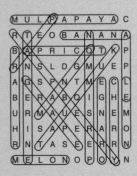

The remaining letters spell out COLDEST SEASON, a clue for the word WINTER.

Jelly Roll

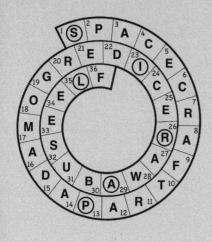

Inward answers:
SPACECRAFT / RAP /
ADAM / OGRE / DICE /
RAW / ABUSE / ELF

Outward answers:
FLEE / SUB / AWARE /
CIDER / GO MAD /
APART / FARCE / CAPS

The circled letters spell
out the word SPIRAL.

Candy Sampler

1. STRAYING (STINGRAY)
2. HIDEOUS (HIDEOUT)
3. REPLACE (FIREPLACE)
4. UNCLE (UNICYCLE)
5. QUART (QUARTZ)
6. BELOW (ELBOW)
7. EASEL (WEASEL)
8. AGENT (MAGENTA)
9. INCH (CHINA)
10. HEART (EARTH)
11. EGGNOG (GONG)

The unused word is TIN.

Chocolate-Chip Cookie

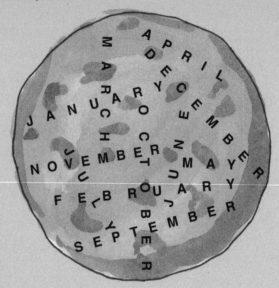

The missing month is AUGUST.

Make Your Own Sundae

After Step 3, your word list should look like this:

ETARIPSPIRALAUGUSTWINTER

Step 4:

ETAIPSPIALAUGUSTWINTE

Step 5:

ETAIPSPIALAUUGUSTWINTE

Step 6:

EAPSPALAUUGUSWE

Step 7:

AEPSPALUAUUGSWE

Step 8:

APPLAUSE

ANSWERS

Page 2

BRAT	CODE	PASTA
RACE	OVEN	ASHES
ACES	DEED	SHARK
TEST	ENDS	TERSE
		ASKED

Page 14

One jockey and one horse together have six legs, so 108 legs would mean there were eighteen horses in the race.

Page 23

Cros<u>sword</u> puzzles.

Page 27

WISECRACK	CHOCOLATE	QUALIFIED
ASTRONAUT	PARAKEETS	TRADEMARK

Reading down the fifth and eighth columns reveals the phrase COOKIE CUTTER.

Page 32

PLATE, PASTEL, STAPLER, PLANTERS

Page 37

All these words are the names of colors with the first letter removed:
EBONY, PEACH, PINK, BLACK, OLIVE, GOLD, GRAY, and ORANGE.

Page 41

STRESSED and DESSERTS are the longest words that spell another word backward.

Page 56

6	3	2	1	5	4
4	1	5	6	3	2
1	2	3	5	4	6
5	6	4	2	1	3
3	5	6	4	2	1
2	4	1	3	6	5

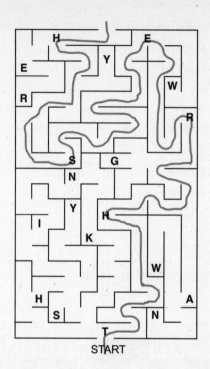

START

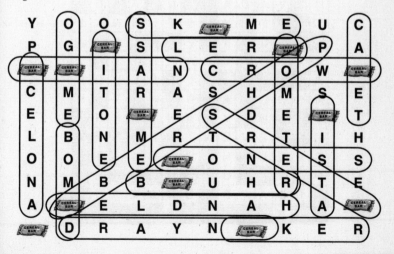

Page 90

EBW: elbow or eyebrow

JYK: jaywalk or joystick

KAP: kidnap or kneecap

LYX: lynx or larynx

QUZ: quiz or quartz

VYL: vinyl or volleyball

VDO: video or voodoo

HZL: hazel or horizontal

YGT: yogurt or youngest

HCF: handcuff or handkerchief

Page 119

The three values are $21, $35, and $44.

Page 137

• I have one eye and a sharp toe. What am I? **NEEDLE**

• Sometimes I have two eyes, and sometimes I have four, and my life often hangs by a thread. What am I? **BUTTON**

• Most people put me out at night yet do not lock me out. What am I? **LAMP**

• My coat is very thin indeed, but you wear me around the house. What am I? **PAINT**

• I get shorter the longer I stand. What am I? **CANDLE**

• You must break me before you can use me. What am I? **EGG**

• My legs are strong, but I will not run and play. You sit upon my lap for hours every day. What am I? **CHAIR**

• Scratch my head and it's no longer red. What am I? **MATCH**

• I'm round in the daytime and long at night. What am I? **BELT**

• If you beat me, I will yell. What am I? **DRUM**

• I will not burn in a fire, and I will not drown in the water. What am I? **ICE**

• Sometimes you can't make a move without me. What am I? **A DIE**

• I'm the end of time and space. In fact, I'm the end of everyplace. What am I? **E**

• If you turn me around, I can no longer see. What am I? **MIRROR**

• Throw away the outside, cook the inside. Then eat the outside and throw away the inside. What am I? **CORN**

• I'm full all day but empty at night. What am I? **A PAIR OF SHOES**

• I may be small, but I fill my house from top to bottom. What am I? **SNAIL**

• I am full of holes, but I can still hold water. What am I? **SPONGE**

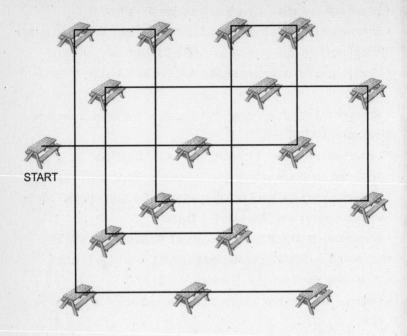

START

Turn the page for an excerpt from

THE PUZZLING WORLD
OF
WINSTON BREEN

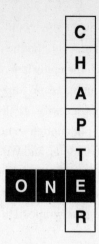

WINSTON BREEN WAS solving a puzzle, but then Winston Breen was *always* solving a puzzle.

The living room was filled with friends and relatives, all celebrating the tenth birthday of his little sister, Katie. Helium balloons bobbed about, pretending to be party guests. It was bright and sunny, and Katie and her numerous girlfriends had spent the day shrieking like crazy and running around the backyard. Winston talked to his relatives, ate hot dogs, and busied himself with the large message board his parents had placed in the front hall, rearranging the letters HAPPY BIRTHDAY KATIE into HIPPIE HAD BRATTY YAK.

Now, Katie sat cross-legged on the floor, smiling in anticipation: It was time to open the presents. Sitting that way in her new party dress, she looked like the child princess of some faraway country, surrounded by admirers and, most especially, the gifts they had brought. Winston tried to remember if he had taken birthdays so seriously just two years ago. He guessed that he had. Certainly when it came time for the presents, anyway.

Winston's present was at the bottom of the pile, so it would be a while before she got to it. He thought she would like it, even though he had bought it just yesterday. Panicked that he had forgotten about the party, he had bicycled through the chilly late-afternoon air to Penrose's Curio Shop. After spending his usual long time exploring the crammed, rickety shelves and chatting with Mr. Penrose, he had come across a small wooden box, just big enough to hold with two hands. It was carved with a pattern of diamonds, and Winston envisioned his sister keeping . . . well, *girl stuff* in it. He didn't know what. She could figure that out. Anyway, the box seemed like just the thing, and now it was sitting here with the other gifts, wrapped in the same red wrapping paper his parents had used.

While Katie opened her new toys and clothes, Winston picked up a stray scrap of wrapping paper, printed with a pattern of different shapes. His first thought, as usual, was to wonder if there was a puzzle buried among the circles and squares and triangles. Even if there wasn't, looking for a puzzle was a lot more fun than watching his sister ooh and ahh over a new pair of pants. He sat back and furrowed his eyebrows while the party continued on around him.

It took some time, but he saw it: A puzzle! Good! As he smiled with satisfaction, however, he became aware that someone was staring at him. He glanced to his left and saw Mrs. Rooney, a fairly new neighbor from down the block. Her eyeglasses were on the tip of her nose, and she was staring openly at Winston like he was a newly discovered and perplexing kind of insect.

Winston knew what she was going to say before she said it. He'd had this conversation, in one form or another, a thousand times before. And sure enough, she said, "That's a piece of wrapping paper."

"Yes . . . it is." He glanced at his mother, who smiled sympathetically. She'd had this conversation herself, many times, on behalf of her son.

Mrs. Rooney said, "You were staring at that piece of wrapping paper. For a long time."

"I was looking for a puzzle," Winston said simply.

Mrs. Rooney glanced at the bit of paper. All she saw, of course, was a scrap of garbage. "A puzzle?"

"I like puzzles," said Winston. Sometimes he thought he should just make up a sign, so that when people asked him why he was staring so intently at that billboard, or that road sign, or the plaque on that statue, he could just wave the sign at them: *Don't mind me. Everything is fine. I'm looking for a puzzle.*

Mrs. Rooney seemed to decide that Winston was probably not insane. Now she just looked curious. "Did you find a puzzle?" she asked.

"Oh, yes. See?" He handed her the paper.

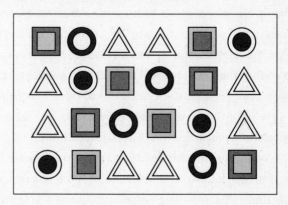

"You can draw a line that touches every shape exactly once and ends up back where it started. The line can't cross itself and has to touch the shapes in this order: circle-square-triangle, circle-square-triangle. Can you see it?"

And soon, while the party continued on around her, Mrs. Rooney was frowning intently at that same scrap of wrapping paper. Winston sat back, smiling. The only thing better than discovering a puzzle was stumping somebody else with it.

Katie had finally gotten to Winston's gift—the last present in the pile. Winston leaned forward. She tore off the red wrapping paper, revealing the box. Eyes gleaming, she opened the lid. There was nothing in it. Katie looked blankly up at Winston.

"You bought me an empty box?" she said.

"A *nice* empty box," said Winston, a little offended. When Katie continued staring at him, he added, "You can keep things in it." Although that, he thought, should have been obvious.

"It's lovely," said their mother, Claire, who was sitting next to Katie on the floor. "It's a lovely keepsake box. Say thank you, Katie."

She didn't. She stared at her brother for a moment more and then closed one eye and peered at the box like a detective looking for clues. She opened it and felt around its smooth interior. Meanwhile, the party began to shift to the next phase. Winston's two aunts began clearing away paper plates and plastic cups. Several other relatives thought another slice of birthday cake might be a good idea. Katie's friends, fueled by cake and punch and then forced to sit still while Katie opened her gifts, now blasted outside to play on the lawn. The birthday girl, however, was oblivious to all of this. She held the box up to the light and felt its underside, frowning a studious detective's frown.

Winston watched this with a frown of his own. "Katie," he said, "the box is the gift. There's nothing in the box."

"You're up to something," said Katie.

"I'm not!" Winston protested. He wasn't sure how to defend himself—so many times in the past, he *had* been up to something. Last year, Winston had hidden Katie's birthday gift in the toolshed and had given her clue after clue until finally, sweaty and exhausted, she found the thing two hours later. Katie tried getting revenge on his birthday, but he had marched through her clues in less than ten minutes, and she was so angry she wouldn't talk to him for the rest of the day.

So it was certainly possible that Winston was playing some kind of puzzly trick with this empty box. Nonetheless, their father said, "Katie, just say thank you. It's a very nice gift."

"I just want to know what the trick is with this box!" she said, lifting the lid again and poking around inside.

"There's no trick! I promise!" said Winston.

There was a faint snap—the sound of a tiny piece of wood breaking. "Aha!" said Katie, with triumph. And she lifted out a part of the box.

"What did you do?" said Winston, in disbelief. He had paid over ten dollars for Katie's gift, and she had broken it in less than thirty seconds. Incredible!

"You hid something in here," said Katie. "I knew it!"

Winston's father, Nathan, leaned over to look. "It has a false bottom," he said, amazed. "The box has a secret compartment."

Winston drew closer. Sure enough, Katie had found a way to remove the floor of the box, revealing a handful of . . . well, what? They appeared to be thin wooden strips with letters on them. What on earth were they?

"What is this, Winston? I don't want to go on another puzzle hunt this year." But when Katie looked up into Winston's face, she saw immediately that he hadn't done this. His expression was one of bewilderment—his eyebrows were arched practically to the top of his head, and that was a look he wore only when faced with a *really* hard puzzle. She looked back into the box at the little wooden strips and then turned the box over and dumped them out.

Four small, thin rectangles fell to the floor. They were made of wood, and each had some kind of inscription in block letters. The partygoers in the living room were utterly quiet as they watched this performance. Even some of the restless kids had crept back in to see why everyone was so fascinated. Winston picked up one of the wooden pieces. It said:

LINE

"Line," he said. Why was the *I* in a different color? Heck—why were these words here at all, hidden away in the bottom of this box? He looked at the others.

BALL   R   PLACE   S

WAY

"Winston?" said his mother. "You didn't do this?"

"I swear, Mom."

"Then who did?"

"I don't know," he said. "I have no idea." Winston gazed at the mysterious little strips. BALL. LINE. WAY. PLACE. Simple, everyday words, but what were they doing here? Why those extra letters, the *R* and the *S*? And why the discolored letters in WAY and LINE? Was that done on purpose?

"Ballerina," said Uncle Roger, suddenly. He had been sitting in the

6

overstuffed armchair, looking like a bored emperor. Now he clearly thought he had cracked the whole case wide open and was sitting up excitedly. When he saw that everyone was looking at him with great puzzlement, he said it again, louder: "Ballerina!"

"What about a ballerina?" said Winston's father.

Roger rolled his eyes. "Nathan! Look! You got BALL and then some empty space and then an *R*. What word could that be? Ballerina! That's it!"

Nathan Breen seemed unconvinced. "Well . . . okay. But if that's right, then what does it mean?"

Roger blinked. "Well. Um. I don't know."

Another relative, Aunt Regina, suddenly said, "High!"

Winston thought she had said "hi," even though she had been there for hours and had greeted the whole family with big lipstick kisses upon her arrival. But he didn't want to seem rude, so he cautiously said, "Hello."

Regina shook her head. "No, no. High! You can put the word *high* in front of all these words!"

They looked. Highway—that made sense.

Winston said, "Highball?"

Regina colored a little. "It's a . . . drink for grown-ups."

"Wait a second, wait a second," said Winston's neighbor, Mr. Bernstein. He was a nice man, but also very loud. And also very fat. "Golf!" he said. "It has something to do with golf!"

Uncle Roger couldn't believe his ears. "Golf? How do you figure that?"

Aunt Regina looked irritated. "Hey! What about me? Look! Highway, highball, highline, and . . ." She trailed off. "High place. I thought that was a word. Wait a second . . ." She stared at the floor and tried to recover the answer she had grasped so firmly just a moment ago.

Winston's mother asked, "What's a highline?"

Winston said, "I've never heard of it."

Regina looked up. "Isn't that a word?" She looked sorry she had ever opened her mouth.

Mr. Bernstein, however, was suffering no lack of confidence. He felt he had waited long enough. In a loud voice he said, "I'm telling you, it's golf! Look! You PLACE the BALL on a tee, right? Right?" He looked around for support.

One of Katie's friends, a thin blond girl named Monica, spoke up. "It's a knot."

Winston said, "What is?"

"A highline knot. It's what you use to tie a horse to a post. My parents like to go horseback riding, and they take me, and I'm going to have my own horse someday." She smiled broadly.

Aunt Regina was pleased. "A highline knot! I knew it."

Mr. Bernstein was going to get through his theory if it killed him. "And then you hit the ball in a straight LINE down the fairWAY."

"Fairway is one word!" said Uncle Roger.

"So?"

"So that doesn't work! I'm telling you, it's got something to do with a ballerina!"

Aunt Regina sighed deeply. "Well, I give up. Winston, what's the answer?"

Winston looked surprised. "How should I know?"

"Wait, you mean you really didn't put that puzzle in there?"

"No! Really!" Winston was exasperated. Didn't they see that he was just as perplexed as everybody else?

Winston's cousin, Henry, was eighteen years old and was one of Winston's favorite people. He hadn't said anything up to this point, but now he jumped in, in a calm voice that somehow seized everyone's attention. "Look, let's say for a moment that all four words have some-thing to do with golf. What would that mean?"

"It would mean that golf is the answer to the puzzle," said Mr. Bern-stein, as if he thought Henry was playing dumb on purpose.

Henry shook his head. "But what would that *mean*? The answer to the puzzle is golf. Fine. So what? That's not very satisfying."

Mr. Bernstein said, "Maybe Winston bought Katie golf lessons."

Katie said with surprised distaste, "Golf lessons?"

"All I did was buy the box!" said Winston.

Henry waved off this possibility. "No. I've solved a lot of Winston's puzzles. If he gave Katie golf lessons—which I really, really doubt—the answer to the puzzle would be something like, 'Happy Birthday! You have ten free golf lessons.' There wouldn't be any other possibil-ity. All these ideas we're hearing, they're all too . . ." He tried to think of the word.

"Vague," Winston's mother offered.

"Right," said Henry. "Besides, I think it's pretty clear that Katie doesn't golf." Katie nodded vigorously in agreement. "No. Winston says he has nothing to do with this, and I believe him." Winston, grate-ful, smiled at his cousin. Several others in the room still looked skeptical.

"So what do you suggest?" said Uncle Roger.

"Well," said Henry. "I guess I'm suggesting that we all have some more cake. Winston will solve this. Give him time."

But Winston couldn't solve it.

He sat staring at the wooden pieces as the party went on around him. Occasionally others would sit with him for a few minutes, help-ing to think up possible solutions. Should the letters all be scrambled together to form some new phrase? (PALS WILL CANE BARLEY was the best they could do, and that seemed unhelpful.) Maybe the wooden pieces should be stacked on top of each other or arranged in some way. (Nope.) Uncle Roger came by, determined to make his ballerina theory fit somehow. He suggested drawing a *line* on a map, from the local ballet studio to . . . well, he didn't know. They got out a map of the town but couldn't figure out where such a line should be drawn or how that might get them closer to an answer. Mr. Bernstein came over several times, and each time Winston had to gently inform him that golf probably didn't have anything to do with it.

After a while, Winston wasn't sure if the puzzle had an answer at all.

Everybody agreed, as the party wrapped up, that Winston had *not* planted the puzzle himself. He was clearly trying too hard to solve it.

"Well, if you didn't create it, who did?" asked Henry. The party was now over. It was evening, twilight, and the house had been restored to its proper order. Henry was staying at Winston's house that night, before driving back to college the next day. The two of them were out on the patio with the wooden pieces on a little table between them.

"I wish I knew," said Winston. His brain hurt—he could actually feel it throbbing, like something out of a science-fiction movie. And he was tired. Sitting in this lounge chair with his feet up, he thought he could easily fall asleep out here.

"Someone put those pieces in there," said Henry. "Maybe someone who knows how much you like puzzles. They thought it was your box. They didn't know you were giving it to Katie."

Winston considered this. "But . . . how did they know it had a false bottom? I didn't even know that."

Henry stared ahead, trying to work around that one. Finally he said, "All right. That's a good point. Put that aside for a minute. Who had access to the box?"

"Well, my whole family, I guess. I brought it home and put it in my room and didn't wrap it until last night."

"Is that all?"

"No—Malcolm and Jake came over and were in my room for a while." Mal and Jake were his two best friends.

"Could it be one of them? Or both of them together?"

"I guess." Winston was doubtful. "I did leave them there when Mom asked me to help her with something."

"Well, then!"

"But if they created a puzzle they wanted me to solve, why not just hand it to me? Why put it someplace where I might not ever find it? And, like I said, how did they know about the secret compartment?"

"Maybe they were going to put it in the box, but then they found the false bottom, so they decided to put it there instead. Maybe they thought you knew about it."

Winston sighed. It was possible, but just barely. He couldn't imagine either of his friends taking the time to engrave letters on thin strips of wood. What would be the point? If either of them had created a puzzle, they would do what Winston did all the time: Jot it down on a piece of loose-leaf paper. "Well, I'll ask them," he said.

They sat there as the twilight turned to full dark. It was starting to get chilly, but Winston was too tired to move. He picked up the pieces again—he couldn't help it—and flipped through them. BALL. LINE. WAY. PLACE. Plus those extra letters. Totally bizarre.

Henry got up and said, "Well, I'm wiped out. I've got to do some reading for school, and then I'm hitting the sack."

"Okay. Good night."

"You know, you usually have a puzzle for me. Didn't have time to create one this time?"

"Hmm?" Winston was back to staring at the wooden pieces.

11

"Nothing, nothing. Good night." Henry started into the house. "Hey. Where did you get that box, anyway?"

"Penrose's Curio Shop, in town."

"Penrose!" He came back out.

"Yeah." Winston looked up at him blearily. Henry suddenly looked like he was lit from within by a great big lightbulb.

"Isn't that the old guy you told me about? The one who likes puzzles almost as much as you?" Henry was practically jumping into the air. "He's the guy who runs that crazy shop where you can buy anything?"

"Yeah." Winston still wasn't getting it.

"Winston, you nut! You must be totally exhausted if you don't see it. Penrose put that puzzle in there!"

Winston's eyes widened. Of course! He couldn't believe he had missed it. Penrose was the oldest man in the world (or seemed so to Winston), and his brain was stuffed with riddles, word games, and brainteasers. Penrose always had a stumper for Winston, whenever he dropped by the shop. How could he have missed it?

"You're right! That must be it. I'll go there tomorrow," said Winston.

"Will he tell you the answer?"

"If I ask. But, no, I want a hint. I want to solve it myself."

"All right. But when you finally get it, you better tell me. This is driving me nuts. Good night, kid." Henry went inside.

Winston smiled. Penrose! It made perfect sense. Although, if this puzzle was Penrose's creation, it was his nastiest one yet. All this time spent on it and not the slightest bit of progress had been made. But trying to solve something was always fun. That was Winston's opinion, anyway. And he smiled as he thought of the puzzle he had snuck onto Henry's pillow in the guest bedroom earlier that day.

Dear Henry,

Each of the words in this list can be found in the grid, reading across, down, or diagonally, and either forward or backward. Some of the words will cross the shaded middle row, whose letters are all missing—you'll need to fill in these letters. When you've found all the words, the middle row will spell out the title of this puzzle.

AFGHAN
AKITA
BASENJI
BEAGLE
BICHON FRISE
BORZOI
BOXER
BULLDOG

CHIHUAHUA
COLLIE
CORGI
DOBERMAN
MALTESE
MASTIFF
NEWFOUNDLAND
POINTER

POODLE
SALUKI
SAMOYED
SHEEPDOG
SHIH TZU
TERRIER
WHIPPET

D	N	A	L	D	N	U	O	F	W	E	N	R
T	G	C	H	I	H	U	A	H	U	A	E	A
S	B	N	E	S	E	T	L	A	M	I	G	F
C	B	O	X	E	R	D	A	R	R	U	B	F
O	L	I	R	A	C	K	E	R	Z	P	G	I
R	P	J	B	Z	I	B	E	T	L	O	Y	T
I	I	E	A	D	C	I	P	P	E	D	O	A
K	N	S	G	H	H	Y	E	P	I	L	D	M
U	T	A	L	S	G	E	V	I	L	E	L	O
L	E	B	E	K	H	F	F	H	L	D	L	Y
A	R	D	L	S	O	X	A	W	O	S	U	E
S	E	S	I	R	F	N	O	H	C	I	B	D

13

ANSWERS

Page 3

Page 13   The center row spells out "Gone To The Dogs."

D	N	A	L	D	N	U	O	F	W	E	N	R
T	G	C	H	I	H	U	A	H	U	A	E	A
S	B	N	E	S	E	T	L	A	M	I	G	F
C	B	O	X	E	R	D	A	R	R	U	B	F
O	L	I	R	A	C	K	E	R	Z	P	G	I
R	P	J	B	Z	I	B	E	T	L	O	Y	T
G	O	N	E	T	O	T	H	E	D	O	G	S
I	I	E	A	D	C	I	P	P	E	D	O	A
K	N	S	G	H	Y	E	P	I	L	D	M	
U	T	A	L	S	G	E	V	I	L	E	L	O
L	E	B	E	K	H	F	F	H	L	D	L	Y
A	R	D	L	S	O	X	A	W	O	S	U	E
S	E	S	I	R	F	N	O	H	C	I	B	D